A Ghost's Tale

Willow Valley Cozy Mystery

by

Sigrid Vansandt

In memory of Maggie and all the wonderful dogs who've given us their perfect friendship, undying loyalty, and constant love. We miss you.

A Ghost's Tale

Prologue

Imagine, if you will, dear reader, you are standing upon a narrow, rock-strewn path bordered, on one side, by an enormous, wide valley stretching out into the distance and, on the other, by rising, snow-tipped mountains intermittently veiled by low hanging banks of mist.

Below you, a river, engorged with the runoff from thawing ice fields, rushes around boulders plummeting over a jagged precipice dropping hundreds of feet into a deep, primeval chasm creating a roar so thunderous you can feel it in the soles of your feet. The scene and its sounds mesmerizes, and with so much water rolling and hurrying towards the far off waiting sea, you can't help but be aware of some similar power coursing through your spirit egging you on to another destination.

Breathe deeply. Surely, this must be as close to heaven as any mortal can physically be.

You walk on, paying special attention to the many stones strewn about and the narrow path. This is no time to tumble. The rugged beauty of the region and the lack of human structures impresses a feeling of timelessness and loneliness alike, but in a place like this, you can't help but be aware of the fragility of life, especially your own. Life and death walk together, close friends in constant communion with one another and sacrifice is the crux which existence balances upon.

Across the wild, dancing fields of bluebells of this ancient highland valley, faintly at first and increasing in strength, comes a voice singing a mournful tune. It waxes and wanes with the ever whipping Scottish wind. At times, the haunting tune is lost among the tall, stately pines covering the lower hills, and at other, the song rambles and reels, picking up strength as it rides the rushing current of the river below. In front of you, above you, and from an impossible distance across the valley, the singer's words begin to take shape.

"Oh bonnie Beast, I love you!" comes the tune clearly now. "Oh bonnie Beast, I love you true! You are my sweetest, darling doggie ever! Oh bonnie Beast, how I miss you!"

The hymn or perhaps it's a lovesong fades away. Did you imagine it? You strain your ears to listen, but like a ghost, the tune evaporated upon intense inspection. Only the wind continues her lonesome murmurings.

"Where are you, you wee, wanderin' mongrel! Come to the hand that feeds yee! Ungrateful Beast!" booms a voice making you jump causing pebbles to scurry over the path's sloping edge.

"Ah, Beast! It is too hard to bear. My heart is breaking! Come home, come home," the voice cries and moans.

An unwholesome chill ripples up your spine and a clammy sweat breaks across your forehead. You shake yourself, trying to make your mind make sense of what you've heard. Was it the wind roaring as it will in these high mountains or did the lowering fog heavy upon the pass confuse your senses? Hard to be certain in a country so full of mysteries, full of tragedies and without doubt, full of ghosts.

"I willna' tramp through this foul weather much longer, Beast! Come to me, my dear old dog that I love! Ohhh!"

The voice wails as it whirls around you, trails down and away through the craggy hillside leaving you stunned, unsteady and frozen to your marrow.

Goosebumps rising on your arms and the hair along the back of your neck pricking warns of the closeness of unnatural elements. On such a lonely, barren spot, with no other humans to ask if they, too, heard the song and the cry, you quicken your footsteps, turn up your collar against the wind, and make your way as hastily as possible down to the low lands and the comfort of warm-blooded, living creatures who inhabit the villages below.

In a short time, you find yourself warming a stool in a dark-timbered, low-ceiling Highland pub. Built but a few years before the Battle of Culloden, it is run by a congenial publican and his no-nonsense wife who bustle busily about the cozy bar and wooden tables meeting the needs of the locals, hikers, and curious tourists.

"Tis the saddest of stories," the publican of The Howling Hound will tell you as he hands you something strong and warm to drink. His expression sympathetic, his tone thoughtful.

"Many a traveler has heard the old Laird of Lochbar's lonesome calls for his best dog and friend, Beast. He lost the poor, Cairn Terrier one bitterly cold and snowy evening coming home along the old footpath high above the waterfalls. Heartbroken at not being able to retrieve his faithful friend, he was never the same. One night, the old Laird was found frozen to death, lost no doubt in one of the terrible winter storms blowing down from the mountains. 'Tis a sad and desolate place. It's no wonder you, alone up there, heard the Ghost of Lochbar's soulful cries."

The publican will turn away and tend to other guests as you are left to ruminate over the haunting tale and to make sense of your experience. After your second hot toddy to steel your nerves, dear reader, you will climb the inn's creaking wooden stairs wishing only to find your bedchamber along the drafty, ill-lit passage and put yourself to rest in one of the low-beamed, antique rooms. Crawling deep into a feather bed, you'll pull the coverlets tightly under your chin listening for signs, like a nervous child, for any still roaming, dead departed souls who might wish to also lay claim to this sleeping space.

Don't let the howl of the wild wind as it rushes past your well-shuddered windows keep you from your dreams. Blow out the candle, curl up tight under your warm, safe blankets and shut your eyes. Let the crackling of the fire in the grate whisper to you a lullaby about long ago legends, valiant heroes, and myths full of magic and mystery.

So, if you are ready, let this winter's bedtime story begin.

—Fitswilliam Carruthers, Laird of Dunbar

Chapter 1

Across the September night sky, another spider vein of lightning lit up the cloud-layered horizon. A thick and oppressive humidity was descending over the town of Willow Valley. All of southern Missouri was in for a whopper of a storm.

Large, heavy raindrops pummeled the half-ton pick-up truck's windshield as it plowed through the congested evening traffic. Even with the wiper blades whipping frantically back and forth to handle the deluge, it was difficult for Roxy Davidson to make out the signposts to the private, elite enclave of Meadowmere Place, Willow Valley's oldest and most beautiful neighborhood.

Her massive, modern wonder-truck moved like a sleek, unperturbed metal hero, and though the storm might batter it, Roxy knew the truck's internal cab was the perfect, indomitable sanctuary. It certainly cost the same as someone's starter house, but it was worth every penny if it handled dirt roads, hauled hay and looked fantastic going down the road.

As Roxy drove through the dignified stone pillars flanking the entrance to Meadowmere Place, the storm appeared to subdue itself as if it had been fussily hushed by the stately homes and the noble oaks lining the elegant neighborhood's narrow, cobblestoned streets.

"Leave it to Root Wad to ask me to come over in this weather. He knows I'd rather burn that contract with Titan than sign it," Roxy grumbled out loud.

The pretty, forty-something woman steered her truck up the driveway to the back of a three-story masterpiece of Victorian residential architecture and put the gear shift in park. Looking up through massive hundred-year-old trees with their limbs intertwining to create a thick canopy over the house, Roxy hesitated at the idea of opening her door and stepping out into the heavy downpour. Instead, she turned, picked up her cell phone and read again the text message from her brother, Harry Sweeny, she received earlier that day.

"I wish Root Wad would return my texts. I don't want to have to deal with Deidra tonight or listen to her drone on about how if only Posh Pups wasn't such a millstone around their necks."

Roxy was well aware of how her brother's wife, Deidra, was ready to be done with the family business. For that matter, so was Roxy's husband, Teddy. As for Roxy, she loved Posh Pups and was ready to take it from being a regional company to one with a national presence.

She studied the phone's screen in her hand. It showed her brother's original message requesting her to meet him at eight o'clock this evening at his house to look at the contract. It also showed her four unanswered replies asking if he could wait until tomorrow.

But Harry was a baseball fanatic. She knew in all likelihood he was probably ignoring his phone to watch his favorite team make mincemeat out of their National League rivals. Baseball was sacrosanct to Harry and he hated talking during a game.

"I can't sit here all night. Better get on with it," she said, swinging the driver's door open and dropping at least two feet to the pavement below.

The wind picked up and overhead the oak trees groaned and whined like old men who are weary with the fast pace of the world around them. Roxy skirted the front of the truck and hopped over the brisk, stream of rainwater running from a drain spout along the sidewalk.

Letting herself in through the wrought iron garden gate, she picked up her speed trying to leap over deep puddles in the paved path to preserve her expensive suede ankle boots. With each misstep resulting in a fresh dousing, she let loose a string of curses.

"Stupid brother! Always has to have everything his way like a whiny baby!"

Finally, achieving the top step of the house's broad, round veranda, Roxy stomped her feet to remove the moisture still clinging to her footwear's fine, velvety nap.

"Harry," she muttered under her breath, "you owe me a pair of Saint Laurent boots."

Each of the porch's outdoor ceiling fans, three in all, circulated and hummed as one wind gust after another rushed around the curved structure with ever-increasing energy and intensity. Reaching for the doorbell, she pushed the button repeatedly while all the time studying the vegetation's crescendoing sways and swirls out in the garden and surrounding street.

"Should've checked the radar," she said as she pulled her jacket tighter around her body. "Temps are dropping. A good sign it is whipping itself into a twister."

No one came to the door. She remembered the difficulty Harry was having with his renovation work on the Victorian. The doorbell may be broken. Either way, her frustration with Harry and the growing storm were building in tandem. Self-preservation demanded she seek a safe shelter soon. Roxy searched her brain for a memory.

"I bet it's still there!" she said, her voice lost in the roar of the wind.

Running over to a substantial fern anchored within an ornate, concrete urn, she dug down to one side of the potted plant. Above her, the large oaks, typically inflexible, started to bend and arch overhead with the pliability of bamboo reads. Searching frantically with her fingers, she found the key and pulled it out from the urn's underbelly and ran back to the front door.

With a heightened sense of fear from the escalating storm and the growing darkness, she fumbled with finding the lock, but finally found the tiny opening, turned the key, and let herself inside and slammed the door behind her. Leaning against the door, she took a deep breath and let it out then slipped the key into her jacket's pocket.

"Sorry, Deidra." she grumbled out loud as she tried to see in the rooms low light, "I'm gonna probably drip all over your oriental rugs, but it's better than facing a tornado out in the open. Stupid Root Wad! Why on God's green Earth did you tell me to come over here, and like an idiot, not be here to open the door?"

Wet from head-to-foot, Roxy stepped into the Victorian's exquisite foyer. A velvety silence filled her ears. Only the muted, occasional creaking of the house, as wind gusts buffeted its sides, gave her any indication the storm was growing in ferocity. The tomb-like quiet was a testament to the methodical attention to detail Harry and Deidra had demanded during the house's renovation.

"Harry! Deidra?" Roxy called into the gloom.

Walking in the direction of the back den where her brother loved to lounge in front of his theater-style television, she was increasingly aware of her uneasiness.

For the most part, the house lay in darkness until the occasional flash of lightning back-lit the interior space.

"Harry?" she almost whispered, peeking in between the two pocket doors of his den. "Are you in here?"

The only denizens of the den were the pillows perfectly arranged, standing at attention, waiting to provide comfort when their people came home.

A real sense of apprehension began to rise in Roxy. Something wasn't right. It felt like the house was watching her, waiting to reach out and touch her. A soft brush against her leg made her let out a frightened scream and jump back from the velvety touch pressing herself against the hallway's wall.

Looking down, and in the low light, it was nearly impossible for her to make out her brother's chocolate-colored Labrador Retriever.

"Pickles! Goodness! You gave me a scare! Boy! Am I glad to see a friend."

Bending down, she gave Pickles a good head rub and an immediate wave of relief rolled over her.

"Where are your people, old guy? Are you scared of the storm?"

Roxy knelt onto one knee and gave the gentle, doe-eyed dog a loving pat and double ear scratch.

"Don't worry, I'm sure stupid Root Wad will be here soon. Come on let me put you in your bed and I'll get you a treat from the jar."

The grateful Labrador beat his tail against the hardwood floors, rose onto all fours and followed her into the kitchen. Roxy was well aware of where the hallowed treat jar sat on Deidra's kitchen counter. One thing good about Harry's wife, in his sister's opinion, even though she was a bit high maintenance, Deidra did love animals.

"Everyone has a saving grace, Pickles," she said using the chicken jerky treat to lure the dog back to his bed in the laundry room.

Once she had him laying down, Roxy pulled the shades to block out the lightning flickering outside and wrapped an old flannel blanket around the dog. With another a good pet, she kissed the top of his head and nudged another piece of jerky between his paws. In return, he offered some more tail wagging to show his appreciation causing his blanket to rise and fall with each gentle thump.

"You'll be fine now, Pickles. Get some rest. I'll turn on your heating pad. Keep the old rheumatism at bay. That'll make it nice, won't it?" she said soothingly.

The grateful dog licked her hand and put his head down between his paws securing the safety of the prized treat under his muzzle. Roxy flipped on the heating pad, stood up and let herself out of the laundry room pulling the pocket door almost shut.

Through the windows, she saw the porch swing going back and forth with the wind. It occurred to her an inside light had been turned on not lit when she walked through the hall a few minutes ago. The corner of her mouth turned up in a smile at the thought that her brother had finally arrived. She peeked back in the den.

"Root Wad, where have you been..."

A whooshing sound was the last thing Roxy Davidson heard. Her body fell to the left, hitting the floor and coming to rest crumpled on its side.

If it's true, what she'd said earlier about everyone having a saving grace, for Roxy, it was her love for animals. Pickles, hearing the thud of something large hitting the ground, used his paw to open the laundry room door and padded back toward the den.

Slowly sticking his head around the corner, he watched as a figure bent down over Roxy and took something from her pocket. It stood up, turned away, and disappeared into the front of the house.

Once he was sure it was gone, Pickles went to where Roxy's motionless body lay on the floor. Smelling blood and death, he softly whined and gently pawed her shoulder, but she didn't respond.

Like all dogs, he knew what was needed. He lay down beside her, resting his soft chin on her outstretched arm and stayed with her, loyal and loving to the end.

Chapter 2

The storm lashed Harry "Root Wad" Sweeny's state-of-the-art SUV as he drove down the interstate toward Willow Valley and home. Though the weather was terrible, at least he was only dealing with a few semi-trucks and the occasional car trying to fight their way through the deluge.

"When I get home I'm going to crawl off in my den, turn on ESPN and pray Deidra hasn't found the bag of chips I hid behind my recliner," he muttered under his breath.

The thoughts of his man-retreat brought on a feeling of momentary peace for the tired Posh Pups CFO. Releasing his intense grip on the steering wheel for a moment, Harry flexed his aching fingers.

The wind and rain had been buffeting the SUV for over twenty minutes, and to have any visibility at all, Harry had been forced to go at a snail's pace. In this kind of storm, the physical and mental effort needed to keep even a heavy vehicle on the road was exhausting.

His cell phone was finally quiet. It had been dinging with text messages and voicemails from his sister, Roxy, for over an hour. The last thing he wanted was to fight two female fronts at the same time: one, his sister and the other, Mother Nature herself. Both were capable of powering through any situation to get what they wanted, but tonight, Mother Nature pulled rank.

Harry was beginning to think the old girl might have a tornado up her sleeve. Like anyone who'd ever lived in the

Midwest, Harry knew to take Mother Nature seriously when she's playing the twister card.

Each time Roxy's caller ID showed up on his Suburban's video information screen, Harry declined to answer. He preferred to keep his eyes on the sky for signs of rotation or on the road to stay in his lane.

"I don't want to hear one more woman whining about business. Between Deidra wanting to be rid of it and Roxy wanting to take it to the next level, I'm wondering if I might be ahead of the game if I run off to Alaska and live like a hermit."

A powerful gust of rain and wind broad-sided the vehicle practically moving it into the oncoming traffic.

"Hell! Maybe, it *is* a tornado!"

He leaned closer into the steering wheel and squinted up at the sky to see if the clouds above him were rotating. Instantly, his peripheral vision caught the movement of something hovering directly ahead of him in the middle of the road.

Slamming hard on the brakes, Harry watched in horror as his Suburban plowed through a human figure. A face, his sister's, rushed at him like a gust of powerful wind. He felt himself thrust backward into his seat as the vehicle's tires caught the side of the highway's gravel and came to a gut-wrenching stop.

"Roxy?" he breathed. "No. No way. Oh, dear God! It couldn't have been."

He took a deep breath and tried to peer out through the windshield as his heart was beating like a jackhammer in his chest.

"Oh my God! What if she was trying all this time to get me to come help her?"

With the car now stopped on the side of the highway, Harry jumped from the Suburban into the slashing rain and ran back along the road from where he'd just come. Practically blind from torrential sheets of water pouring from the heavens, he repeatedly wiped his eyes in an attempt to see into the darkness. A lightning shard crackled across the darkening sky briefly illuminating the lonely stretch of highway. A semi-truck barreled past lashing him with a spray of water.

"Roxy!" he yelled. "Roxy!"

No human reply came back to him only the rain hitting the asphalt and fresh rounds of thunder. His mind struggled to make sense of it all. Did he imagine it? Instantly, a new more horrible thought rushed over him.

"Oh, God! Oh, please dear God, no!"

Running back to the vehicle, he steeled himself and bent down. He looked under the SUV, but there was no one...nothing.

Taking a deep breath, he blew it out spraying rainwater from his mouth like a human geyser. Completely soaked and beginning to feel the first signs of shock, Harry mentally shook himself and remembering the flashlight in his safety bag, he quickly opened the back hatch and found it. Taking to the road's shoulder, he walked the same stretch again.

"Roxy!" he yelled, flashing the beam of light down the road's side and into the ditches.

There was no sign of any human, either dead or alive, anywhere along the road. Even the usual traffic was sporadic. Most travelers were probably waiting out the worst of the storm in safe harbors like restaurants, gas stations or truck stops.

The pelting rain slowed and with it, Harry's fevered search. He was cold from being wet and feeling disoriented, he returned to the still open Suburban's rear hatch.

He found the duffle back with his gym clothes and climbed into the roomy, open area of the vehicle's back end. With a weary effort, he pulled the hatch down, taking off his wet clothes and trying to dry himself off with the towel he always carried in the gym bag. Soon, completely changed, he sat for a moment staring through the back window and watching the hundreds of rivulets of water make their way down the outside of the glass.

His mind looped again and again with the image of Roxy standing in the middle of the road.

"I've had Roxy so much on my mind, maybe I just thought I saw her," he said softly, trying to comfort himself.

But slowly the image of his sister and her expression came back to him.

"She wasn't terrified like someone would be who was about to be mowed down by a car. Roxy looked sad, so sad," he said out loud.

Crawling up to the front driver's seat and taking his phone, he dialed Roxy's number. Nothing. He mentally chastised himself for not answering her calls earlier. He tried Deidra's number.

"Hey, Baby," came her soft voice over the phone. "When are you going to be home? This storm's a hell mess."

"Deidra," Harry replied. "I've seen the most horrible thing."

"What, Sugar?"

"I thought I saw Roxy standing in the road. I nearly hit her with my car. Well, I thought I *had* hit her, but she's nowhere. Nowhere on the road."

His voice rising at the end with confusion and anxiety.

"Have you been drinking, Harry?" Deidra asked, sounding like a wife who was quickly moving from loving to perturbed.

"No! Absolutely not!" he exclaimed. "I was thinking about her and our stupid fighting over the business. Could my mind play some kind of horrible trick on me?"

No answer came immediately from his wife.

"Deidra?" he asked.

"She wasn't at our book club meeting tonight which is odd for Roxy. Harry, did you look…" she came back, but hesitated to finish, "around…on the road…for a body?"

"Of course I did. I can't find anything — anyone."

A truth dawned on him.

"Come to think of it I never heard my car *hit* anything."

"Darling, you may have dozed off a bit and imagined it," Deidra came back, her tone much more sympathetic. "Where are you?"

"About an hour from home," he answered.

"I've got to run into Puggly's and pick up some things for dinner then drop off the quarterly financials for the foundation at Lynn's. I'll probably beat you home, but with this weather, it should be about an hour before I get there. Be careful driving the rest of the way, Harry. I love you."

Deidra hung up leaving Harry still sitting in his car on the side of the highway wondering what he'd seen. Finally, with a shrug and a sigh, he turned the car back onto the blacktop. Only drizzle hit the windshield now.

"I guess the worst of it is over," he said to himself with a shudder and continued down the interstate toward Willow Valley.

Chapter 3

Teddy Davidson filled his glass with tomato juice and vodka. Picking up the video he'd rented, he headed for the living room, but his burner phone came to life with a pulsating buzz. He grabbed it from the kitchen counter, recognizing the number, flipped it open with a greasy grin.

"Hey," he said silkily into the receiver. "I just made it home. Don't tell me you miss me already?"

A woman's voice on the other end of the line came through making Teddy's mouth twist into another salacious smile.

"Yeah, I got drenched," he answered. "The rain was so heavy, it was hard to see to drive."

He listened for a moment, his expression turning dark and said, "I promise to work it out. You'll have to be patient. Yes, I want to meet again. Ok, I'll be there."

He snapped the phone shut and tucked it into the pocket of his jeans. Out through the kitchen window, he saw fragile leaves flinging past, caught up in the storm's powerful, merciless gusts. Three plastered themselves against the window's glass panes, clinging there as if begging for help from their fate. Seconds later, the wind's invisible, fiendish fingers plucked at their edges, they quivered and flapped, and without remorse were ripped back into the wind's grasp and were gone.

A loud bang brought Teddy around making the three Golden Doodles, Betty, Rue, and Bea go crazy with barking.

"Shut up!" he yelled, unnerved by the noise. The dogs scuttle back down the hall to Roxy's bedroom, a place he wasn't welcome these days.

Something, he thought to himself, a limb, must have fallen against the house.

"Better investigate," he said, picking up the Bloody Mary drink and heading off in search of the sound. The dogs, he knew, wouldn't come back out. They loved him about as much as he loved them. If they were looking for reassurance from him, they were out of luck.

The house was partially lit throughout as he'd deliberately kept it dark because of the storm. In the last five years, lightning had hit the house three times wiping out their electronics. Teddy wasn't taking any chances. Replacing tv's, wifi routers, HVAC systems were expensive. Money was tight, meaning his budget for playtime and playthings was severely restricted, but this was about to change. Teddy smiled at the possible reversal of fortune.

The bang had come from the living room area. As he went in that direction, he thought he could see a shadow pass toward the other hallway leading down to Roxy's bedroom.

Some instinct in him halted his progression down the hall. Not sure of his eyesight in the darkness, Teddy didn't move. He waited, trying to catch a sound. Was it an intruder? Surely not in this storm.

From Roxy's bedroom, he heard the three Golden Doodles whining. He was instantly aware of the prickling of the hairs along his arms and the back of his neck. Frozen in the hallway, his mind flashed to the handgun in his truck's glove compartment. He waited, straining to hear any further indications of human movement in the house. Nothing. It wouldn't do to stand there forever. The three dogs intensified their noise.

"You're on your own, girls," he thought to himself as he turned around to go in the direction of the garage, his truck, and the gun.

But as he rounded the corner, he stopped in his tracks. In the doorway, was Roxy, her head dripping with blood. At first, she didn't seem to see him. Her entire focus was on her dogs now at her feet.

In that instant, he knew what she was *and* what she wasn't.

"Can't be," he said. "Not possible."

Aware of a swimming feeling taking hold of his brain and a sudden clamminess of his skin, Teddy's knees buckled under him. He was aware of everything happening in slow motion. Roxy, the dogs, the blood on her temple, and him struggling to hear her words.

Teddy didn't get time to answer her back. Instead, he hit the kitchen floor in a faint with her voice echoing in his head, "Why Teddy? Why me?"

Chapter 4

The rain had slowed from a torrential downpour to a steady deluge. Wesley King hovered near his bedroom window watching for his friend-with-benefits to show. The darkness and the rain was making it difficult to see the back driveway where he'd told her to park.

Their relationship was bizarre. He wasn't allowed to call or text her. She refused to give him her number and, likewise, never called him on her phone.

When they met, it was because she sent him a SnapChat telling him when to be somewhere. If he tried to SnapChat her back, she always ignored him. It was off-putting at first, but he found himself enticed by her coldness and besides, it also kept things from getting messy, until now.

Normally, Wesley would never have a woman to his home, simply because he still lived with his mother and brother. On the day before, however, and much to his pleasure, he'd learned Presley, his younger brother, was driving to St. Louis, at least three hours away, to pick up their mother from the airport. Rosalie had been in Los Angeles meeting with a client and hadn't made arrangements for a driver to shuttle her home. This hitch in his mother's plans had given Wesley room for invention.

He proposed the idea about coming to his house the night before at the motel they frequented along the interstate. She'd shrugged, appearing bored by the idea, flicking the invite off. Her indifference always threw him.

He found it odd, unlike his other women who showed interest and curiosity about his privileged lifestyle and beautiful home, this woman only laughed and said the interstate hotel was good enough for what they were doing.

The rebuff stung. It was the first time *he* felt cheap, a play-thing for someone else's pleasure. Most of his life, and in his casual relationships, women were the ones carrying *that* baggage around.

This woman, however, was way out of his usual options for a lover, so he dropped any hangups he might have or the injured-ego attitude. He may be the boy-toy in this rare instance, but Wesley was by no means stupid.

It came as a shock when an hour before tonight's storm, he received a call from her on the house's landline. She told him she would meet him after all — at his house.

He was thrilled. The thought of her kept him twitching the curtain and walking the floor of his bedroom. She was everything a man like himself wanted in a woman. Her body was amazing, almost like something out of a teenage boy's dream and when they were together, she fired demands at him like a drill sergeant.

Unlike the majority of the women he played around with, she was devoid of any interest in cuddle-time or wrenching promises of fidelity from him. In all, she was perfect.

It was if he'd met a female version of himself. Like Narcissus, who'd fallen in love with his own image, Wesley had met his match and he knew he was sinking deeper into the same intoxicating malady reserved for other people — love.

He'd never dated a woman older than himself. She'd turned the tables on his usual macho, in-control modus operandi. In fact, and this was another of her exciting traits unlike other women, she was utterly indifferent to his feelings, needs or requests. She was in total control, and tonight, Wesley was like her dog who sat at the door all day waiting for his mistress to arrive.

At the sound of a loud bang on the back door, he quickly glanced out the window to see if her car had pulled up. He ran down the stairs and through the beautifully designed kitchen his mother had spent months laboring over to make perfect, he reached the mudroom's door. Flinging it open, he saw her standing there drenched, but delicious-looking all the same.

"Come in, baby," he cooed as she walked in through the door.

Reaching out to help her with her wet overcoat, she held up her hand to stop him. Unspeaking, she scanned the room with her eyes, but if he'd expected her expression to register admiration for the luxury and beauty of his mother's designer kitchen, he was quickly let down. She said nothing but only walked past him through the kitchen.

For the first time, he realized she was barefoot. Even with her coat dripping and leaving puddles of water where she'd been, Wesley didn't move. He waited patiently, reverently like a good boy trying to show his teacher he remembered how to behave.

"I don't need your help to remove my coat, Wesley," she finally said. "I can do it myself."

Turning around to face him and locking her gaze on his, she slowly pulled the overcoat's belt through its buckle. He practically salivated with expectation.

When the coat dropped to the floor, he was oblivious to where it had come to rest for his eyes were riveted to her exquisitely formed naked body standing there in the half-light. A tantalizing smile playing at the corners of her mouth, as she said, "Tough night out there. I'm cold. I'd like to take a hot shower…first."

Wesley, feeling intoxicated from drinking in the vision of her, forced himself to lift his gaze back to her face.

"Come with me. I'll set you up," he said, his voice sounding hoarse like he'd only used it for the first time all day.

She let him lead her up the back stairs. Knowing she was behind him completely naked and almost feline in her quietness, both thrilled and unnerved him. When they arrived at his bedroom suite, he went into the bathroom and turned on the shower. Handing her two fluffy towels, he watched as she pressed them to her chest and buried her nose in their soft nap.

"Your laundry smells wonderful. Do it yourself, Wesley? Bet not," she said, the corner of her mouth curling up in a teasing, sarcastic smile.

He'd done well, for she lifted her face and offered him a kiss which he interpreted as having warmth and gratefulness at its core. Emboldened by this, he wrapped his arms around her, feeling her skin's delicate softness. A desire to protect her, even own her, infused his being.

As much as he wanted her, deep in the primordial recesses of his brain he was drowsily aware of a faint warning signal tapping out a S.O.S code for danger.

Chapter 5

"I'll be right over," Sheriff Zeb Walker said and hung up the phone.

Rising from his office chair, he grabbed his weather-proof jacket and yelled down the hall of the Willow Valley's police building, "Kirchner! I need you to call Pineville!"

"Sure thing, sheriff," Tommy Kirchner, his deputy, said as he materialized within Walker's office door. "What's up?"

"Deidra Sweeny has found her sister-in-law, Roxy Davidson, dead in her house. I want Sebastian, the head of forensics, to be called out. Get a hold of him and tell him to bring his team. The address is 21 Weller Street, Meadowmere Place. Meet me out front. We'll take my truck."

Deputy Kirchner disappeared from the sheriff's door and Walker heard him talking with Sarah, the dispatcher. Grabbing his set of keys from the wall hook, Willow Valley's Sheriff took long, quick strides down the hallway toward the front entrance. Mentally, he was organizing his thoughts.

Roxy Davidson was dead and Deidra Sweeny sounded hysterical. Dog Days, the most important annual event of the year in Willow Valley, was about to start. He'd heard talk about Posh Pups being sold to an outside company.

Could the buy-out have anything to do with Roxy's murder?

Outside, the fresh, oxygen-rich evening air left behind from the storm made Zeb pause and take a deep breath. The need to breathe was an unconscious response to his shock at hearing about Roxy's murder. They'd gone to school together since kindergarten, even double-dated during high school.

A memory of Roxy pitching softball when they were kids flashed through his mind. He recalled how she always sent a Christmas card addressed to not only himself but Popcorn, his miniature poodle, too. Roxy was someone good, someone thoughtful and, now for some horrible reason, she was dead.

He hit the unlock button on his keys and climbed into the police SUV. Kirchner bounded out of the station's front door and jumped into the passenger seat beside him.

"They're on their way, sheriff," he said and murmured the next sentence. "Roxy Davidson dead. Do you think it was a robbery gone wrong? She was such a nice person from what I knew of her. It's too bad."

Sheriff Walker put the gear shift into reverse and gunned the gas backing the vehicle out of its spot.

"We're going to find out, Kirchner," Walker said, his voice low with emotion. "And when we do, the person responsible for her murder is going away for a long, long time. That's my promise…to an old friend."

Chapter 6

The next morning.

"Get out of my rose bush this minute, Fritz!" Sonya Caruthers practically cried as she stomped her foot in sheer frustration.

That morning when she'd walked out onto her front porch, tears sprang up in her eyes at the devastation wrought by the storm. Plant carnage covered her garden. Limbs down, flower beds mangled from the hail, and hundreds if not thousands of leaves were strewn around her yard. Fritz, her ghost companion, was only adding to her agitation.

"You may be a spirit, Fritz, but you're shaking loose what the storm didn't already demolish!"

No answer came from the red rose bush as it shook and twisted appearing to be thrashed by unseen winds. All other trees and plants in Sonya's once perfectly manicured garden remained unmoving in the fresh, still morning air.

Willard, Sonya's terrier, appeared to be convinced as well of the unseen, unnatural presence in the bush. With lots of yapping and running to and fro around the agitated plant, he proclaimed his protective loyalty to his mistress.

"Fritz! If you ruin my gorgeous rose bush, I'll personally find a way to contact your wife, Mary, and have her put a bounty on your head with a Scottish hag. You're in enough trouble as it is," Sonya said, her voice rising steadily as another deluge of delicate red petals fell to the ground.

"Hah!" a deep, male voice boomed from inside the rose bush. "I'm not afraid of Mary McGregor Dunbar or any vile sea hag she might conjure up against me!"

"That's debatable," Sonya scoffed. "It's your fault if I throw my lot in with Mary. Now, come out of there and stop acting like you're the wronged party in this affair."

With a marked effort to get her voice under control, Sonya swallowed hard. It wouldn't do for a passerby to see her arguing with an unnaturally moving rose bush.

"I have a right to thrash about in this garden especially when you've turned me out of the only home left to me!" Fritz came back.

Willard increased his growling, barking and darting at the bush again.

"Of all people, Sonya, how could you turn that vicious, man-eating, she-wolf, my wife, against me?"

Sonya knew the Laird of Dunbar, dead over two hundred years, was throwing a tantrum. He'd had a marvelous time last night kicking up his heals and enjoying the fury of the storm. So much fun, no one in the house had slept due to his antics. Singing bawdy drinking songs, ripping around the upper floors, and howling along with the wind, Fritz had been feeling his afterlife oats all night.

For a while, Sonya had tolerated his high spirits knowing, as she did, ghosts love a good thunder and lightning storm. The abundant natural power in the air gives them a surge of vitality, like being alive all over again, but when Sonya had finally asked him to quiet down, he left in a huff saying something about how the living were a dull lot and sucked the fun out of being dead.

She assumed Fritz nipped off to one of his other haunts, but that hadn't been the case at all. This morning, during her walk with Willard, Sonya learned how poor Mrs. Townsend, her neighbor across the street, had run out of her house in the middle of the heaviest part of the downpour last night screaming she was being chased by a luminescent flying pancake. Without a doubt, it had been Fritz, and because of these constant high jinks directed at her neighbors, Sonya had had enough.

Fritz was lucky the tiny octogenarian woman hadn't been hurt or had a heart attack, and Sonya had informed him after hearing what he'd done, he had to leave her house until he made amends to Mrs. Townsend. Being dead didn't give him special privileges when it came to behaving. He'd taken the reprimand poorly.

"I know what you did last night," Sonya pushed on, "and this is only your home when you behave respectfully to my things, to our friends, and our neighbors. You need to make it up to Mrs. Townsend. Otherwise, I'm simply disappointed in you and we will have to rethink our arrangement. You took it much too far."

The rose bush slowed to a complete stop and a thin mist congealed near a wrought iron table in the corner of the garden's lawn. Soon, Fritz's entire form sat at one of the chairs. He looked bedraggled and downhearted.

"I'm not worthy of your hospitality, Sonya. I feel like a cur," he said, his Scottish brogue adding a heart-melting sadness to his voice. "You'll not have me underfoot a moment longer. I'll go to the shack until I've mended my ways."

Sonya considered his dejected look and tone. Her heart softened like it always did when she knew he was truly contrite. The shack he spoke of was down along the coast of Alabama. Fritz had found the abandoned fishing cabin years ago and he liked to go there and soak up the sultry heat to make him feel more alive. She always knew when he'd been there. His Scottish brogue showed signs of vowel elongation and he took to wearing a white, Panama hat and Seersucker suits.

"Fritz, I've not asked you to leave. I've asked you to be kind to Mrs. Townsend. Whatever's gotten into you, I don't know, but there's more to this than what the storm blew in last night."

Sitting quietly, he sighed.

"Sonya, I'm feeling old, and I'm wondering why I haven't passed on to my reward. Sometimes when the wind and thunder roll in, I feel strong, robust, like I'm a young man again. There are days I miss being alive. Maybe, I need to jump on the up escalator and accept whatever's going to be doled out to me. I'm nervous to go. I've lived a wanton life, to be sure."

Sonya started to say something but halted. A throat being cleared behind her froze her into silence. Turning around slowly with an inward cringing feeling, her gaze came to rest on the bemused but handsome face of Sheriff Zeb Walker.

Across town Teddy Davidson, Roxy's widow, sat with his head in his hands and his backend in a well-padded, leather wingback. Nelson, his attorney and friend, was throwing questions at him regarding the last twenty-four hours of his life.

"So you worked at the race track garage until six o'clock last night and you went straight home. Can anyone verify the time you left?"

"I've told you," Teddy came back, "my pit crew manager left at five o'clock and I was the only person in the office. No one was around. Besides, can't the police have my phone tracked or look at the security footage from the parking lot?"

"We need to get the story straight," Nelson replied. "It's a murder investigation, buddy. The police are going to go over it again and again to test you. Now, did you see Roxy at all yesterday?"

"Yes, in the morning. She took the Golden Girls for a walk, you know, her dogs. The last time I saw her, I was leaving through the gate. I waved…"

Teddy's voiced broke on the last word and he quickly hung his head trying to handle the sudden, powerful wave of uncertainty flowing over him. His reaction was surprising even him. After a few moments, he forced himself to regain composure and cleared his throat.

"Sorry, Nelson. I can't believe she's gone," he gulped.

Chapter 7

He looked up at the friend he'd known since middle school. Their eyes locked for a fraction of a moment, but Teddy's shifted over to where a bottle of Scotch sat on a long credenza.

Nelson nodded and stood up. Going over to the credenza, he opened a sliding panel and took out two crystal, squat tumblers and filled them with the golden liquid. In a few short steps, he crossed the room back to Teddy and held out one of the drinks for him to take.

Teddy made a clearing sound in his throat and swallowed half the glass.

"Thanks, Nelson. I'm sorry. I'm not being much help."

Taking another pull from his glass, he leaned back into the deep, comforting wingback which sat across from Nelson's expensive, antique carved wooden desk.

"It's a horrible thing, Ted," his lawyer said. "No one can wrap their minds around it. Roxy was such a spit-fire, so full of life. I remember one time she got mad at me. We'd all been over to The Whole In the Wall to celebrate someone or other's birthday, and I made a mouthy comment about women getting fat when they're pregnant. I never saw it coming. Your wife turned and popped me right in the gut saying, 'It's not fat, it's a baby and it'll grow up. When will you, Nelson?'"

Nelson smiled and chuckled. The two men were quiet for a moment.

"Tell me again about yesterday morning," the lawyer resumed.

For what seemed to him like the hundredth time, Teddy related his story.

"Roxy always took her girls, the Golden Doodles, for a long walk every morning. She'd told me at breakfast she wouldn't be going into the office because of the press engagements for Dog Days. As you know, Roxy was the main spokesperson for Posh Pups."

Nelson shrugged, took a sip from his drink.

"So, you didn't talk to her at all after breakfast yesterday?"

"No, but I did get a text from Harry wanting me to meet him for lunch. He wanted to talk about Posh Pups."

Nelson pushed on.

"What did you do for the rest of the day? Did you go out for lunch with Harry? Can anyone confirm your whereabouts after work?"

There was a definite hesitation in Teddy's response.

"Well," he said, trying to find the right words. "I had lunch with Harry, who was his usual holier-than-thou self. He asked me about some personal stuff, you know, family gripes. Babette Nichols came in and she sat with us for a few moments. Harry left and she and I talked about the upcoming Dog Day events. Babs left and I went back to the garage. The rest of the day, I worked and when the storm was beginning to move in and I...I..."

"That's all?" Nelson asked. Teddy could feel him watching him with a hawk-like intensity.

Teddy looked up at him over the rim of his glass. He considered the truth and veered with a touch of vagueness to the left of it.

"After leaving the garage, I drove through and got a sandwich at Big Brother's Burgers then headed home. The storm was in full swing and I wanted to get the computers and televisions unplugged. We had a direct hit last spring and I didn't want a repeat."

He watched Nelson's face and then continued.

"I went to the basement, drank a beer and fell asleep on the sofa. The next thing I know, a deputy was banging on the door. Roxy's dogs were going crazy."

Nelson put his drink down softly on his desk and turned his body around in his chair. His stare was cold and direct.

"Ted, I know this is a hard time and I also know you loved your wife, but I get the feeling, call it professional intuition, there's another woman in the picture. We need to be on the offense with your testimony. What kind of family issues were you and Roxy having? Don't hang me out to dry on this, you're not going to shock me with the truth. I've heard it all."

Teddy mentally wrestled with what exactly was the truth and how not to be too forthcoming with it. Staring down into the glass and watching the Scotch swirl inside, he drew a long breath, held it and made a decision.

"Nelson, I…I've been with someone. I love Roxy of course. I mean—loved her. The other woman was…," he looked for the right words, "something on the side. I did it out of boredom. Roxy was always so busy with things. I kind of got shuffled to the side most days."

"Who was it?" Nelson demanded more than asked, his professional side exerting itself.

"Babs."

"Babette Nichols," Nelson said quietly, the corner of his mouth twitched up in an appreciative smile, but was quickly subdued. "How long's it been going on?"

"It's only happened a few times. I was so tired of Roxy never being around. She wasn't exactly keeping our bed warm for me. Babs is gorgeous and came on really hard."

"Was anyone privy to this info besides you and Babs?"

"I think Roxy knew. She might have told Harry. When Babette came over to the table yesterday, I nearly choked on my food. Harry got up, threw some money down on the table and went to the restroom. He came back and said he needed to go because he had a meeting with a vendor."

"I'll have to give Harry a call," Nelson reasoned. "How are things over at Posh Pups?"

"Harry's got this potential deal with a buyer for Posh Pups and Roxy's been against it from the beginning. I'd love nothing better than to sell that barnacle of a business, but I'm tied to it if I want to keep driving the circuit," he paused considering his glass as a smile slowly spread across his face. "I just realized I don't have to worry about that anymore."

"Harry wants to sell Posh Pups?" Nelson asked, his eyes narrowing.

"Well, as much as Harry wants anything different than what his old man wanted. Old Sweeny was a ball buster. Doted on his wife and daughter, but treated men like dirt. Harry and Roxy were at odds about selling the business. She wanted to buy him and Deidra out."

"Why didn't you?" Nelson asked.

"We didn't have a lot of money, my friend. Stock car racing is an expensive hobby. Roxy wanted to pull back on my spending. I told her we needed to sell the business."

"You're in deep water, Theodore," Nelson said. "Infidelity is a strong motive to kill your wife. You'd better put the quits on any more messing about with Babs. Do you understand?"

"When Babette came over to the table yesterday I was going to tell her we needed to cool it for a while, but we were interrupted by the waiter. The best I was able to do was tell her to meet me last night at her house. We met and well, you know. Things happened. Afterward, she said she had some things to take care of over at her studio, so I left and grabbed a hamburger at Big Brothers."

Nelson sat like a bird of prey watching Teddy as if he was a titmouse scurrying around beneath him. His expression was cynical and brooding.

"We need to be upfront with the prosecuting attorney. If the police find any reason you should be a suspect and believe me, Ted, you are one, the more we show good faith in this, the better for you in the long run."

Teddy jumped in.

"I had no idea Roxy was going over to her brother's house, no idea whatsoever. Last night was some book thing at Kayla's. I knew she wouldn't be home and I could meet Babs without drawing much attention to myself."

He sat back in his chair again and groaned. Turning Nelson's words over in his mind further, he said, "It *was* a break-in, wasn't it? Someone wanting to rob Harry and Deidra's place and Rox was in the wrong place at the wrong time?"

"I'm sorry, Teddy. Nothing was stolen. Nothing. Zeb Walker has declared it to be a murder investigation. You stand to gain half of Posh Pups, which according to this conversation, you wanted to sell and Roxy was determined not to."

"Forever, I wanted Roxy to slow down. I wanted us to get out of Willow Valley. She wouldn't go…she wanted to stay. This thing with Babs surprises even me, but I have feelings for her now and I want to be with her."

Nelson leaned back in his chair causing its hinges to let out a slow, tormented screech. He studied his client thoughtfully and finally responded.

"That, my friend, is what they call having a motive. No, let me rephrase, Ted. In your situation, *that's* what they call having *three* motives for murder."

Chapter 8

Catching her breath, Sonya's heart beat rapidly in her chest as Zeb Walker continued to lean on her garden gate and study her with a good deal of amusement on his face.

Realizing she was blushing and feeling a slight awkwardness at being caught talking to a rose bush, she quickly said, "Good Morning, sheriff. Out checking to see if the good people of Pickwick Place survived last night's storm?"

A dark cloud passed over his face. She watched as Zeb shifted his position uncomfortably and his smile completely vanished.

Sonya made her way over to the fence. His tired eyes and stubbled chin told her he'd had a rough night. With the storm wreaking havoc and emergency calls from citizens, he'd probably lost more than a few hours of sleep.

Walker offered a second weak smile. His gaze darted back and forth between Sonya and the table where Fritz had only moments ago been sitting. She knew he was trying to decide whether she was completely insane or if there was more to her earlier conversation with garden furniture.

"Actually, Mrs. Caruthers, I'm here on official business. Do you have time to answer a few questions?"

"Of course, sheriff. Why don't you come inside? I've got some chocolate, cherry dump cake coming out of the oven in about ten minutes. It's supposed to be a gift of atonement for a wronged neighbor, but we can have a nibble. How about some coffee, and some decent breakfast, too? You look like you need some sustenance."

The weary man nodded appreciatively.

"I wouldn't turn either down," he said. "It's been a helluva night."

He appeared to hesitate.

"I'm sorry Mrs. Caruthers. I hope I haven't offended you."

Sonya chuckled.

"Oh, sheriff, let's get some food in you first. We can decide afterward if you need deportment lessons with Miss Seaton teen's cotillion classes at the community center."

Zeb laughed softly and followed her up the front porch stairs and into Sonya's pretty, Victorian house. Painted yellow with white trim and flower boxes at every window, Number 11 Pickwick Place could have easily graced the front cover of a glossy home or travel magazine.

A high-backed, wooden porch swing with brightly covered chintz pillows hung adjacent to a white, wicker table and chairs which served as an outside dining area during good weather days. Pulling open the screen door, Sonya let Willard run across the threshold first and signaled to the sheriff to follow the terrier's lead.

"He knows it's time for a treat," she said as they moved from the foyer into the dining room. "Willard is nothing if not punctual regarding his treat schedule."

Within a few minutes, Sonya removed the chocolate-cherry dump cake from the oven resulting in the room being filled with a most tantalizing smell. The sheriff sat at her kitchen bar, hunched over a steaming cup of coffee and munching on a bowl of granola with fresh berries. His hostess, with a wicked twinkle in her eye, explained he must eat something decent before plowing into something decadent.

As she put two pieces of cake on sturdy, mustard-colored plates, Zeb explained the reason for his visit.

"Mrs. Caruthers do you know how Meadowmere Place backs up against Pickwick Place?" he asked, as she handed him his plate.

"I do. The houses on my side of the street share the rock wall boundary with Meadowmere Place," Sonya replied.

"Last night, a woman, Roxy Davidson, was murdered at twenty-one Weller Street. She was found dead in her brother's house. By any chance, you didn't hear or see anyone coming down the alley behind your house?" he asked and then taking a sip of his coffee.

Sonya, remembering last night's chaos with Fritz, shook her head ruefully.

"Unfortunately, sheriff, I only heard the storm and some other noises from... well, a guest of mine. But poor Mrs. Townsend had a rough night also. I saw her heading to Mr. Poindexter's," she pointed to her left in the direction of the kitchen window. "She may have been a bit disoriented, but perhaps she or Mr. Poindexter saw something."

Sonya tilted her head and studied the sheriff.

"There's something more to this," she said slowly. "You can tell me, sheriff. I'm discreet."

She watched as he bowed his head and studied the half-eaten cake on his plate as if trying to find the right words. As he looked back up at her, his lips compressed in a hard line. Something in his eyes told her he was struggling with what he had to say.

"Roxy Davidson, the woman who was killed last night, was *seen* by her brother."

Sonya waited for him to offer more, but he said nothing.

"I don't think I'm following you," she finally said.

Zeb scrunched up his mouth to one side and gave Sonya a penetrating look.

"You see, Mrs. Caruthers, there's a bit of a problem. I need someone to help me understand how Harry Sweeny saw Roxy Davidson standing in the middle of Interstate 44 looking very much alive when our county coroner claims that at the same time, she'd been dead for well over an hour."

Chapter 9

"The Golden Paw Award is as good as mine this year, Babette," Mrs. Tamara Lilton said over the phone to her friend. "You're miniature poodles won't have a Husky's chance in Hell of winning this year. I've got the trophy *and* the ten thousand dollar prize in the bag."

The woman on the other end of the line snorted with contempt.

"Poodles are anything but passé, Tamara," Babette corrected and continued in a mocking, tone. "Three of the judges from Posh Pups own them and for five of the last nine years, a poodle has taken the award. My bet is on my breed and your Lhasa Apsos will have to be content with a third place ribbon as usual."

Babette Nicols and Tamara Lilton had a twisted definition for the word friendship. Since they'd met in sixth grade they'd been cohorts. Neither was minion to the other's dark overlord. In high school, they worked more like top-tiered predators who liked to hunt as a team, feeding on their prey together.

Babette was blonde and this had given her a leg-up, so to speak, in the early years when it came to defiling other people's marital relationships, but it was Tamara who in the end achieved the more elevated status in the minds of the two women. Tams had snagged a rising corporate star.

Patrick Lilton had landed in one of the ultimate promise lands for executives, a Fortune 500 company called Titan.

It was a big-box retailer headquartered in St. Louis, Missouri, and Patrick was its CEO.

Replying to Babette's dig regarding her Lhasas' chances at the prize money, Tamara said, "Roxy Davidson loves her Golden Doodles, but she just received two adorable Lhasas. Patrick and I had dinner with her and Teddy two weeks ago. She's absolutely ga ga over her new dogs."

Tamara paused in her name dropping exercise intended to sting Babette and remind her of her social inferiority.

"Oh, I do forget sometimes, Babs, that you probably don't have a clue how global business is run. Suffice it to say, Patrick is interested in knowing more about Posh Pups and the Davidsons invited us to dinner."

Babs couldn't help giving Tamara a good swipe of her own claw.

"It must have been tough playing nice-nice with Patrick's old college sweetheart. Does he still pine for her much? Besides, Tamara, you might be surprised by who I'm friends with other than *you*. Roxy Davidson isn't the only judge on the panel. Teddy, her husband is a friend of mine."

There was a significant pause on Tamara's end of the conversation. Wondering if she'd hit bone, a twinge of a smile plucked at the corner of Bab's mouth. Finally, she heard a condescending laugh come through the line.

"I'm sure any teenage fling between Roxy and Patrick, was just that — a fling," Tamara said. "As for Teddy, he's Roxy's pet, if ever there was one. He practically worships the ground she walks on. He'll only vote for who she tells him to. Besides, I have another trick up my sleeve to win the Golden Paw."

Babs was quiet. She knew Tamara was baiting her, but she didn't want to give the smug witch the satisfaction of actually asking. The uncomfortable silence finally needled Tamara into plowing forward with her tasty secret morsel.

"You do know that Titan, Patrick's company, is considering acquiring Posh Pups?" Tamara revealed.

"Is that why you made such a nice gift of the two Lhasas to Roxy?" Babs asked, her tone derisive. "To butter her up? Nice move, Tams. Help Patrick and help yourself. You've always been so economical in your steps toward world domination."

Tamaras' hearty laugh coming through the phone stopped.

"How'd you know *I* gave her the Lhasas? I never said it was me."

Babette maneuvered cagily through her misstep.

"It doesn't take a mental giant to put two and two together, Tamara. You gave Roxy a gift and you want to make her love Lhasas Apso. Besides, Greta Parks, the other pilates instructor, told me Roxy was talking about receiving some dogs from someone trying to butter her up before the Golden Paw competition."

"Now, now, now, Babsy," Tamara cooed. "You're being so snarky. I'm sure my puppy present to Roxy Davidson was more about me sharing my great love of Lhasas with another devotee of the breed."

"You are so full of it!" Babs blurted out and laughed again. "I've gotta go, Tams. Good luck at the competition. You're gonna need it!"

She put the phone down into its cradle and let out a frustrated scream. Tamara loved taking any opportunity to remind Babette of her social inferiority and it was a bitter pill Babs was tired of swallowing. Winning the Golden Paw award would be a delicious victory.

Catching her reflection in her dance studio's mirrors, a smile spread bewitchingly across Babs' face.

"Tamara," she murmured to herself, "You're about to be dethroned. I can't wait to see your face when you are left standing empty-handed at the awards ceremony and Patrick loses Posh Pups for Titan."

Chapter 10

"An hour *after* she was dead?" Sonya repeated.

Sheriff Walker nodded in the affirmative.

"Yep, and to make it even more unusual, Harry Sweeny said his sister," he took out a notebook and read from it, "looked sad."

"Oh, how awful for him," Sonya whispered.

"Well, it nearly scared Harry to death. He almost wrecked his car trying to slow his vehicle down, but because of the rain, he says he slid straight through her. When he got the car stopped, he searched for her, but she wasn't there."

Sonya shook her head. She'd seen this before with apparitions.

Zeb continued.

"It was Harry Sweeny's wife who called us at around nine o'clock last night, in a state of hysteria. She'd found her sister-in-law's body in a hallway of their home. The dead woman had a contusion to her right temple."

"Did the police arrive before Mr. Sweeny did?" Sonya asked.

"Oh yes," the sheriff answered. "We have a statement from him. He pulled into the driveway as our emergency and forensic teams arrived."

Sonya softly sighed.

"What can I do to help?"

"Harry Sweeny is convinced he saw his sister in the middle of the highway. On the other hand, I have to consider why he would make that claim. He may have something to hide or needs an alibi."

Sonya fiddled with her fork and picked up her coffee to take a sip. She waited for Zeb to decide if he wanted to ask the resident ghost whisperer for her help.

"Harry Sweeny is adamant he didn't have anything to do with his sister's murder. He feels she may have walked in on a burglary. The Sweenys claim to have no clue why Roxy Davidson, the victim, was even in their home last night. She hadn't been invited over and they both had prior commitments for evening. We're checking the phone company's records of Roxy's text messages."

Sonya gave Sheriff Walker an encouraging smile along with a tilt of her head, hoping he'd get to the point of his visit.

"Okay, okay," he finally grumbled. "Would you consider putting out your feelers?"

He made a silly gesture of wiggling his fingers as he said the last two words.

"Are you asking me to see if Roxy is still lingering and if she knows who her murderer is?" Sonya asked, giving him back a snarky look.

She liked seeing Zeb Walker stew a bit. Besides, watching him was enjoyable. He was definitely easy on the eyes.

"Well, this situation reminds me of the Poppy Turner mystery you helped us with last spring. If Harry Sweeny is lying about seeing his dead sister's ghost or if you can dig anything else up, I'd appreciate the help."

"Okay," Sonya replied, offering him a warmer smile, "I will look into it, so to speak. I'm sorry for Roxy and her family. She may have passed over already, but I'll send out a push to see if she's still around."

"Good, and if anyone should mention to you anything unusual about last night, please give me a call," he said rising from his stool. "Oh, and one more thing, you may need to know. Roxy Davidson was in her late thirties and had red hair. Don't want there to be any confusion which ghost we're looking for," he said scratching the back of his head in an expression of slight uncertainty.

Sonya laughed out loud.

"I think I've got it: redheaded and newly departed. Shouldn't have any trouble with that description."

As they walked out of the house, he thanked her for the delicious breakfast. Tipping his hat to her in a pleasant way, she watched from the porch as his police vehicle pulled away from the curb and disappeared down the tree-lined street.

Death, especially one so cruel, was always so difficult to understand, Sonya mused to herself as her gaze turned back to her ravaged garden.

Since her return from Cornwall, where she went most summers to get away from the intense Missouri heat, Sonya hadn't spent any time working as a ghost therapist but had busied herself with getting her house and garden in order for the autumn days ahead.

Taking a deep breath, she let it out and turned her gaze away from the yard. If she was going to help Sheriff Walker and Roxy Davidson, she needed to get in the right frame of mind. This meant using every available asset she had, even the difficult to handle ones.

"Fritz!" she called as she walked into her house. "I hope you're still here. We've got work to do!"

Chapter 11

The sound of a woman weeping woke him from his dream. He struggled to move, but his limbs were like stone, completely cold, heavy and lifeless. As if his body were a dumb thing, unable to respond, he struggled to make it answer his will. Could it be, he wondered, that somehow his mind was detached from his body?

A memory pulled at his consciousness, or was it the lingering effects of the dream? His friend's image weakly took shape in his mind, but the face with its merry eyes and shaggy beard melted before it was completely restored. If only he could remember.

The sobbing resumed, this time he was aware of longing and fear in the woman's crying. He tried to rise, to shake off the lull and pull of the dream. Somehow he instinctively knew the woman belonged to him, though he had no memory of her. With a great surge of will, he forced his being to respond, to wake up, and to throw off the incapacitation of his limbs.

"Why me?" the woman cried. "Why me? I want to go home!"

The spell broke over him. He came free of his resting place and instantly he found himself standing in a beautiful garden. Above him was the bright sun, warm in the early morning sky and around him were flowers, thick grass, and the wind.

Air surrounded his body. He could feel the breeze lifting and playfully whipping through his fur like an old friend grateful to see him after a long absence.

The deep, rich smell of the ground filled his nostrils causing his brain to overload with inexplicable pleasure. True to his kind, he happily lay down in the grass rolling back and forth trying to immerse himself in its delicate perfume.

As he turned over one more time, he saw her. She stood over him, tears still in her eyes, but smiling the way humans do when they've seen something pleasing to them.

"Who are you?" she said softly to him which naturally made him sit up, grin and thump his tail in his best friendly greeting.

She crouched down beside him, and giving his head a good scratching, she joined him on the grass. Knowing instantly she was good because her scent was free of cruelty, he performed his best front paw stretch and jumped up into her lap. One kind deed deserved another so he gave her cheek a good lick.

"Hey!" she said laughing, the skin around her eyes crinkling from her broad smile. "You're just what I needed. It's been a rough day or night, I'm not sure which is which anymore. You wouldn't happen to know where everyone is, would you? Are we the only living things around?"

She gave him a good fur ruffling pat along his back.

He wagged his tail with enthusiasm. Things were slowly coming back to him. Jumping down from her lap, he sprinted around the garden, his ears in the wind and his tongue lolling happily from his open mouth. The woman laughed at his joyful antics.

"What a crazy boy you are?" she called. "Come here, my little man!"

He ran to her. She picked him up and kissed him on the top of his head between his two shaggy ears.

"I'm so grateful you are here," she said. "I'd like to leave my brother's back yard and never come back. Something horrible happened in there, but I can't remember exactly what. Each time I try to leave, fear grips me. You're the first friendly face."

He watched as she looked up at the grand house and studied it for a while. Ever so gently she tightened her hold on him, but finally sighed and returned her gaze down to his.

Cocking his head, he tried to read her thoughts. Her mood lightened almost instantly and her facial muscles relax into a sad grin.

"I always love it when my dogs cock their heads," she said. "There's something so intelligent and caring in that head tilt."

She hugged him to her and he felt such happiness.

"Let's try to get out of here…," she said to him and cocked her head in a way indicating to him she was trying to figure something out. "What should I call you, you little beast?"

He went completely still. That sound she made, he hadn't heard it in such a long time. He looked deeply into her eyes and willed her to say it again. Her expression turned quizzical as their mutual unflinching gaze locked for a brief moment.

"What was it I said?" she asked, her words coming out slowly. "Was it when I called you a *beast*?"

There it was. That word again. It sent him into exciting spasms and he wiggled in her embrace. She laughed as she tried to hold him in her arms.

"I do believe your name must have been Beast. Odd name, but it somehow fits," she mused out loud. "It's like when someone calls a mischievous young boy, Stinker, more out of love than annoyance. Okay, Beast. How about you and I get out of here? I need some answers and sitting around her boohooing won't get me any. Let's roll."

She put him down on the ground and he followed her as she walked toward the garden gate.

"First stop, I want to go back to my own house. I was there but somehow came back here. I want you to meet my girls, Bea, Rue, and Betty. They're my Golden Doodle girls and…" she froze in mid-stride.

Beast instantly sensed another energy coming toward them. His hackles raised ever so slightly and a soft, low growl crept through his being. The woman's smell turned from relaxed to fearful.

"Should we stay here?" she whispered and moved back in the direction of the house, but as they got closer to the structure, she stopped and stood rigid in the yard like she was unsure of what to do.

Beast, with a strong desire to protect the woman, trotted in front of her. He saw a shadowy thing hovering in the vegetation near the garden's stone wall. It watched them and stayed quiet. With a string of rapid, aggressive barks, Beast let the interloper know that he would defend his human.

"I see it, too," the woman said, her voice edged with uncertainty.

Slowly from under a snowball bush came another small dog. It stayed in a low position, more like a crawl on its belly than a trot of any kind.

Remaining rigid, his tail up and his focus intense, Beast was ready to go into battle if needed. The other dog, a brown terrier, thumped its tail in a friendly gesture and gave a short whine. An understanding was made between the two canines and Beast relaxed.

Willard, Sonya's terrier, resumed his normal stance on all four legs and continued the easy tail wag as he approached them.

"Follow me," he said to Beast. "Bring the human, too. I've been watching you both from the alley behind this house. I know someone who can help you…both."

Beast looked back at the woman. His earlier feelings of joy at being alive now subdued. He could sense her returning fear and uncertainty.

"Why should we follow you?" he asked the brown dog.

"Cause I know something neither of you do know," Willard replied with an easy wagging of his tail.

"What's that?"

"You're both dead."

Chapter 12

"Put the tents for the vendors down along the first half of the street. The two big tents, for the indoor arenas, will be set up in the park."

A tall, young man was balling out orders and pointing in the direction of Willow Park, the main location where Dog Days would take place.

"My butts on the line, boys! Put some muscle into it!"

With a gleam in his eye, he watched as the crew unloaded the tents. His attention to detail was rigorous. From his excellent choice of clothes to his well-polished shoes, Presley King was not only a man of exceptional style, but he was also the person you wanted when you had a deadline and Dog Days was one enormous deadline.

It was the biggest event of the year for Willow Valley. Visitors from all over the Midwest would cram into the town for three days of pooch parades, dog grooming demonstrations, and the chance to buy anything from canine cowboy booties to pup treats.

The grand finale was a fashion and talent show sponsored by Posh Pups, the largest regional retailer for dog lovers and their furry canine babies. The winner took home the coveted Golden Paw award and a check for ten thousand dollars. If you were a dog breeder or a dog devotee, ten grand gave you a leg-up on improving your business or you and your dog's lifestyle.

Presley was the key to the event's success and people knew it. If he said jump, people jumped. The revenue generated by Dog Days for the businesses in Willow Valley was enormous. This year, celebrities were involved, causing television news stations from Kansas City and St. Louis to follow the festivities.

One much-loved celebrity was Stace Dee, a cozy mystery writer, invited by Mayor Claxton to bring her beagle, Maggie, to officiate as the Dog Days Ambassador and be the Grand Marshall for the Pooch Parade. The Dog Days committee was ecstatic they'd accepted. Maggie was a beagle with a nose for solving crime, but her real allure was how incredibly cute she looked in her deerstalker cap.

Presley, out of the corner of his eye, watched as a police vehicle approached and came to a stop beside him. He turned and squinted his eyes against the sun to see who it was.

Inside, Tommy Kirchner, Willow Valley's Deputy Sheriff, and his police dog, Sheba, were both wearing friendly smiles. As Tommy rolled down his car window, the air conditioning escaped. It was a welcome relief from the mugginess of the day.

"You got your work cut out for ya, P.K.," Tommy said. "Dog Days is already filling up with tourists. Just had to ticket a lady trying to jump the gun by selling her stuff out of her trunk. She didn't have a retail license yet. By the way, I saw your mom talking with Miss Willa Lemming the other day. They looked chummy almost as if they were coming up with ideas on how to get you to the wedding altar."

P.K., as he'd been known in high school, leaned down into the driver's window with a grin you give to your closest friend. He knew Tommy was ribbing him. His mother wasn't home from St. Louis yet. As for Willa Lemming, she and Rosalie, his mother, weren't on speaking terms since Presley had broken up with Willa two months ago. Both women had been severely disappointed. They both wanted a wedding, but Presley wasn't ready.

He punched Tommy's arm through the window.

"Don't you have tickets to give to unfortunate senior citizens? I see you're still driving around with the only woman who'll have anything to do with you?" he razzed back and pointed to Sheba. "As for Willa and my mama, they can drum up ideas all day long about marriage and babies. I'm avoiding all of the above."

The two men shared a laugh. They'd been good friends since the day Presley had pulled two second grade, playground gorillas off of Tommy. Presley had sent them running with threats of having his older brother Wesley use them as tackling dummies. It had been a good bluff that turned into a great friendship.

"You're gonna hate me, P.K.," Tommy said, his tone turning somber.

Presley's shoulders slumped and he dropped his chin onto his arms now resting on the driver's window.

"Why do I have the feeling you're here officially?" he asked.

"Yeah, it's a pretty sad business. A woman was murdered last night. The home where her body was found shares a corner with Willow Park. We need about twenty-four hours to have the forensic team do their thing so that means you'll have to hold off putting up the big tents for another day."

Presley groaned and gently thumped his forehead against the back of his forearms.

"Dang it!" he said returning to an upright position with a sigh.

"Sorry to hear about the woman, Tommy. We can make it work and I hope you find the person responsible. Can I ask who was murdered? Has to be a neighbor of mine. I live on Weller."

Tommy returned a grim expression with a shake of his head.

"Sorry, bud, but until we have some leads, I've been threatened within an inch of my life to keep it quiet."

"No worries. I'll know by the end of the day anyway. This town holds no secrets for very long."

Presley gave his friend an encouraging smile.

"That's the truth," Tommy agreed. "Let's go fishing when this thing is over. Fish are biting on Indian Creek. Let's do a run down there soon."

Presley gave the deputy a wave as the car pulled away from the curb. Officers were already starting to wrap yellow tape along the park's perimeter. A muddled memory of a female voice coming from his brother Wesley's room last night tapped timidly at his brain. His mother's flight had been canceled out of Chicago, so he'd turned around and driven home in the storm.

"Wesley must have thought he had the house to himself last night. Thank God Mama won't be home until later. I wonder who he had up there last night?" he thought to himself.

A twinge of uneasiness needled at the base of his brain. Time to check up on his older brother. With one last visual review that the placement of the vendor tents was going as planned, Presley texted his assistant, Carrie, saying he had an errand to run and he'd check in with her later.

He headed to his car, got in, started the engine and turned the air conditioning to full blast. The heat in southern Missouri, even in September, can turn you into a puddle of sweat in less than a minute.

"Wesley," he said to his non-present brother under his breath, "I hope you've got the sense to get whoever you're with out of the house before mom gets home this afternoon."

The car's interior cooled as Presley made the turns necessary to arrive at the home he shared with his mother and brother. Though he could easily afford a place of his own, he understood the meaning of responsibility, and in this case, it meant being there for his mother and keeping his brother out of trouble.

The trees were beginning to show signs that summer was giving way to autumn. Leaves the colors of yellow, red and orange where beginning to languidly waft along unseen air currents throughout Willow Valley's old-fashioned neighborhoods until they came to rest bestowing one final, beautiful blessing upon yards, houses, roads and sidewalks alike.

Presley couldn't help feeling grateful each time he drove the familiar, quaint streets of his neighborhood. A low, limestone rock wall running along the right of the road announced the upcoming entrance to Meadowmere Place. Beside the curb sat a compact car with a bright yellow tennis ball sticker on its back window with the name Sam.

"That car wasn't here this morning. Tennis, huh?" he mumbled out loud. "I didn't know Wesley had any friends who played tennis."

Pulling up through his family's driveway, he stopped the car and turned off the engine.

"Well Mama's not here yet," he said out loud to himself, noting her car wasn't in its usual place yet.

Time to check on his brother.

Going inside, he went bounding up the stairs calling, "Wesley! You home?"

A giggle and the soft tone of a woman's voice came from his brother's bedroom, telling Presley that Wesley was not with one of his guy friends, but, as usual, it was a woman. Needing answers, he went ahead and knocked on the door.

Appearing at the half-cracked door revealing initially only one annoyed-looking eye, Wesley slipped quickly out of his bedroom door, shutting it immediately behind him. He was wearing only his boxers.

"Guest?" Presley asked his tone and facial expression equally as annoyed.

"What's up?" Wesley asked, deflecting any direct admission of guilt.

"Who's in there?" Presley demanded. "Is her name Sam? I saw a sticker on the car."

"That's none of your business baby brother," Wesley said smiling and throwing a mock jab at Presley's abdomen area. "A gentleman doesn't throw a lady's name around."

Presley shook his head and replied, "Fine, but I gotta ask you a question. Did you have anyone up here last night? Or, did you go out in the storm?"

Wesley lowered his head and looked up at his brother through long dark lashes. The King brothers were handsome and Wesley appeared to consider his choice of words before speaking.

"I wasn't alone last night, but I didn't go outside. Who goes outside Presley in the middle of a hurricane?"

Whoever was frantically dressing in his brother's bedroom, Presley knew they most likely were able to easily hear the brother's conversation.

In a whisper, Wesley said, "Let me call you later. We can talk then." He made a shewing gesture at Presley. "Now go on and git. I need to wrap things up baby brother." He did a side nod toward the bedroom door. "The lady needs to leave and I don't want you gawking as she goes. Vamoose! I'll be waiting to see your car pull out."

Presley didn't move, but pushed on with his interrogation.

"Wesley, Tommy Kirchner said a woman was murdered last night in this neighborhood. You know how Willow Park backs up on the corner of our property?"

Wesley nodded and his gaze glanced nervously over to the bedroom door.

"Well, they've shut it down for a forensic team. It has to be one of the houses in Meadowmere where the body was found. Did you see anything or did you go out yourself last night? There was water all over the floor when I got home."

"It wasn't me," Wesley said, his tone turning serious. "Go on, Presley. We can talk later. I'll be home all evening."

Presley knew the conversation was over. His brother wanted him out of his hair to wrap things up with the mystery woman waiting to escape down the back stairs. He sighed and let it go.

Giving Wesley a worried look, he said, "Mama's going to be home probably soon. You'd better hurry with the goodbyes. Sure you've got nothing to say about last night?"

The other man shook his head. His gaze melting into warm affection, he reached over and grabbed Presley pulling him into a bear-like hug and answered, "Presley quit being a mother hen. I'll see you later. We can talk then."

Presley gave him a sour, unconvinced look, but not moving away.

Wesley reached over and playfully chuffing his brother's head, he added, "I promise to see you later. When have I ever broken my word to you?"

"Never," Presley grudgingly answered, the corner of his mouth turning up into a half smile.

"Then remember that — never it is."

Chapter 13

Willard took the trip home slow. He knew ghosts were flaky creatures and rarely followed normal human modes of behavior, but the two behind him appeared happy to be led anywhere. Every fifty feet or so, Willard checked to mak sure they were still in tow. Sure enough, they were always there.

Without any problems, they arrived at the back of Sonya's property. Willard's hearing picked up his mistress talking to Pickwick Street's mailman. As he rounded the ancient snowball bush at the edge of the front porch, he caught sight of Sonya talking at the edge of the fence. Wary the two ghosts might evaporate, he took special care to go slow.

Hanging over the garden's front gate where the two humans deep in conversation about all the excitement going on around Dog Days, the storm, and the death of Roxy Davidson. Like all small towns, nothing happened everyone didn't know about within twenty-four hours. Willard could hear Lou saying everyone at Tilly's Cafe thought it was probably one of the tourists or vendors coming into town for Dog Days.

With an encouraging wag of his tail, he told the ghost dog to wait. Trotting up to the fence next to Sonya, he stuck his head between two boards to see if Lou the Chihuahua, the mailman's official mascot, was sitting in the mail truck's window-seat on his perch.

Sure enough, upon seeing Willard's head poke through the fence, Lou offered a few friendly yaps in the way of a greeting. It was obvious he had some gossip of his own to share. He was shaking with excitement from the tips of his twitching ears to the tip of his whirring tail.

"Hey, Willard. Did you hear the news?" he asked.

"No, what's up?"

"The girls, Gigi, Zsa Zsa, Mimi, and Chéri are back in town!"

"So?"

Lou's shakes intensified at Willard's casual indifference to his announcement.

"Dog! Are you deaf? I said, the girls are back in town. Don't you want to see them again this year?" Lou asked, his bark tone going up an octave.

"Nah, I'm still licking my wounds from last time we had anything to do with those she-wolfs. Besides, I've got work to do. Can you get a message over to the two beagles, Lewis and Clark for me?"

"The girls are not she-wolfs, Willard. They are Miniature Poodles!" Lou barked.

Willard was sorry for his pal's confusion at his indifference. Last year, they'd enjoyed a great three days getting to know the cast from Poodles Galore who came as an entertainment venue for Dog Days.

With a sigh, Lou laid his head upon the mail truck's window seal, and after a short pause, he said sullenly, "Okay what's the message for Lewis and Clark?"

"Tell them to bring Marnie for a visit to Sonya's. I've found two ghosts over at Pickle's house. You know, the old dog who lives on the other side of the alley. I think the boys might be able to tell me more about what's going on over there. Can't beat a beagle's nose."

Lou gave Willard a peevish look.

"Alright, I'll do it. I probably won't see them until tomorrow. We've already delivered over at the campground today. Will ya at least think about visiting the girls tomorrow? They're staying at the motel out on fifty-nine highway. We could jump on one of the buses that drop off over there."

"Nah, Gigi is snippy and a drama queen. You go on without me, Lou. I'm a hot-tempered Scott. Best to leave the french ladies to the Latin lover types like you."

Lou nodded sagely in agreement at Willard's truth.

Larry, Lou's human, was walking back toward the mail truck, and Sonya made her way inside the house.

As the truck pulled out into the street, Lou caught sight of Beast poking his head through the slats next to Willard. The Chihuahua toppled from his perch causing Larry to run up onto the curb and bounce off it again. Willard's eyes brightened and he panted a huge dog smile as the box-shaped vehicle wobbled from one side of the road to the other in Larry's attempts to reinstall Lou back on his famous perch.

"Come on," Willard said to Beast. "It's time to meet Sonya. She should be able to help you both. Make sure the human stays with us."

But before the unusual threesome finished climbing the porch stairs, Sonya appeared at the screen door and came through. With an expression of delighted wonder, she held out her hands in a welcoming greeting.

"Hello," she said drawing out the word. "How wonderful for Willard to have brought you here. Please come inside. You'll be safe here. I think you must have questions and I can help you."

Chapter 14

Mrs. Rosalie King looked much younger than her actual years. Elegantly dressed, pearls at her neck and skin still smooth except for laugh lines at the corners of her eyes, Rosalie, like her sons, had style and beauty.

As Presley and Wesley's mother, she'd been the perfect domestic goddess when they were growing up. It had been easy. Her husband, Morris, had been an orthopedic surgeon. Money hadn't been an issue allowing Rosalie to build her own small business using her natural flair for interior decorating to dress the best houses in Willow Valley and beyond.

Her talent and practice had come in handy. When Morris died from a heart attack, she'd put the insurance payout into trust funds for her boys and paid off the family home in Meadowmere Place. She opened up an interior design firm that grew to enjoy both local and international clients. Rosalie was in demand from St. Louis to San Francisco and Bali to Brazil. If you wanted your house decorated by her, you'd better arrange for a private car or jet. She didn't come cheap.

The problem with the King parents' success was it was a hard act to follow. Though Presley was doing well, Wesley was comfortable living the life of a privileged man-child. So, as Rosalie King's taxi pulled in through her house's front gates, she scowled. Wesley's car was still in the driveway even though he should be at work.

"He's supposed to be at the school," she said through semi-clenched teeth. "What is it going to take to get him motivated! Maybe, if I chuck him out on his backend, he'll learn how to work."

After the taxi came to a stop beside Wesley's convertible BMW, she got out and waited for the driver to retrieve the luggage. Something sparkled on the driveway, catching her attention. Rosalie cocked her head to one side in a gesture of recognition and confusion.

"That's Wesley's watch," she half muttered. "It's completely crushed."

On the ground between her car and his, was her son's watch half mashed into the cobblestones of the drive. Bending down, Rosalie reached out and picked up the timepiece's remains.

"Wesley," she said, her words a whisper, but thick with sudden uncertainty.

She knew he loved that watch she'd given him at Christmas. Odd that he would leave it like that. A tiny sliver of fear rose in her mind and stabbed at her memory. Once, at a picnic when the boys were only five and seven years old, they'd disappeared. Now as then, her intuition told her something was wrong. When she'd gone looking for them, she found them wandering off into a parking lot following a soccer ball. A man was driving a large truck and unable to see them in between the other parked vehicles. If Rosalie hadn't screamed when she did, Presley would have surely been hit.

Turning her eyes up to where she knew Wesley's bedroom was, she hurried into her house.

"Wesley!" she called.

The house echoed back her voice. Nothing moved except the striking of the grandfather clock in the front room telling her it was six o'clock. Heading upstairs, she came to her first born's bedroom. The door was wide open and inside, the bed was a rumpled mess. At least things looked normal.

In the space of time it took her to go from the car to his bedroom, her mind threw out simple, comforting possibilities for why his car was home, but he was not.

"Presley," she said the name like it was a life-line. "He'll use the app on his phone to find his brother."

Rosalie knew, like most older people, the young had unique ways of staying in touch. Her sons had an app on their smartphones which allowed them to locate each other. She'd asked if they would share their locations with her, but Wesley just laughed and quickly made his escape.

Pulling her phone from her jacket pocket, she tapped the name Presley on her contacts. She waited for his sweet voice to come on the line.

"Oh, I'm so glad you answered, baby," she said, her tone worried and a bit shaky.

"Hey, Mama," came his gentle reply. Of her two boys, Presley was most like his father. He always treated her with protective kindness.

"Honey, I can't find Wesley. His watch is in the driveway completely crushed and…"

She hesitated and continued, "His car is here. Will you look for him? On your phone thing. You know what I mean."

She waited, anxiously on the phone for his reply.

"Hang on, Mama. I'm sure Wesley's fine. He was just there. Most likely, he's out with Clay or Zak. Let me call you right back. Will you be okay for a minute?" he asked.

"Yes. honey. Thank you."

Rosalie tapped her phone to end the call and stood in the middle of her oldest son's messy room. Wesley had been a difficult child to raise from the beginning. In elementary school, he'd been rebellious and frustrated with learning. Later, in middle school, he found football and things turned around. Throughout college, he'd been a star player.

Unfortunately, a car accident his senior year ended any hopes for playing pro ball. That's when the real trouble started. Losing his dream of the NFL shut down his confidence and he spiraled into deeper problems.

It broke Rosalie and her husband's heart to see Wesley crumple-up inside. They tried everything to boost his confidence, inspire an alternative direction, but he struggled and the wrong crowd became an escape mechanism.

Three years after college, he'd been in two drug treatment programs and working for a building contractor. The loss of Morris, his father, was like losing the family's spine. Rosalie for the first year was trying to find her feet and the boys, especially Wesley, were lost souls.

Eventually, they did rally. Presley finished college, Rosalie found her talent for interior decorating also provided an excellent income and even Wesley found a coaching job at one of the high schools. They clung to each other and for the first time in the years after his car accident, Wesley was making some progress.

Spying a picture of him with his father hanging on the wall beside the bed, Rosalie walked over and lifted it off its nail. A tender smile warmed her worried face.

"You rascal," she said, her words so soft they were more of a maternal blessing than an inditement.

Her cell phone rang breaking her fleeting moment of respite from worry.

"Presley?" she answered.

"His phone is in the house, Mama. Did you hear it ring?"

The earlier tightness returned to her chest.

"No, I can't hear it," she said. "Will you call his friends for me? I'm so worried. Should we call the clinic or even the hospital, Presley?"

"Mama, it's just Wesley being Wesley. He's fine. Go make yourself a nice cup of chamomile tea, get in your pajamas and I'll be home in about twenty minutes. Wesley is probably with his new girlfriend. I saw him earlier today and they were together."

Complete relief flooded Rosalie's mind and body at Presley's interpretation of the situation. Wesley was truly a lady's man and his coterie of female liaisons were legendary. He'd probably left the phone behind so whoever he was with, she wouldn't see the incessant incoming texts from other women. Rosalie shook her head.

"Presley, you're right. He's a mess. If you hear from him, sweetheart, tell him to call me. I want to know he's okay."

"Get yourself a bite to eat, Mama. I'll see you in a bit."

She ended the call and feeling relieved, she sighed. The rumpled bed and clothing scattered about the floor caught her eye again and she smiled.

"Oh, Wesley. What am I going to do with you?"

The question spurred her into action. It wasn't Karen's day to clean so Rosalie stripped the bed, grabbed the things off the floor and took the sheets to the washing machine.

"I'm going to clean his room from top to bottom, and when he gets home, we're going to have a come to Jesus conversation. He's going to straighten up and fly right."

In thirty minutes Rosalie's motherly ministrations returned her son's bedroom to hospital cleanliness standards. Not a speck of dust, a strand of hair or the smudge of a fingerprint remained.

Proud of her work and secretly hoping Wesley would appreciate her loving attention to his needs, she shut the door.

"He's going to be annoyed, I know, but," she said with a sparkle of maternal love in her eye, "he'll also like having it nice."

Rosalie went downstairs, made a comforting cup of chamomile tea and waited for her sons to come home.

Chapter 15

For a short moment, Sonya doubted her eyes. It had to be Roxy Davidson. She studied the face, hair, and contusion on the woman's right temple.

"It's okay," she said to the uncertain visitor. "Please follow me. I'll help you if I can."

An unknown yap brought Sonya's attention immediately downward. At the redheaded woman's feet sat an adorable ghost dog looking almost like Willard's twin except for the color of its fur.

"How wonderful!" she exclaimed. "I've never seen an animal who was a ghost. Please, please both of you come in inside."

Willard trotted through the door first to encourage Beast to follow. A few seconds later the woman and her companion crossed the house's threshold.

In the living room, Sonya bent down and gave Willard a loving pat and a good ear scratch.

"You've done a wonderful job. Thank you. I don't know what I'd do without you." Turning to her new guests waiting patiently for her direction, she said, "My name is Sonya. You're welcome to stay here as long as you want."

The two spirits wavered in strength and began to dematerialize. Sonya pushed on.

"How can I help you?"

The woman's image was fading, but as she came closer, her expression contorted with pain. Turning her head, she showed a brutal wound stretching across the temple area. Though Roxy didn't speak, an anguished voice emanated from her.

"Someone hit me."

"What is your name?" Sonya asked.

The woman's eyebrows knitted and for an infinitesimal moment it was as if she wasn't able to remember, but finally, her face relaxed.

"My name is Roxy…Roxy Davidson. I don't remember…"

She gingerly touched the wound on the side of her head.

"I don't know what happened to me."

Sonya held out her hand to the woman. This simple act of compassion gave a renewed strength to the ghost's image.

"It's going to be okay, Roxy," Sonya said gently.

Roxy nodded and looked about the room. She reached out to touch a quilt hanging on the back of a chair but her hand filtered through both objects. Tears welled up again in her eyes.

"Am I dead?" she asked.

Sonya hesitated, took a deep breath, and nodded in the affirmative. The truth's impact hit home. Roxy let out a soul-wrenching groan and covered her face. Her crying made the ghost dog fret and run about whimpering at her feet.

Reaching over, Sonya touched the place where Roxy's arm appeared, effecting a powerful reaction upon the apparition's material strength. Her image warmed again to life.

"I know you are scared and sad. You *will* be okay. The truth is, you're going to be more than okay," Sonya said. "You're about to know unimaginable bliss."

Chapter 16

It was extremely unusual for a newly crossed-over spirit to be so aware of their death. Roxy may even remember her killer, but first things first. The soul was more important than the body's death.

"Roxy, I've visited with many ghosts in my life," she said. "Most want to pass on to the place where their loved ones are waiting for them. Some are called to be with God. There are those who, because a tragedy or unresolved issues hold them to this reality, can't or won't cross over. Normally, when our bodies die, we see a great light beckoning us toward it. Do you remember experiencing this?"

"Oh yes!" Roxy's voice whispered through the room, her image fading.

"What kept you here?" Sonya asked softly.

"I had to stay. My brother, my brother…"

Sonya waited for her to finish, but Roxy's energy was quickly declining. Willard, who'd been sitting patiently on his bed under the piano, got up and trotted over to where his toy box sat. Taking a ball, he went and dropped it at an unoccupied spot in the room. The ball started moving back and forth as if some invisible paw was batting it around.

The simple gesture of offering the toy to Roxy's companion appeared to give her renewed energy.

"My brother is in danger," she said.

Sonya didn't immediately answer. One had to be careful with words.

"Roxy, if you knew your brother would be safe, would you be able to pass over?" she finally asked.

No response came for a short time, but she finally answered.

"Yes, I need to know he'll be safe before I can go." Pausing, as if considering some other addendum to her decision, she added, "Also, I want someone to tell my girls I love them. Teddy needs to take care of them."

Sonya nodded as Willard's ball scooted about the floor. The ghost dog companion was enjoying his new toy. Roxy's last sentence gelled in Sonya's mind.

"Your girls?" she asked.

"Bea, Rue, and Betty, my Golden Doodles. I call them my Golden Doodle Girls," Roxy said, her face lighting up with a smile and her silhouette coming more in focus.

Relieved children weren't let behind, Sonya softly chuckled.

"I'll make sure to let your husband know your wishes regarding the girls, but for now, back to your brother, Roxy. Do you fear for his life?"

"Whoever…" Roxy hesitated, "*killed* me, I felt something when I died. It was like the person was covered in lust, covered in greed…"

Her voice trailed off and she again touched the wound on her temple.

Roxy's impression, Sonya knew, wasn't unusual. Many people upon death had a moment of utter clarity and understanding of the true nature of the people around them. Often if their death experience involved being murdered, they might lock onto their killer's thoughts and feelings.

Knowing her priority was to Roxy's soul, Sonya thought quickly. She had to convince the spirit that someone else would assume the great responsibility of protecting her brother's life.

The fact he might be in danger wasn't something to take on lightly. One had to be completely certain of one's capabilities.

Taking a deep, steadying breath, Sonya quieted herself and gave real consideration to the promise she wanted to give Roxy.

Comfortable with her answer, she said, "I will make sure your brother has protection. I will see to it he is safe."

Roxy weakly smiled.

"You are sure?" Her bodiless voice weary and uncertain.

Sonya replied "You have done what you needed to, Roxy. You made someone aware of a danger to your brother. Let me take it from here but I have one last question. Do you have any idea who might have killed you?"

The wavering ghost shook her head from side to side.

"I don't know who it was but Pickles might."

Sonya didn't push any further. She wanted to make sure Roxy's spirit was taken care of properly.

"You need to ask for the light to come, Roxy. When you see it, go with it. All will be well and you will feel a great peace when it appears."

The early evening sounds, crickets and cicadas beginning their lullabies, filtered gently in through the open windows. Sonya's gaze fell to the ground to see the toy ball roll ever so slowly to a stop. As if signaling the quiet completion of the physical's pull on living matter, the last sunbeam of the day broke through and filled the room with a soft, golden radiance.

Wishing Roxy's well, Sonya watched as the spirit attach to and departed with the loving warmth of day's last light. A delicate breeze came in through the window, circled the room, and left the same way it entered.

"She's gone," Sonya whispered looking down with a tender smile for Willard.

"My dear," Fritz's familiar voice came from behind her, making Sonya jump, "I saw it! I saw her go! It was… sublime," he breathed. "Maybe I should have hopped on that sunbeam, too."

"I'm glad you were here Fritz," she said turning toward the voice to see if he was in his favorite spot. Sure enough, he was comfortably sitting cross-legged atop the baby grand piano.

"I am, too," he said coming more into view. "She left behind the wee dog, though."

Sonya, quickly turning her head back to where the ball had come to a stop earlier, saw the ball and the dog were gone. Willard, however, was still at her feet.

"The dog is still here?" Sonya asked Fritz.

"Yes, and if my eyes don't deceive me, he's the spitting image of one I used to know. A lovely man, he did belong to once. Together we spent many a day fleeing from dragons in the Weem Woods."

Trying to calculate the century and the place Fritz might be referring to, Sonya sighed softly and shook her head.

"Dragons, Fritz? Really?" she said, sounding extremely dubious.

"Sunny," Fritz said, calling her by his favorite pet name and slipping into his tall-tale tone of voice. "The Laird of

Lochbar and I survived not one of the fire breathin' scaly, windbags but *two*. And as always," he said, his voice building with drama and excitement, "if it were not for the sturdy, fearless loyalty of Lochbar's dog, we might have been burned, lashed and hung out for the birds to pick at our entrails. On our last trip into the Weem Wood, one of the foul hydrae tried every wicked trick in her arsenal to separate us from the living, but she never caught us in her clutches. The brilliant terrier at your feet always knew when the crafty creature was going to drop down upon us. I do believe, Sunny, the ghost dog Willard brought home is Lochbar's pride and joy — Beast."

Immediately, a firm bark came from an untenanted place in the middle of the living room's floor.

"How on Earth did a ghost dog from Scotland end up being the companion to Roxy Davidson?" Sonya asked, more to herself than of Fritz.

"Well, how did we find each other, Sunny?" Fritz returned, his tone poetic and a bit shmoosey.

"I saw you in a hotel chandelier in Montreal," she answered, her tone wry.

"I saw you first from the Grand Ballroom's piano top *then* I positioned myself in the chandelier. I thought it was a magical moment, the first time we clapped eyes on each other."

Fritz broke into singing "Some Enchanted Evening".

Ignoring him, Sonya said firmly, "Beast," and looked around for the dog.

Together the invisible canine *and* the invisible ghost answered.

The canine barked whereas Fritz exclaimed, "I most certainly was not!"

"Not you, Fritz," she explained. "I'm trying to see if the dog will show itself to me once more."

The Laird of Dunbar called out, "Beastie! Show yourself!"

In front of her eyes, a shaggy Cairn Terrier with his coat a wheaten color, stood ready and alert on all four short legs. Willard immediately trotted over, and the two dogs went about greeting each other.

"He wasn't very clear before, but now, why he's adorable!" Sonya gushed. "The two dogs are almost twins. Look, Fritz! One is black and one is cream."

"Wheaten," Fritz corrected. "I wonder if he misses old Fergus?"

"Fergus?" Sonya echoed.

"His master, and one of my best pals."

Sonya bent down to encourage Beast to come to her.

"I think there's some sort of connection between the families, Fritz. Tomorrow I'm off to the library to read up on the Sweeny family. This dog is here as a protector, a spirit who stays close to a family or person during times of trouble or danger."

"Well," Fritz added. "Fergus died looking for Beast. This has me thinking. I'll be gone for a while, Sunny. I'm off to see the Hag of Dunbar, also known as my wife. She might know where I can find Fergus. Can I take Beast with me?"

"If he'll go, but I doubt if he will. He's here for the Sweenys," she said with her hand still out to the dog.

"Beast, come here!" Fritz commanded. "I'll take ya with me, home. Together we'll find old Fergus. They say he's still up there wanderin' about looking for ya."

Instead of coming to Fritz, Beast, with his head slightly down, walked toward Sonya. Once within her range of touch, he sat down. His coal-black, intense gaze never leaving her eyes.

"He won't go with you Fritz, dear, not for now anyway. I think he has unfinished business with the Sweeny family. When the time is right, he might follow you."

"I'm off, Sonya. I'm going to look up old Fergus," Fritz said, his tone sounding more cheerful than earlier. "Fergus and I may have time to rouse up a dragon like we used to in the days of our youth."

"I didn't know there were goblins or dragons in the early nineteenth century," Sonya said teasing.

"Woman! I've been talking about my wife and Fergus' wife. Those two women had tongues tipped with fire and tempers forged in Hades. Mary and Antonia found our drinking place in Weem Woods. If old Beast hadn't warned us of their coming, we'd been strung up by our heels and our stash would ha' been tossed into the loch."

Sonya nodded as she internally kicked herself for even remotely considering the idea of dragons in nineteenth-century Scotland.

"Do me a favor, Fritz?" she asked.

"Anything, dear Sunny!" he said.

"Don't, absolutely DON'T, do anything to annoy either of those two women. Neither I or Willow Valley is ready for a hydra or a dragon. Do you understand?"

"On my word of honor, if I see the Spit Fire of Dunbar, I will be as charming a gentleman ever walked the shores of Loch Lomond."

Using his best 1930's Hollywood leading man voice, probably taken from an old pirate film, he declared, "Fear not, lass. You can count on me. I'm off to find the faithful Fergus and bring him here to you!"

With a rakish tip from his hat and a blast of cool air, he was gone.

"And that," she said with a sigh and looking down at the two terriers sitting at her feet, "is what I'm afraid of."

Chapter 17

Posh Pup's home office was empty of people except for Harry Sweeny and his wife Deidra. They'd sent their employees home after telling them of Roxy's murder. Even if Dog Days was in full swing, the shock was too much for such a close-knit family business.

"I can't focus, Harry," Deidra said, slumping back in her chair.

They'd been working desperately to understand the company's position now with Roxy gone. It was a bit of a panic situation, simply because Harry was convinced Teddy would try and hock his shares to the highest bidder.

"My brain won't stop replaying last night," Deidra said, the tears pooling in her eyes. She covered her face with her hands and continued. "How can you concentrate on those spreadsheets? We've been here since noon and it's past seven o'clock. I'm exhausted."

Harry lifted his face to meet her gaze and blinked his red-rimmed eyes. He looked like a man who'd been caught in a nightmare and wasn't able to wake himself up. There was almost a numbness to his expression as if his ability to find the words, or the will to answer his wife, was something foreign and lost to him.

"Honey," she said, "we need to go get some sleep. You look unwell. This is ridiculous."

"We can't go home," he said, his voice sounding hollow. "She died in our house, Deidra. Someone killed her there. How can we ever go home to that house again? I'll never be able to walk inside without being reminded of the horror of her lying dead in the hallway."

He put his head down upon his folded arms and broke down sobbing. Jumping up from her seat, Deidra hurried around the desk. Turning her husband around, she tenderly wiped his eyes with her thumb.

"It's going to be okay, darling. I promise. We won't go back to the house. I'll manage this. But for now, we've got to do something besides sit in this office."

Pulling him into her, she held him close to her chest and made a decision.

"We'll stay in the old carriage house in the back. It hasn't been used in forever, but it has everything we need. That way Pickles can still have the yard. Come on, Harry. Get up. We're going home and getting some sleep."

As she tugged him up from his chair, the phone on the desk rang. Grabbing the receiver, she answered, "This is Deidra Sweeny, how may I help you?"

For a minute or more, she made the usual responses and finally hung up.

"Who was it?" Harry asked, still holding on to her.

Taking a deep, reassuring breath, Deidra thought for a quick moment. The call was so bizarre, she wasn't sure where to begin.

"Some woman named Sonya Caruthers. She says she lives on Pickwick Street not far from our house. Have you ever heard of her?" Deidra asked.

He shook his head and stood up, "No, should I have?"

Together they walked toward the door of the office. As they passed through, Deidra flipped off the lights and they continued down the darkened hallway unspeaking for a few moments.

"Funny thing is, Harry, I *have* heard of her. Women at my pilates class and at our book club meetings have mentioned her. She's some kind of medium or person who talks to ghosts."

"Oh, God!" Harry exclaimed. "Sounds like a crackpot, Deidra. What's wrong with people? All the crazies crawl out of the woodwork when something like this happens. What did she want? Money?"

"Well, she says she has some good news and some bad news for us. Which would you like first?"

Harry shrugged and shook his head.

"Surprise me," he answered his tone flat with a hint of sarcasm.

"The good news, according to this Sonya person, is supposedly Roxy has passed over peacefully."

Harry made a scoffing sound and said, "Oh really?"

"Yes," Deidra replied, and added, "Wanna hear the bad news?"

They stepped out into the night air and walked toward Harry's car.

"Sure. Why not? What's one more awful thing to have to swallow?" Harry said. "Hit me with it."

"This Sonya says you are in danger."

As Harry held the car door open for his wife, Deidra became increasingly aware of an unwholesome tingle crawling up her spine. She scanned the empty parking lot the same way a mother bear sniffs the air for dangerous predators in the wild.

"On who's authority?" he asked.

90

Deidra looked up at him. As his wife, she well knew Harry's feelings on anything to do with life after death. He was a confirmed cynic.

"That's the interesting part, darling. This Caruthers woman says Roxy told her so."

Chapter 18

Day Two

"You're welcome to come over to my house or, I live around the corner. I can come to you, as well."

Sonya paused waiting for the reply from the other end.

"Okay, I'll be there in a few minutes," finished with the call, she put the phone receiver in its cradle.

The phone call had come as a surprise to Sonya. Deidra Sweeny, who'd only used practically monosyllabic words on the phone the previous night, had called Sonya before she'd finished her first cup of coffee that morning.

"Come on Willard. We're off to visit the Sweenys after I grab a shower. I have a feeling they're in need of direction. I've seen it before. Having a tragedy in your home makes for a difficult transitionary time for the people left behind, not to mention the house itself. Poor things!"

Hurrying up the stairs with Willard on her heels, Sonya slipped into the bathroom and turned on the shower to warm up the water. Back in her bedroom, she pulled her favorite dress from the closet and grabbed a pair of comfortable high-top sneakers.

"I'm extremely surprised they called me, Willard," she said to the terrier curled up below the bathroom sink on a pink, fuzzy bath mat. "Last night on the phone, I had the distinct impression Mrs. Sweeny must have thought I was some kind of nut. Oh, I know, what you're thinking — that's the norm, but I think we're needed and we have to keep our promise to Roxy."

Done hypothesizing with a now snoozing terrier, Sonya stepped into the shower and was soon out. Fresh as a spring daisy and equally as pretty, she tied up her curly hair in one of her favorite, colorful scarfs and wearing a uniquely Sonya outfit composed of a knee-length, bright blue tunic dress and hot-pink leggings, she grabbed her satchel, flung it across her shoulder and made for the back door.

Thinking it was best to drive her scooter instead of walking, she headed for the shed where it was kept.

"Oh, no!" she exclaimed upon seeing she'd left the keys again in the ignition. "I'm such a feather brain, Willard. This is the third time this week, I've not removed the key. It's only a matter of time before it gets stolen by a thief."

Done chastising herself, she pulled the Vespa from its garage and strapped on her new purple helmet. Willard was lifted and safely ensconced in his basket. He allowed Sonya to put on his goggles and helmet, and within minutes, the two of them were zipping along back alleys and side streets until they arrived at the front of the Sweeny's lovely Victorian house.

"Hmmm," Sonya mused looking up at the stately, old mansion. "More than a few deaths have happened here."

She shook her head slightly.

"But for the most part, they were all happy passings."

She continued to assess the energy of the house.

"There is something else, Willard. I think the Sweenys are afraid to stay in the house anymore. They find the house repugnant. Oh, what a pity! Dark deeds leave such negative energy. Maybe there's something we can do."

Realizing the Sweenys might be watching her from one of the windows, Sonya quit talking out loud to herself. If they already thought she was a bit of a loon, it wouldn't do to push their buttons further. Leaving Willard in his basket, she took the Vespa's key from its ignition, mentally congratulated herself for doing so and opened the storage place under her padded seat.

"Let me get the helmet locked up, Willard, and we can go through the gate."

As Sonya opened the scooter's seat, voices coming toward her caused her to look up. She saw a lithe woman with an athletic flow to her movements and a man built like a football player appear from behind the back of the house. They were walking toward her down a brick pathway.

Sonya offered a friendly smile at their arrival but received a tight, uncertain one in return from both parties.

If Deidra Sweeny was second-guessing her decision to invite the resident ghost guru over for a visit, Sonya wasn't sure. The man, however, opened the gate for the woman to come through so they were at least going to meet with her.

"Mrs. Caruthers?" Deidra Sweeny asked, giving Sonya a flitting assessment.

"Hello, Mrs. Sweeny," Sonya replied, offering her hand. "Thank you for letting me come for a visit."

"Of course."

She indicated with a brief movement of her hand the man standing to her right.

"This is our security person, Mr. Alfonso. He's just started with us this morning. The break-in and my sister-in-laws'…death have made me particularly nervous. If you don't mind, Mr. Alfonso will need to pat you down and check your purse. I'm sorry for the inconvenience."

"Oh, of course not," Sonya said and thinking to herself what an excellent turn of events it was for Harry Sweeny to have private protection. Remembering Willard, she added, "I hope you don't mind, I've brought my dog."

Deidra Sweeny's gaze dropped to the sidewalk. At finding nothing there, her expression registered perplexity.

"Oh, I'm sorry," Sonya said, "he's here."

Stepping to the right a couple of feet, Sonya revealed Willard still setting quietly with his two front paws resting on the basket's edge and wearing his favorite plaid bow tie for a collar.

The excited terrier gave a cheerful bark-greeting followed by his best doggy smile and tail wag. As he hadn't been relieved of his driving goggles yet, Willard was a sight few people, with any love in their hearts for dogs, could witness without feeling joy.

It was exactly the response Sonya had hoped for and the one Deidra Sweeny appeared to experience, too. The younger woman's face broke out in a huge grin. There was a definite crack in the ice.

"Well, aren't you the cutest little man!" Deidra exclaimed followed by a laugh. She came up and patted Willard on his shaggy head. Turning back to Sonya, she smiled broadly.

"I needed something life-affirming right now. Thank you, Mrs. Caruthers."

Mr. Alfonso did his brief check of Sonya, her bag and Willard's fur.

"It's all fine, Mrs. Sweeny," he said.

Deidra's shoulders visibly relax, and opening the gate to go back into the yard, she said, "Please, won't you both come through? Willard is welcome to come inside as well. My dog, Pickles, is out here somewhere. He's our old Lab and very gentle. My husband and I are staying in the carriage house at the back of the property. We don't feel comfortable being in the main house right now, as you can imagine."

Sonya's brain grabbed on to the name, Pickles. That was the very name Roxy had told her last night. She filed the piece of information away for another time.

With a glance back up at the house to her left, Sonya tried to get a feel for the mood of the place. She'd been right. Like a loved child who'd fallen from grace, it had a smear of darkness and rejection over it. But with the right approach, the house's situation could be remedied.

"I know my phone call must have come as an unusual surprise to you, Mrs. Sweeny," Sonya said, hoping to allow Deidra the opportunity to express her qualms about the visit.

"Well, to be honest, your phone call was a bit... unexpected."

"I can imagine," Sonya said good-humoredly. "Maybe what you'd like to say is my phone call was a bit weird."

Both women shared a short, congenial laugh.

"It's not every day you get a message...from the dead, Mrs. Caruthers," Deidra said, slowing her pace up the brick path. "You see, Roxy's death has been horrific. My husband, Harry, is struggling terribly. The night it happened he may have seen his sister. I don't know if he dreamed it or if she'd been on his mind and he fell asleep at the wheel briefly, but when you called last night and said Roxy had shown herself to you and Harry was in danger, I couldn't get it out of my mind. Harry, quite honestly, thinks you're a charlatan, but I'm scared. I came home last night and hired a full-time security person after you called."

Sonya simply nodded, and said, her tone understanding and kind, "Thank you for letting me come."

The group arrived at a charming dwelling matching the architectural style of the main Victorian house, but at least a hundred yards to its back. It was two-storied and nestled in among two massive, ancient Holly trees with garage doors below and an apartment above.

A climbing rose bush with flowers the size of tennis balls, most likely similar in age to the Holly trees, clung and clambered beautifully over most of the carriage house's facade imparting a feeling of sweet tranquility and grace.

"This is our new place for a while," Deidra said with a shrug. "It's small, but in a way we enjoyed staying here last night. It reminded me of our early days when we lived in a studio together in St. Louis."

Sonya watcher Deidra as she continued to gaze up at the carriage house's upper story with a wistful, yet melancholy feeling about her expression.

The manicured gardens were quiet. Even the usual insect noise was strangely silent as if all nature in the immediate area of the genteel Victorian had, out of respect for death, put a moratorium on all liveliness or unnecessary noises.

Deidra turned and said, "I'm sorry, Mrs. Caruthers. I'm so tired and find I'm saying the most random things today. Roxy's death has brought about so many endings for us. I wish I could sleep for a week."

The unvarnished statement made Sonya want to offer some sort of comfort to the younger woman.

"We'll never know what purpose Roxy's death is meant to serve, Mrs. Sweeny. Truth is left to our Creator to determine, but I can tell you this with absolute certainty: death isn't an ending. It's more like a bump in a long road littered with more bumps. All living things come and go down the road but we're never alone. Never. Love is always around us. Our brains sometimes get in the way of what our hearts always know. Roxy passed over to a beautiful place and her last concern was for her brother. I'm glad you let me come over. I made a promise and I intend to keep it."

Deidra Sweeny's face was utterly still except for a tiny twitch in one of the muscles above her eye, most likely brought on by fatigue. If she disagreed with Sonya's interpretation of life and death, her stony expression revealed nothing.

"You made a promise?" she asked. "To Roxy?"

Sonya nodded.

"Yes, I did. She believed Harry was in great danger and I promised to make sure he was safe."

Deidra visibly blanched. Sonya saw the finely sculpted lips quiver ever so slightly.

"Well," Deidra said taking a deep breath and letting it out, "you'd better come up. Sounds like we've got a lot to discuss."

Chapter 19

Patrick Lilton was subtle. No one thing stood out about him and this, for him, was deliberate. He was fit, well-groomed and clean shaved. Six feet tall with perfect teeth and a winning smile. He appeared to be like thousands of other businessmen, except he wasn't.

As CEO of Titan, the goal was to swim at the top of the food chain, but without drawing too much attention to yourself from the other sharks in the same pool who wanted to have you for their lunch.

Feeding frenzies were the norm, and Lilton had gotten to where he was by making sure others were the meat du jour even if it meant chumming the water around his ladder-climbing competitors.

On the weekends, he started his day early, at 4:45 am with swimming for thirty minutes in his lap pool. This was followed by two hours working in his home office until his wife and daughter woke up. It was a family ritual to have breakfast together when he was home.

Most days, Patrick drove into St. Louis to work unless he was traveling. He slept as soundly at forty-thousand feet as he did in his bed at home, and he went through at least one passport a year.

Sixteen years ago, he'd married Tamara. She was pregnant with their one-night-stand. He could have shrugged his shoulders and told her to prove it was his, but after a quick mental appraisal of the potential within the situation, a skill he excelled at, Patrick asked Tamara to marry him.

Tamara was beautiful and driven, the perfect corporate wife for a rising corporate star. Titan preferred married men on their VP roster. It was a good time to shed the single life, so he did. The rest was history. He became Titan's first CEO to assume the title under the age of forty.

The real surprise, for Patrick, had come with the birth of the child. He was stunned, and thrilled by the adorable infant they named Samantha. Something powerful and raw took root in him. Watching Tamara with the baby, her loving care of it, stirred within him a monumental feeling of protection and love toward his little family. He never looked back. He was a committed husband and father from that point on.

Done with his swim for the morning, he decided to work from home due to a meeting later in Willow Valley with Harry Sweeny.

A soft knock brought his attention up from his computer.

"Come in," he called.

As the heavy, paneled door slid open, Tamara appeared. He saw immediately she'd been crying. A quick look again at his watch, he realized it was nearly ten o'clock. Why hadn't anyone come to get him for breakfast?

"Tamara," he said, "what's wrong? Why are you crying? Has something happened?"

She walked in and pulled the door closed. Turning to face him, she simply stood in front of him wearing a thin, silk nightdress the color and luster of pearls. Her hair was loose and hanging in thick, messy waves about her shoulders.

"Patrick," she said with a sniffle, "I want a divorce."

To his credit, he didn't flinch. Boardroom skirmishes build nerves of steel, but a twinge of tightness caught at his throat.

"Why?" he said swallowing hard.

Coming forward, she sat down in the leather chair across from his desk.

"You're in love with Roxy Davidson. You've never loved me. To you, I'm only Sam's mother or someone to take to business dinners. Everyone is always hinting at how much you loved Roxy. I'm sick of it. I figured it out at dinner the other night why you're trying to buy Posh Pups. It was for her, wasn't it? You're trying to save her from a ridiculous husband and from losing her business. This entire town knows Teddy Davidson spends more than Roxy earns."

A wave of relief washed over him. He chuckled.

"I don't love Roxy. I love you. Where is this coming from?"

"I think you were having an affair. I saw the way she was flirting with you. You were both exchanging these glances only lovers do."

He looked at his wife, who'd begun to cry again. Getting up, he walked around the desk sitting down on its corner in front of her.

"How could you think I'm having an affair? It's business between Roxy and me. Nothing more. Our past helps for sure. She's being difficult about selling Posh Pups. I did a bit of low-key flirting to loosen her up. I'm not going to sleep with her. I don't find her in the least bit attractive."

Tamara compressed her lips into a thin, tense line.

"I *think* you would sleep with her if you could. I'm tired of living in the shadow of your high school sweetheart. I'm tired of living with a man who's never loved me. I'm tired of everyone thinking you only married me because I was pregnant. I won't be pitied by you, by those people down in that town, or Babette Nichols!" Tamara cried, pounding the arm of the chair with her fist. "I want a divorce, Patrick. I won't play second fiddle to a dead woman."

He heard her last words, but he didn't respond immediately. Standing up, he asked her again.

"Dead woman? Who are you talking about Tamara?"

"Roxy. She's dead, Patrick. They found her in her brother's house last night. She's dead."

He blinked, trying to ingest her words. Tamara got up and turned to leave, but grabbing her hand, he held her in front of him.

"Dead? Roxy is dead?" he asked looking into Tamara's eyes for confirmation of his question.

"That's what I said. I just got the call from Babs. She heard it from the other pilates teacher at her studio who also cleans for the Sweenys. Everyone knows. It's a small town, after all, Patrick. Babette couldn't wait to rub it in my face how broken-hearted you must be."

He gave Tamara a strong tug, pulling her in between his two legs and wrapping his arms around her.

"Now you listen to me," he said, his tone authoritative, but with a grin across his face. "I don't give a damn what Babette Nichols thinks and neither should you. I love you, Tamara. Our marriage may have started differently than other's, but I wouldn't trade it for anything in this world."

He pulled her to him and brushed her hair back from her shoulder. Looking back into her eyes, he stood up and kissed his wife.

"Did Terence take Sam to school?" he asked, his voice low.

An uncertain, tentative smile pulled at the corners of Tamara's mouth. She shrugged saying, "He took her to school about an hour ago. Why?"

"Good," he said pulling her into him and kissing her a second time as he ran his hands down her back. "I'm going to own Posh Pups, darling. It's time to celebrate — in bed."

Chapter 20

It was lunchtime and the coffee drinkers at Tilly's Diner were well into their third cups of coffee and the last round of a heated debate over who had offed the Davidson woman.

Usually, during the annual event of Dog Days, they would be joyfully grousing about the tourists. Common complaints were the same each year and heatedly discussed with vigor.

The lack of parking spots along Main Street, how the tourists were using Willow Valley's sidewalks like garbage cans, and the uppity, entitled attitude of dog show people were all some of their favorite grumpings.

But a moratorium on these more banal annoyances had been declared. A murder had happened. One of their own had been killed in the town they all called home.

At first, the boys were sure the killer must be some near-do-well brought in like a flea on the back of Dog Days, but one of the less vociferous coffee drinkers, Carl Fessler, which made him a sage of sorts to the others at Table Number Three, had offered up his take on the murder in Meadomere Place.

"Had to be someone from the town," he said, slow and sure, like the way one would expect a turtle to talk. "Had to be someone who knew the Sweenys. My daughter, Kayla, goes to Junior League with Deidra Sweeny. Kayla took food over this morning and Deidra told her whoever killed

Roxy Davidson must have used the key hidden under the plant near the front door to get inside. The key is gone."

The news hit Table Number Three's members hard. Furtive gazes flitted from face to face. What if the killer was a Willow Valleyian? One of their neighbors, or… someone eating in Tilly's?

They regarded each other suspiciously. The killer could even be someone sitting at their hallowed table. Fortunately, Earl Higginbotham, the undeclared Head-of-Table, did the decent thing, he shifted the guilt back where it belonged, on the outsiders.

"Well, if you ask me," he began in a stentorian voice, "my bets on it being someone from St. Louis. The Sweenys are always having parties at their house. Anyone of those party people could have seen Deidra or Harry fiddle with the key in the plant. The Sweenys have money. I bet it was a break-in to loot the place."

Table Number Three continued with a tenuous feeling of uncertainty. Earl, sensing the nagging unease, wasn't going to let his knights go down the dark road of doubting one another. He made another stab at bringing them around.

"Boys," he said lowering his voice conspiratorially and leaning in toward the table's center. Each of his subjects, in turn, following his lead except Bo Clyde, a retired veteran of the Korean War who rarely followed Table Three protocol. "I'm not supposed to say anything, but I ran into the sheriff early this morning down at Puggly's Grocery. You fellas keep it to yourself, hear?" he asked.

They each, in turn, nodded their assent, except Bo Clyde. Earl's voice dropped to a whisper causing Clyde to lean in slightly so to hear, but still retain his dignity.

"When I asked Walker when they were reopening the park for Dog Days, he said as soon as they'd taken statements from all the vendors camping along the park."

The faces staring back at Earl didn't appear to comprehend the value of this juicy tidbit of information. He grimaced at their obtuseness.

"Don't you see what that means?" he asked, shaking his head, his scraggily eyebrows arched in incredulity.

Some at Table Number Three squinted, some pursed their lips, and Bo Clyde leaned back with a dubious grin, folding his arms across his chest.

"It means the sheriff thinks whoever killed Roxy Davidson must be one of with those vendors lined up along the park! God knows, the Sweenys knew every one of those vendors. I bet every one of them has been to a party at their house at least one time or another!"

Earl leaned back in his chair confidently folding his arms across his puffed-out chest.

As the light dawned, each man nodded at Earl's brilliant deductive reasoning. Again, it was some damned outsider who was most likely the murderer. Earl's reasoning was extremely sound, if not more palatable.

"All the sheriff needs to do, in my opinion," Earl explained, "is find the vendors camped along the park who have been to one of the Sweeny's parties. Clear as day, boys, clear as day."

There was firm solidarity again at Table Number Three. They sipped coffee, relaxed and offered warm smiles to one another. Suspicion had been banished and even Bo Clyde slapped the table at Earl's well-argued explanation. The Fessler theory was shut down. Higginbotham had saved the day.

The good feeling ramped up upon the recognition of the sheriff's truck pulling into a parking spot in front of Tilly's. They waited with expectant faces as Zeb unfolded himself from his police vehicle and with a bronc buster's easy stride, walked slowly into the cafe.

"Hey sheriff," Marsha said as he sat down at the bar and removed his hat. "You're in here late today. Want the lunch menu?"

"Think Tilly would make me an egg sandwich, Marsha? I need something hearty," he asked.

"No problem, Zeb," she answered. "Till is in a good mood today. She won at canasta last night. We'll get your food right out."

With Marsha gone, the men at Table Three watched Zeb's back. He sat hunched over with both elbows leaning on the bar. It was obvious he'd not slept much the last two nights. Chances were good he might offer up some inside info with the right prodding.

"How's the investigation going Zeb?" Bo asked, his tone affable, but with the right amount of seriousness in it to indicate his appreciation for the tragedy of the situation.

Zeb turned around on his stool, his manner easy. Giving the men an inscrutable grin, he answered, "Well, Bo, it's a sad situation."

Table Number Three's faces respectfully stern at the sheriff's use of the word sad, all nodded in agreement and made the usual sounds of agreement.

"Sad, yes very sad," they murmured separately.

Bo pushed a bit further.

"It's a terrible thing. Got any ideas who might have done it, sheriff?"

Zeb shook his head, the side-to-side movement almost imperceptibly, his mouth a grim line.

"We've got some leads, but I'm not at liberty to discuss it. You 'all understand, of course?"

They all did and nodded again in firm compliance with Zeb's statement as the cafe's phone rang. Only Bo looked put out by Zeb's official position.

"Tilly's," Marsha answered. "Sure, he's here. One minute, I'll get him."

"Hey, Zeb, you gotta call. It's your office."

Handing him the phone, Marsha disappeared into the back. A hush fell over Table Number Three. They watched and listened intently to Sheriff Walker's extremely even yet uncertain sounding responses.

"Go ahead. Yeah, my phone's not working. Tell Betty, my secretary, to call County and have them get me a new one. Who's the message from? Caruthers? At her house? Got it," he said.

The men at the table shot knowing glances around the table. It was common knowledge, the Caruthers woman was a few bricks short of a full load.

"Okay," the sheriff said. "I've got to tell the mayor's office they can put up the big tents. We've cleared the park for the event, but when I finish, I'll go visit with her."

He put the phone down on the bar and hollered, "Marsha! I got to go!"

Coming out of the kitchen's swinging door, the head waitress expecting this turn of events, handed Zeb a brown paper bag.

"Figured you'd have to run. Till put it in a to-go sack for ya."

"Tell her thanks, Marsha. Here's what I owe," he put a ten-dollar bill down on the counter.

"Nope, she said it's on the house, but when you have time come by some evening and play a few rounds of canasta."

Zeb looked down at the ten-dollar bill laying innocently on the bar and shook his head.

"That little woman back there will get that and more," he said looking back up at the waitress with a charming grin.

The sage Marsha nodded, her mouth pulled up in one corner expressing the wryness and the truth of his statement.

"Cleaned me outta yesterday's tips last night."

"Tell her I'll be by as soon as I can and you keep the ten. It's a tip for knowing I'd need this to go."

As the sheriff grabbed his brown bag meal and headed through the diner's front door, Earl Higginbotham called out, "Got a break in the investigation, Zeb?"

"Maybe, Earl!" he called back to the men waiting hopefully for a tantalizing newsy morsel, "If you believe dead women do tell tales."

Chapter 21

"What in the world do you two want? You're acting like you've got something important to tell me."

Marnie Scott, the owner of the Whispering Pines RV and Camping Resort, was having a normal human-canine conversation with Lewis and Clark, her two beagles.

A bright afternoon, the sunshine came through her camper's kitchen windows warming the cozy space. Putting the mail down on her banquet's table, she watched, Larry, the postman, continue putting mail in each of her long-term tenant's boxes.

"You both sure enjoyed yapping it up with Lou," Marnie said shaking her head good-humoredly. "That Chihuahua! Why in the world does Larry dress him up like a postman? Poor dog."

Sitting down, she intended to go through her mail, but it was not to be. Lewis, putting both of his front paws on Marnie's knees, panted cheerfully while Clark went over to where the leashes hung on a hook and barked once never taking his eyes off the adored instrument of his freedom. The boys wanted a romp and the autumn woods were calling.

"When you're beat, you're beat," Marnie said with a chuckle. "Better to give into you now than deal with your antics later."

She took down the halters and the leashes and walked to her door.

"Okay, let's take a stroll into town. I'd like to see all the tents. Larry says some of the vendors have set up for Dog Days and we can buy you both a treat," she said giving the two brown, furry heads a loving rub.

A few minutes later Marnie and the boys were hiking down a favorite wooded path leading to Willow Valley. It was a nice short cut to town, and with the leaves beginning to turn and a blue sky above, the trio was in bright spirits. Looking up at the sparkling and golden light filtering in through the upper canopy, she drew a deep breath of fresh air.

"Okay, you're free," she said bending down to release the dogs from the leashes.

Happily running ahead, giving full vent to their beagle noses' powerful desire to sniff everything, the two dogs were in aroma nirvana.

Off to her right, but more deeply in the forest, Marnie caught sight of a figure standing and regarding her. She couldn't tell from its clothing and the distance between them whether it was a man or woman. An immediate feeling of unease and the awareness of her aloneness overtook her.

Lewis erupted into a barking storm causing her to quickly shift her gaze to where he was digging at a huge pile of limbs and forest debris. Snorting, with his nose near to the ground, the beagle continued to push his muzzle deeper into the brush pile.

With a quick glance, Marnie looked back to where she'd seen the figure, but it was gone.

"Did I imagine it?" she said softly to herself. "It may have been only a shadow."

Uncomfortable, but distracted by Lewis' repeated barking, she continued scanning the area to her right, but whether it was a shadow, a trick of the light, or a person, it was gone now.

Clark joined Lewis and both dogs were working in tandem pulling at the brush pile.

"Come on guys!" Marnie called. "Leave whatever is in there alone!"

But once a beagle has its nose on something, it's a difficult proposition to sway it from its quarry. Clark hunkered down and was working his way into the thicket of limbs, rotten tree trunks, and fallen leaf debris.

"Clark! No! Don't go in there!" she yelled. "There might be a skunk or snakes!"

She took off running in his direction. Her hurried feet made crunching sounds as they fell upon the leaf-strewn forest floor. Closing in on the brush pile, she slowed her rapid approach and came to a complete standstill.

Her heart raced. Not from the sprint, but because of what Clark had managed to pull free from the tangled mass of forgotten forest brushwood.

"Drop it, Clark! Oh dear God, Clark! I said drop it!"

With a sinking horror, she watched as Clark let his quarry go and with Lewis, trotted over to her, tails low and almost tucked. Once they arrived, she put her hands out in front of her.

"Sit!" she commanded, forgetting to give them their usual reward of a good pet. Swallowing hard, she tried to control her panic and took the leashes from her coat pocket. With shaking hands, Marnie clicked the bolt snap into both collars. Once the dogs were secure, she took out her cell phone and tapped 911 with shaking hands.

"Hello? Yes, I need the police. Meyer Woods. There's a human hand…"

Her words died, as a feeling of nausea welled up in her. Looking back where she'd seen the obscure figure only moments ago, fear helped her find her voice.

"I think there is someone dead out here. I'm scared. Please hurry!"

Chapter 22

"Good afternoon," Zeb said with a tip of his hat to Sonya from the other side of her front gate.

He'd finally made it to her house to hear the information she called about earlier. Sitting at her porch table, Sonya waved him to come on up.

"Have a cup of coffee with me and a fresh cinnamon roll. I made some for the Ladies Auxiliary bake sale. Shouldn't sell something you haven't taste-tested, right? They're raising money for the Willow Valley Animal Shelter at Dog Days. Would you care for one?"

Remembering his last meal was the egg sandwich at lunchtime, Zeb said, "I've heard about those rolls of yours. Deputy Kirchner has put on a few pounds. I think it's because he spends a good deal too much time patrolling Pickwick Place."

Sonya laughed and selected a good-sized cinnamon roll for the sheriff.

"Tommy and Sheba have become great friends of mine. I believe he has a sixth sense for when I'm baking."

Handing the sheriff his plate and pouring him a hot cup of coffee, Sonya settled down across from him.

"So, sheriff, I've got two interesting bits of information to pass along to you. First, guess who I met last evening?" she asked.

Zeb heard the excitement in her voice. He took a stab at the obvious.

"Roxy Davidson?"

Sonya's shoulders slumped a bit as if he'd taken the wind out of her big reveal.

"Yes," she said, sounding less disappointed than he expected. "She came to me. Well, my dog, Willard, found them and brought them here."

With his mouth full of wonderful cinnamon, sugar, and bread, Zeb concentrated on not choking even though he had an intense desire to laugh at the idea of her dog rounding up ghosts and delivering them to her house.

Instead, with infinite physical control, the sheriff managed to grab his napkin, cover his face and only cough a few times without any loss of his dignity.

Once he'd swallowed, he managed, "Your dog brought Roxy to you?"

"I imagine you think I'm batty, but yes, Willard did bring them to me. Anyway, we found out a great deal. Unfortunately, Roxy didn't see her killer, but she thought Pickles might know who it is. I've since heard from Deidra Sweeny their dog was in the house. Interesting, don't you think?"

Zeb took a drink of his coffee and looked across the table at the pretty woman. He thought to himself how attractive and intelligent she was, but something was unnerving about Sonya Caruthers. There she sat waiting with an expectant expression upon her face for his answer. Why would she want to know about the Sweeny's dog?

"Okay, I'll bite, Sonya…" he said. "Why do you want to know about the dog?"

"Simple," she said sitting up straight. He noticed how her eyes twinkled with excitement. "The dog will remember the killer. There's a chance he saw him or her, but certainly he'll know the killer's smell. Mark my word, the dog will be your best asset in solving this case."

"Well, I've never heard of a dog being used as an expert witness, but there's a first time for everything," he said.

He saw the fleck of disappointment in her eyes. He decided to give her something to chew on.

"We didn't find any fingerprints other than the Sweeny's and Roxy's. Deidra Sweeny said she'd left Pickles, their dog, to have free run of the entire house as was their custom. She also said Roxy hadn't been to their house in over a month. The addition of Roxy's fingerprints on the laundry room's door handle tells us she may have tried to put the dog in his bed."

"Pickles is a Lab. Must have a good nose, right?" Sonya asked.

"Perhaps, but for the most part he's old and has some rheumatism," Zeb said and changed the direction of the conversation. "Sonya, who were you referring to when you said 'we' and 'them'?"

Sonya tilted her head to one side. He wondered if she was trying to remember what she'd said. Her face brightened.

"Oh, yes. You are good, sheriff! What an excellent memory for details!"

He colored from the warmth of her compliments.

She continued, "I was with Willard of course at the time when Roxy and her dog arrived. Fritz may have been around, but one never knows about him, what with his constant comings and goings."

She stopped and smiled expectantly at him as if her last statement explained what happened.

"Fritz?" he asked, not sure he wanted an answer. "Who is Fritz?"

"My spirit companion," she said matter-of-factly.

Zeb worked hard to keep his facial expression deadpan.

"O-kay—," he said, drawing out the word.

He thought a change of approach a better tactic.

"Well, what about the Sweeny's dog, Pickles? Why was he with Roxy?"

It was Sonya's turn to look askance at him.

"Pickles?" she said, sounding confused, her head to one side.

Then she laughed. Her laughter was infectious. He wanted to share in her merriment against his own will. And out of the blue, it hit him. Sonya Caruthers was beautiful. His stomach dropped and he blushed. Immediately, he forced his gaze from her face and back to his cinnamon roll.

"Not Pickles," she said, her tone sweet. "Beast, the dog from the Highlands of Scotland. Somehow Beast is attached to the Sweenys. He's a ghost dog, you see, sheriff. He's come to protect them."

Chapter 23

The desk of Harry Sweeny was piled with baseball memorabilia, coffee cups, some ribbons, probably for the Golden Paw runner-ups, and a picture of his wife Deidra hugging their dog.

He'd spent the day studying the contract Titan's CEO, Patrick Lilton, had sent over for him to read. It was unusual to be in negotiations with the CEO of any company, but he and Patrick had known each other since high school. They'd had the occasional run-in at local restaurants and of course there was the time Roxy dated Patrick during high school. They'd spent a few family dinners together during those early years when Harry and Roxy's parents were still alive.

It was an excellent offer for the acquisition of Posh Pups, but Harry's attorney had brought two other extremely healthy contenders to the table in the last month. Titan wasn't the highest bidder, but it was the safest bet. For even considering the sell, Harry felt like a traitor to his father, who'd built the business, to Roxy, who had fought the idea of selling, and to the community of Willow Valley, who depended on it financially in many ways.

His phone buzzed beside him showing a text from his secretary. Patrick Lilton was here for the meeting. Shaking his head, Harry tried to clear the mental and emotional cobwebs from the last two days.

"I guess one shouldn't look a gift horse in the mouth," he said under his breath, adding, "better get him in here."

Posh Pups' office building was modest in size, so Patrick Lilton's arrival at Harry's office door was quick. To Harry, he looked like he'd deliberately dressed down for the meeting. Blue jeans, a checked Oxford shirt, and some leather loafers. The idea being conveyed must be that firm of Titan wasn't the cold, impersonal retail giant who eats smaller companies for tax write-offs, but instead your neighbor, friend, and regular guy.

One thing Harry knew for sure — Patrick Lilton was anything but casual, nor was he interested in hanging with the common man. Harry smiled at his cynical thoughts.

The man in the doorway nodded.

"Hope your smile means you like what you've read in the contract?" Patrick asked.

Standing up, Harry walked over offering his hand saying, "Come in Patrick. Thank you for meeting me here today. I'm sorry to not get back with you sooner."

Lilton held up his hand for Harry to stop.

"I heard about Roxy and I'm so sorry, Harry. I wouldn't have expected any response under these kinds of circumstances, but I am glad we were able to meet today. The board is excited about the possible acquisition of Posh Pups, and I don't have to tell you it's a business very close to my heart."

Harry nodded and coughed. Was the heart reference a Freudian slip about Roxy or deliberate? She'd dumped him for Teddy. God knows why.

"Have a seat, Patrick."

He indicated a comfortable chair across from his desk.

"Would you like some coffee? I'm afraid I'm an addict," he continued with a laugh indicating with a nod of his head the menagerie of cups cluttering his desk. "It's not usually this bad, but, well, since Roxy's…," he paused and coughed again, "I'm trying today to do the job of two people."

"I wouldn't mind a cup, if it isn't any trouble," Lilton replied.

Making the coffee gave Harry some time to think. He was exhausted from the last two days. Roxy's murder, Dog Days, this contract negotiation with Patrick, had turned his brain to mush. There wasn't anything left in him to try and be cagey or slick with his handling of Titan's offer. All he had left was to be direct.

"You take it with anything?" he asked.

"No, I like it plain."

"Good, so do I."

Handing Lilton his cup, Harry walked around to the other side of the desk.

"How do I know you won't sell this business or run it into the ground as a tax right-off?" he asked sitting back down and looking at Lilton over the brim of his cup.

"It's good business not to, Harry. You and Roxy have brought Posh Pups a long way from Sweeny Farm & Feed."

The mention of the old family name for the business brought a quick smile to Harry's face, but also a pang to his already guilt-ridden heart. He listened as Patrick continued his pitch.

"You've added three more brick-and-mortar stores in the last two years bringing you to a total of fourteen in a five-state radius. Online sales have increased forty-four percent since 2014 and our research shows your customers give Posh Pups a ninety percent satisfaction rating. Plus, Titan wants to build a stronger presence in the pet industry and it doesn't hurt you've done an excellent job of sourcing your products from American made companies. That's good press for Titan. If you're worried about the Willow Valley shipping warehouse, don't be. I've got no intention of turning my community against me by shutting down an employer who provides over three hundred jobs. The house Tamara built isn't something we ever intend to leave, so best not to burn bridges where you live. Posh Pups will keep its brand, only coming in under Titan's umbrella."

Harry nodded and offered a hint of a grin.

"Your offer sounds more than fair, Patrick. I've got to talk to Teddy. He's a tricky bastard. I know he's been wanting to be rid of the business, but now Roxy is dead and he holds her shares, I've got no idea what he'll do."

The other man said nothing for a moment.

"Harry," Patrick said, "when we first talked a year ago, I would never have thought you'd even consider selling Posh Pups. You and your sister weren't exactly on the same page, but you came to me and asked if Titan would be interested. I'd assumed you'd already offered the business to your sister and she didn't have the funds to buy you out."

Taking a steadying sip of coffee, Harry tried to think of the right words to say before plunging forward with his answer. Family was family, even if Teddy was a despicable ass.

"I'd offered to sell my shares to Roxy three years ago. She didn't have the money, but we'd never agreed on a long-range plan for my buy-out. My sister did not want to sell the business, but I'd wanted out almost since the day dad passed away. It was a contentious situation at best. The truth is Roxy was dealing with a real cash flow problem at home if you get my meaning. She needed Posh Pups to keep Teddy's lifestyle up and for a long time I was willing to keep going so she wouldn't have to suffer. Deidra has had enough. You don't know this, but last year, I had a minor scare with my blood pressure. That's when I let Roxy know I was done."

"If it was a cash flow problem with Roxy and Teddy, why didn't she want to sell it, make a killing over it? I know you've been approached by at least two other retailers. You and Roxy wouldn't have had to worry about money ever again."

"True," Harry replied. "But Roxy loved this business. She wanted to take it to a national level and add a new twist. Each Posh Pups location was going to have a state-of-the-art doggie daycare, veterinary clinic, and animal welfare assistance. It would have been an enormous capital investment. I saw myself being dragged along in Roxy's whirlwind for another ten years so I started to seriously consider how I was going to get out from under it all."

Neither man said anything for a few moments. The room was alive with unsaid thoughts until Patrick spoke.

"You talk to Teddy, Harry, and let me know. I will tell you though that he and I talked this morning about Titan buying his shares. I told him I wouldn't undercut you, but he made it clear he's also looking at other buyers."

Patrick paused and stood up from his chair putting his coffee cup down on the table beside him and continued.

"I want this business, Harry. Your family built a good thing here, but I think I can make it better. Sounds like you've got a wild card in Teddy. I'll look forward to your answer. In the meantime, if there is anything you and

Deidra need, just ask. Tamara and I have your family in our thoughts and prayers."

Harry showed Patrick to the main front door and watched him drive away. As he walked back to his office, Patrick's revelation regarding his brother-in-law ate at his mind.

"Teddy was so bereaved by his wife's death, he'd found time to already call Lilton about selling his shares," he said under his breath. "The lying, cheating ass. I'd like to kill him."

Chapter 24

With one side of his mind fighting a new attraction and the other wrestling with an insane conversation, Zeb had an uncontrollable urge to get up, walk away from Sonya, go home, and soak his head.

She was watching him closely.

"Sheriff?" she asked, her tone concerned. "You're worn out, aren't you? I bet you haven't slept since the night of the murder."

He shrugged, trying to keep his movements easy as if he wasn't bothered by lack of sleep or outrageous conversations.

"To be honest, most of what you're saying is, well," he hesitated to finish. He didn't want to say something to upset her.

"Crazy sounding?" she asked, finishing his unsaid thought.

Their eyes met. Her expression was full of humor and compassion for his awkward position.

"Trust me, sheriff. There are times when what I say even makes me cringe. I wish there was an easier way to explain things to people, but unfortunately, it is what it is. There is a ghost dog. His name is Beast. My ghost companion is a high maintenance, drama-king slash laird from Scotland. Roxy is gone. She passed over and it went well. I visited with the Sweenys today and they are, in my opinion, completely innocent of any wrongdoing. I want to see Pickles, their dog. May I have access to the Sweeny's main house? Harry and Deidra weren't sure if it would be okay with the police, so I didn't go in after our visit."

Zeb sat dumbly across from her. His brain feeling like ants were running through it the same way they do in a child's toy ant farm. He knew giving Sonya Caruthers, a known medium, carte blanche to visit the Sweeny's home to investigate on his behalf would be professional suicide on his part. On the other hand, he remembered how her talent had aided his investigation in another earlier murder. He needed this murder solved. The county was breathing down his neck.

An idea slowly came to him.

"I'll tell you what, Sonya," he said. "I think it might be a nice gesture to bring the Sweenys some of these rolls. Deputy Kirchner is going over to their guest house later to talk with Deidra Sweeny about the missing key. While he's talking with her, you'll have time with their dog and can check out the house. We can keep it between us. Sound okay with you?"

She smiled and nodded.

"There's one more thing. Harry Sweeny is in danger, sheriff. Roxy knew it and I've promised her I'd make sure he would be protected. Whoever killed her may have a reason for wanting her brother out of the way, too. I feel it's something to do with their business or their wealth. Roxy said she felt the killer's greed and lust. Today when I spoke with Harry, he described seeing Roxy during the rainstorm and he, too, had the same impression. He didn't remember the feeling until we talked, but the company they own, Posh Pups, will have some problems facing it. Roxy's husband, according to Harry Sweeny, wants to sell his shares. Also, if you interview Teddy Davidson, please ask him what his intentions are toward Roxy's three dogs."

Zeb nodded almost dumbly They'd been looking into Teddy Davidson's alibi and his motivations. Everything Sonya was saying, except for the three dogs statement, made sense to him. He knew people killed most of the time for either greed or love. Different sides of the same coin. But what was slightly annoying was how much Sonya knew and how she was asking *him* to get information for *her*.

"Maybe I should hire you to do all our investigations," he returned, sounding a bit peevish. "I don't have any proof Roxy Davidson was the intended victim, Sonya. She may have been killed by someone breaking into the Sweeny's house to steal from them. That is a greedy action, too."

"Nothing was taken, correct?" Sonya asked.

"No, but the killer's original objective may have been to ransack the house for valuables. Roxy came in, she saw them and they killed her. We need more proof."

They were both quiet for a moment.

"I know one thing for sure, Roxy believed her brother was in danger," Sonya said.

Zeb replied, "We've considered putting an officer on protective duty for the Sweenys."

Sonya looked up at him, giving him a warm, kind smile. She reached over a patted his hand in the same way an old friend might offer a simple comforting gesture.

"There's no need," Sonya said simply, removing her hand and picking up her cup, taking a dainty sip.

He was bewitched. In her eye, he surely saw a twinkle.

"Do you know something Sonya you'd like to share with the police?" he asked.

"They've hired a security man. Mr. Alfonso. Patted me down today to make sure I wasn't carrying a weapon. Nice man, but cold hands."

It was like emotional ping-pong. Within seconds, he went from feeling like a balloon full of helium to now feeling a sudden sharp stab of intense dislike for a man he'd never met. With his mind muddled by all these spasmodic emotions, he felt like exploding. As an act of self-preservation, he got up from the table and lifted his hat.

"Guess I'd better go meet the competition," he said, kicking himself the minute the last word dropped from his lips. "I mean, well you know, the competition for the police. We will put a man on the Sweenys as well. Gotta keep our promises, right?"

Rattled, he shook his head at her.

Sonya looked up at him, her expression surprised.

"Uh, well, yes. That is very kind of you, sheriff. Are you already leaving?" she asked, her tone disappointed.

He nodded, saying, "Got to get back to the investigation. Have some more statements to go over. Goodbye. I'll keep in touch,"

Zeb Walker turned and walked toward Sonya's garden gate, the entire way feeling like a man who'd been sucker-punched, straight in the one place he'd promised himself he'd never let anyone get near again, his heart.

Chapter 25

"Pineville's done with the forensic work. You're free to do what you want with the park," Tommy Kirchner was saying to Presley King as they stood outside a smoothie place sipping green, foamy drinks. "Dog Days starts tomorrow, so I can imagine how pressed for time you are."

"It's been crazy. We need the tents up by the end of the day. The workmen have a stage and bleachers to erect and I've got at least fifteen sponsors who've paid to have their company's logos emblazoned along the main tent's inside walls. And if Dog Days wasn't enough stress, Wesley didn't come home last night and my mom is about to have a conniption."

Deputy Kirchner screwed up his mouth to one side and took a long drag from his straw. He felt bad for his best friend. He knew Presley and his mother, Rosalie, had spent many a day and night over the last ten years worrying over Wesley.

Trying to make light of the situation, Tommy said, "He's probably out with one of his many girlfriends. Don't worry. Tell Rosalie, I'm going keep an eye out for him."

Presley shrugged.

"You're right. I've got too much work right now to go hunting for him."

Tommy's work cell phone rang. As he picked it up, the police radio in his car buzzed into life requesting his immediate response.

"Hey, I gotta go, buddy. Both of us better get to work," Tommy said and headed to his police car tapping the green answer button.

"See ya!" Presley called from behind him.

Immediately upon answering his phone, Tommy heard the serious tone in Sarah, the dispatcher's, voice.

"Deputy Kirchner, you're to respond to a 10-100 at Meyer Woods. Sheriff Walker is also en route."

Tommy spoke into his receiver, "On my way."

Within ten minutes, he was maneuvering his vehicle down a dirt road originally built as a fire break alongside Meyer Woods.

An unusual sensation of fear had taken root in his stomach. The dispatcher said it was a 10-100, meaning a dead body had been found. His intuition kept trying to shoot up the most obvious flare, but he refused to look at what it wanted to reveal.

Soon, he was within the part of the forest bordering Willow Valley and coming into view, he saw someone waving. In front of a massive pile of brush was Marnie Scott, the owner of the Whispering Pines RV Park, and her two dogs, Lewis and Clark. Tommy pulled up beside her and recognized the signs of shock apparent in her face. He jumped out of his car.

"Marnie, come on," he said soothingly, "get inside my car and sit down."

He didn't wait for a response, but took her hand and guided her around the vehicle. Her expression was flat and he noticed the clamminess of her skin.

"It's a dead person, Tommy," she said finally as he got her to sit down in his passenger seat. "It's in the brush pile. The dogs found it. I don't want them to go near it again."

"Marnie, you're going to be okay. I want you to stay right here. Do you understand?" he asked, looking her in the eyes and keeping his voice gentle, but firm.

She nodded and he noticed she had a death grip on the two dog's leashes.

"I'm so sorry. I couldn't look," she said. "Oh, God! Tommy," she continued, her voice rising in hysteria, "It's a man's hand. He's got a ring on. One like they wear when they play football. You know, like if they've won an important game."

Her words made his stomach constrict. Tears filled her eyes as Tommy heard the engine of another vehicle swiftly approaching.

"I need to go over there and look, Marnie. Will you be okay for a few minutes?"

She nodded her willingness to stay put, but before he could leave her, Sheriff Walker's utility vehicle pulled up next to him and stopped. The sheriff got out and walked over to Marnie.

Zeb asked, "Marnie, are you okay?"

She shook her head.

"We've got it now, Marnie," he told her.

He reached into the back seat of Tommy's vehicle where a blanket was kept for this kind of purpose. Taking it out, he wrapped her up in it and gave her a squeeze.

"Better? I want you to sit here. Don't get up. I'll be right back. Okay?"

Marnie nodded.

"I'll be fine, Zeb. The hand has a big ring on it. Like the one you see the football players wear."

"I'll take a look."

"Sir," Tommy said after swallowing hard, "Wesley King's mother and brother said he didn't come home last night."

The sheriff nodded saying, "Where's the body?"

"There."

Tommy pointed at the brush pile.

"Sorry, but I arrived only a few seconds before you. Haven't had a chance to check for signs of life."

"Stay back here," Zeb said. "Fewer feet around the site, the better."

He watched Zeb walk over, kneel and reach in between the limbs and twigs of the brush pile with his hand feeling for a pulse in the person's arm. Finally, he shook his head, got up and came back over.

"Whoever is in here, he is dead and not only has someone tried to conceal the body, I think they intended to destroy it. Do you smell gasoline, too?"

The smell was strong.

"Yes, I do," Tommy answered. "Sir?"

But Zeb continued his instructions.

"We need to keep as many feet from tampering with the area including our own until the forensic team has a go at it."

Tommy tried again, "Do you think it was Wesley King?"

Zeb turned and gave the younger man a hard look which softened as he must have realized the connection Tommy had with the King family.

"No way to tell, Tom. I'm sorry, very sorry if it is. I need you to take Marnie's statement. She's calm enough. Better to catch any information from her now, before she has time to double think herself. Take her home and come back."

"Do you want me to call Pineville?"

"No," Zeb said, sounding weary. "I'll call Pineville and have them send forensics out here. Looks like we've got another homicide. Two in two days in Willow Valley. This must be some kind of record."

Chapter 26

Babette Nichols turned the closed sign in the window of her pilates studio to open. Soon they would arrive, but not for another thirty minutes giving her time to catch up on some accounting.

Women vied to get a slot in this particular class. The next session was the one Roxy Davidson, Deidra Sweeny and of course, Tamara Lilton attended, three of the five women in Willow Valley who, if you had their ear, could get things done for you.

The other two star attendees were both from monied families who'd lived in the area for fifty years and like to throw money at community projects the same way someone on a park bench might toss popcorn at pigeons.

There were a few more women who came as well, but if you wanted to rub sweaty elbows with the female power elite of Willow Valley, this was the only pilates class in town.

Babs had a love-hate attitude toward her clients. They paid a premium price for this particular class, and yet she also despised them because, in her opinion, they were privileged snobs. There was one saving grace for Babs in the situation. In her mind, she looked better than they did. The time spent with them, for her, was always a nice confidence builder.

An electronic bell dinged indicating an arrival. Looking up, to her surprise, she saw Teddy Davidson standing in the door with a bouquet of yellow roses, smiling.

"Hey, baby!" she gushed coming over to him. She was well aware of his thirsty gaze as it took in her perfectly proportioned and taut body.

"What brings you by? This isn't the best time. My class starts soon. People might talk!"

She finished the last sentence with a flash of sarcasm in her voice and a giggle.

"I wanted to see you, Babs," he said, sounding weirdly serious in her opinion.

Teddy wasn't the sober type whether in thought or action. So his tone fired a subtle warning signal across her bow. She watched him closely.

"Sure, Teddy. What about?"

"We need to talk."

Babs was an excellent reader of other people's intentions. Teddy's body language and odd display of gift-giving, especially in such a potentially public situation as her pilates studio, was out of order. They'd been keeping their affair on the down-low. She shifted immediately into her most successful survival mode with men.

"Sure," she said reaching up, wrapping her arms around his neck, pressing her body into his and kissing him on the mouth.

Finished with her first tactical maneuver, she said soft and low, "Those flowers for me?"

Teddy had reciprocated the kiss with great gusto. She could feel the initial tension in him melting. Pulling away, she initiated stage two by going on a relationship offensive.

Like any pro, she knew how to play the person, not the situation.

"Teddy, I love the flowers, but I think it might be time for us to cool our…" she made a flippant wave gesture of her hand, indicating hopefully to him she was trying to dust-off an invisible thing she may be losing interest in with each passing minute.

"What should we call them, Teddy? Our get-togethers? I'm…I am not comfortable with the situation. It feels," she scrunched her nose, the same way people do when they smell something unpleasant, "dirty since your wife's death."

She offered him a chilly smile.

The maneuver of being the first person in the relationship to go cold was always an excellent move for anyone wanting to recapture the other person's attention. Babs waited to see Teddy's reaction as she inspected the yellow roses he still held, all be it now limply, in his hand. It hit her, yellow roses! He'd brought them as a token of apology before he dumped her.

"I…I…I didn't know you felt *that* way. I came here today…" he stammered.

His voice trailed off. She heard the emotion in his voice.

"Why *did* you come here today?" she asked, sounding peeved, but unsure.

He looked back up at her, "I came here today to tell you nothing is standing in our way now. Roxy's gone and I've removed the problems keeping us from having the life we've talked about."

Babs was shocked. She stared at him. How could she have got it so wrong?

"Why *yellow* roses?" she squeaked.

He shifted his gaze down at the bunch of flowers. As she watched him intensely, his expression was one of surprise, like he'd forgotten they were still in his hand.

"Oh, well, you said you liked my yellow race car. So, I thought you liked yellow."

A wastebasket sat within reach. Tossing the flowers into them, he turned and pushed on the door's handle to leave.

In her mind, Babs wrestled with three conflicting thoughts. First, the man was a sweet simpleton, but a rich one which made him perfect. Something akin to affection sprung up in her heart. It scared her.

Second, if she had it right, he wanted to take their relationship out of the closet, bring it into the light. She had honestly thought from his demeanor, he had come here to dump her. Most rich men usually did. They never left their wives. It was too expensive, but Roxy was conveniently out of the way.

Third, going public would bring the entire town down on them. Roxy was dead…beloved by all who knew her, except herself and Teddy. They'd be like lepers.

The door shut. He was gone.

"Wait!" she called, catapulting herself through the door and finding he'd already made it to his truck. "Teddy! I'm sorry!"

He turned around, looking like a wounded pup.

"You're sorry?" he asked. "What do you mean?"

"I mean, I thought you'd come to…to end it," she said. "I was scared. I like you, Teddy. I don't want this to be over."

"Why did you say you did?"

How to explain it? Her mind worked fast. Best to go with the easiest truth.

"I thought you were here to dump me. Yellow roses are usually a gift you give to a friend. It's a way someone can say, 'I want to be only friends'. Do you see why I went on the defensive?"

His face broke out into a smile.

"Well, girl! You gotta not read so much into everything!"

He laughed and grabbed her in a lover's hug and kissed her in the parking lot for God and all of Willow Valley to see, including Tamara Lilton, who was pulling up in front of the studio.

"I guess the cat's out of the bag, Teddy," Babs said laughing with a cock of her head in the direction of Tamara. "They're gonna crucify us. You understand, right?"

"Who cares," he said. "With the money I'm gonna get from the sale of Posh Pups, we can blow this town and kiss those clawing cats," he gave another nod in Tamara's direction, "goodbye."

Chapter 27

Sonya put the sandwich down in front of Marnie and refilled her cup of chamomile tea.

"Try and eat something, honey. You're shaken up from what you saw. You need a bite to eat and the tea will calm your nerves," she said trying to use an even, comforting tone.

Taking up the fork, Marnie picked at the edge of the homemade bread of the sandwich. She put a modest bite in her mouth as she sat gazing through the bay window at the three dogs, Lewis, Clark, and Willard, running about in the garden.

"I don't even know who it was, Sonya," she said. "I told Tommy to bring me here, to your house. I didn't want to go home. I hope you don't mind. Moving here and building up the RV park hasn't given me much time for getting to know a lot of people."

"I'm glad you came here. To be honest, I think two heads are always better than one," Sonya said soothingly. "You and the boys are welcome to stay with me. Quite honestly, I wouldn't mind having someone with me for a few days. At least until they find who's responsible for these murders."

Marnie nodded and sipped her tea. Soon, she returned to eating her sandwich with more interest. Neither woman spoke for some time. Sonya's phone rang, bringing them back from their mutual silence. She tapped the accept button and lifted the phone to her ear.

"Yes?" she answered. "Oh my goodness! Lana, I completely forgot! I'm so sorry."

There was a long pause as she listened and her eyes darted over at Marnie.

"Yes, she's here. Uh-huh, it's been a terrible shock. No, she didn't see who it was. They're not releasing the name of the victim. I will. Yes, I'll be there definitely tomorrow. Thank you, Lana, and again, I'm so, so sorry for not remembering."

Putting down the phone, Sonya took a deep breath and let it out.

"You forgot your hair appointment?" Marnie asked, a faint smile pulling at the corner of her mouth.

Sonya nodded.

"Lana must already know about the body in Meyer Woods. How the talk does get around in this town. Who in the world told her I was the one who found the body?" Marnie asked.

"Lana said Trudy, the receptionist at the funeral home, was there to have her color touched up. Carl Brackmen, the funeral director and county coroner, was on his way to Meyer Woods to sign the death certificate and collect the body. Trudy saw you in Tommy's patrol car as she was going over to Lana's shop. She put two-and-two together and realized you were the one who found the body. With Lana being Zeb's mother, she probably thought it was okay to talk to her about it."

For a minute, Marnie sat quietly and reaching over, she grabbed one of the no-bake cookies sitting on a plate in front of her.

"Sonya?" Marnie said softly.

"Yes?"

"Do you think the killer was still there in the woods? Do you think they saw me find the body?"

Not wanting to distress Marnie further, Sonya shook her head.

"I doubt it. I would think a killer wouldn't hang around after disposing of someone. They would want to get away as soon as possible."

Marnie sat quietly, not moving, only staring out at the three dogs romping about in the yard. The cookie she held was poised halfway between plate and mouth. Sonya watched her face.

"What is it, Marnie? Did you see something out there you're afraid to talk about?"

Slowly, Marnie turned her gaze away from the window toward Sonya.

"What if the killer *thinks* I saw them? You see, there was such a smell of gasoline. I…I think they intended to light the pile of brush, but I came along. They were probably watching me the entire time."

Marnie shivered and put the cookie back on the plate.

"Did you?" Sonya asked. "See anyone?"

A look of fear took shape in Marnie's eyes.

"No. I didn't recognize anyone, but they might *think* I did," she said.

Confused, Sonya shook her head.

"I don't understand, Marnie. What are you trying to say exactly?"

"I mean, I saw someone out in the woods. It was only a figure, and when it disappeared, what with the bright colors of the fall trees and the sunlight, I thought I'd imagined it."

"Did you mention it to the police?" Sonya asked.

"No, because I wasn't sure, but my head is clearing. If this killer thinks I saw them, they might also think I would be able to identify them. Sonya, I'm scared."

Sitting back in her chair, Sonya sighed and thought to herself, "Thanks to Trudy, everyone in town knows you were the one in Meyer's Woods who found the body," but she didn't dare say it out loud.

"I'm leaving," Marnie said standing up abruptly from the table, making the dishes and silverware clatter like wind chimes in a sudden breeze. "I'm taking the boys and going to my Aunt Maureen's in Atlanta for a few weeks. I'll let Dale, my handyman, run the RV park. He'll love being in complete control. As soon as they've caught the killer, I'll pack up the camper and head back north."

Sonya smiled. She already knew how this was going to go, but it was the first gut reaction and Marnie needed to work through the initial fear.

"Honey, sit down for a minute before you go flying off to Atlanta."

She patted the seat where Marnie had only seconds ago vacated.

"You need to take a moment and remember this: you can't leave town after finding a body. The police probably won't let you. If you're afraid, you need to stay here with me. We've got plenty of watchdogs. Willard plus Lewis and Clark will let us know if a squirrel so much as crosses the road out in front of this house."

Marnie hesitated, but finally sat back down.

"A squirrel, possibly, but I'm talking about another sort of nutter," she added. "One who walks on two legs."

Sonya gave a soft laugh.

"I don't think there's anything to worry about, Marnie. Let's try it out and I'll ask Deputy Kirchner if he'll keep my house on his surveillance rounds. Sound good?"

"Okay, but I have one request if I'm going to stay here," Marnie said picking up the half-eaten sandwich lying on her plate and beginning to eat it.

"What?" Sonya asked while biting into her second cinnamon roll. It had been a rough day for any diet.

"Don't cook anything while I'm here. No bread, no rolls, no cakes or cookies, understand?"

Taken aback, but her mouth now full, she managed a, "How come?"

Mumbling also through a mouth half-full of bread, Marnie said, "Cause I'll eat every bit of it, and when it comes time to go home, I won't fit through the door of my fifth wheel anymore!"

In unison, the two women swallowed hard and burst into laughter.

Chapter 28

With the sun long since down, the forensic team continued working. Huge floodlights lit the area while men and women in protective clothing moved about the forested area taking samples, collecting photographs and discussing among themselves the crime scene.

Already, the body had been removed from its twig-and-limb tomb and the coroner, Zeb, and Tommy stood in somber respectfulness around the gurney it rested on.

"Wesley King," Tommy said, his voice hoarse with emotion. "This is going to be rough on Rosalie and Presley."

"Did the contusion kill him, Carl, or was he given something?" Zeb asked the coroner.

Carl Brackmen didn't reply immediately. He continued to study Wesley King's face.

With a sigh, he said, "I won't make any assumptions right now, Zeb. Once I've done a post mortem, I'll call you. The body will be at the mortuary until we have an ID from a family member. Rosalie," he shook his head and clearing his throat, continued, "poor woman. She or Presley can call me anytime, even if it's tonight. I'll meet them there."

Brackmen walked away to his van leaving the sheriff and the deputy alone.

"Sheriff, would you let me go tell the Kings?" Tommy asked.

Zeb saw the young man had been on the verge of tearing up since the body had been removed from the brush pile.

"Presley is my best friend. I'd like it to come from me. I promised Presley only today...I'd find him."

A tear broke free finally from Tommy's eye. Zeb reached over and rested a reassuring hand on the young deputy's shoulder.

"These are the toughest ones we ever do, Tom. I'm sorry you have to go through this. If you need some time, you can have it...after Dog Days. We need every man tomorrow."

They were quiet for a moment. Zeb screwed up his forehead making deep lines form across his brow.

"Tom, what did you mean about finding Wesley?"

"Presley told me earlier today, Wesley had been gone since yesterday. I told Presley I'd keep a look-out for his brother. I honestly thought, and so did Presley, he'd gone off with a woman somewhere."

Quiet, the sheriff stood thinking for a moment.

"Go and tell the Kings. Try and ask them about recent conversations or unusual happenings around their home. If they are up to it, ask them when was the last time they saw him. Take both of their statements. We may need forensics over there as well."

"It's going to be a lot to expect from them tonight, sir," Tommy said.

"Rosalie has two sisters living in Tulsa. Tell Presley to call them and get them up here for his mother. That's what family does, pads the shock."

"Yes, sir. I'd better go. I think I'll be up most of the night."

Zeb nodded his head up and down.

"Fine. Be in tomorrow at two o'clock. I'll need help with the parade and I'll need you to go by and see the Sweenys. I want you to take Sonya, er I mean Mrs. Caruthers there tomorrow. I need to know more about the lost key from the outdoor planter and I need Mrs. Caruthers to have access to the main house. Tomorrow, I'm in Pineville in the morning, but afterward, I'll see you at the parade."

"Sonya?" Tommy asked. A swift smile broke across the younger man's face but was quickly snuffed out again. "You wanna fill me in, sir?"

Zeb shot him a steely look.

"Call Mrs. Caruthers tomorrow afternoon after the parade and before you head over to the Sweeny's house. I'd like you to get more information regarding who else besides them was aware of the key in the plant urn. Understand? Let Mrs. Caruthers go about her own business. She's looking into something for me. You won't discuss this with anyone. Understand?"

The last sentence was said without much eye contact on the sheriff's part. With a shrug, the young deputy nodded his assent and walked to his vehicle leaving the older man to watch him go.

As Tommy drove away, Zeb went over to where Brackmen, the coroner was shutting the doors of his van.

"Between you and me, sheriff," Brackmen said, "your killer is a left-hander with a helluva swing. Probably shorter than Wesley, but taller than Roxy Davidson."

"No idea of the murder weapon yet?" Zeb asked.

"On Roxy, the skull fracture was consistent with either a tire iron or a fireplace tool. Same with Wesley King. Your

killer has a favorite implement. These two deaths remind
me of a murder investigation I worked in Springfield ten
years ago. Turned out the killer was an auto repairman who
went bankrupt because two of his wealthy clients refused to
pay what they owed him. He killed them with a crowbar.
This murderer may be in a service role, mistreated by a
monied client or is disgruntled by his financial situation.
Both Roxy Davidson and Wesley King had lots of money."

"Well, it's true they both lived affluent lives paid for by
others. Wesley was a ladies' man living at his mother's.
There's been a few men, husbands, and a few women who
might've liked to take a crowbar to him. As for Roxy, the
story is she was cash short. I don't know. I'd like to rule out
one thing, Carl."

"What's that?"

"Let me know if both victims have had coitus in the last
twenty-four hours, okay? I want to know if they were
involved," Zeb said, shaking his head and looking down at
the ground. "I'm going to wait on forensic's report. Wesley
was a big man and whoever got him out here," he looked
past Brackmen into the darkness of the forest, "had to use
something other than force."

Brackmen sighed and asked, "You think it was a
woman?"

"I think it would have taken a man's strength to have
dragged Wesley into a brush pile and cover him with those
huge limbs," Zeb answered. "No sign of a struggle, and
whoever killed him removed any signs of the body being
moved. It's like he climbed into the pile of limbs and
bashed himself over the head."

Carl nodded.

"Women have always managed to make me do some
pretty stupid stuff. Some of it I'd probably do again…for

the right reward," he said, a goofy grin spreading across his mouth.

Zeb's tired face also spread into a smile.

"Truer words were never spoken, Carl." He paused, and added, "How *is* your wife, Angie?"

"She's in Iceland right now probably sitting in a geothermal spa," Carl Brackmen said, his expression tinged with irritation.

"Good life, if you can get it," Zeb offered half-heartedly.

Carl Brackmen shrugged.

"Good life as long as I can afford it."

In a probable attempt to shift the conversation away from his globe-trotting, expensive wife, Brackmen asked, "You look half beat, sheriff."

"Two murders in two days," Zeb said, "and nothing to connect them, but the same possible murder weapon and geography."

"Geography?" Brackmen repeated.

"Roxy Davidson was at the Sweeny's home when she was murdered. Wesley King lives with his mother whose home is not two hundred yards from the Sweeny's. Can't be a coincidence, can it?" Zeb said more than asked. "I want to know if they were having an affair."

Brackmen scuffed the ground with the bottom of his shoe in a gesture of thought.

"Okay. I'll let ya know. I gotta go, but I'll say this: I don't envy you your job, sheriff. Dog Days, two murders and a killer on the loose. You've got a lot on your plate."

Zeb nodded.

"Thanks for putting it into such stark relief for me, Carl."

"Hey, if I could strap on a gun and help you out, I would, but I'm more of a lover than a fighter. As it is, I've got to go do an autopsy."

Zeb cringed at the thought of opening a dead body and pilfering through its organs.

"I don't know Brackmen," he said. "I think I'd rather work with the living."

"Perhaps," Carl said now sitting in the driver's seat of his van. "But, I prefer working with the dead over shooting at maniacs. You don't wanna switch jobs, do ya?"

"Nah, I'll wear the gun and hunt the bad guys," Zeb said with a slow, tired smile.

Shrugging, Brackmen said, "I guess we're all trying to make a living."

Rolling up the windows of the van, Brackman drove away. His last words reminding Zeb of what Sonya had said about Roxy feeling her killer's lust for money.

As the van carrying Wesley King's body disappeared into the gloom, Zeb made a decision. Tomorrow, he would talk with Teddy Davidson and most likely, Teddy's attorney.

Chapter 29

Day Three

It was a somber feeling in Lana's Beauty Shoppe when
Sonya walked through the door the next morning. Because
it was early, the place was empty of clients.

The usual laughter, gossipy conversations, or easy
comfortableness typical to Willow Valley's favorite female
retreat was nonexistent due to the shock of two murders in
such a small community.

Lana motioned for Sonya to come and have a seat at her
station. As she followed her through, Jaxon and Sabrianna,
two of Lana's stylists, were sitting at the shop's communal
lunch table. They were deep in a heated conversation
regarding Presley King.

"He's over there, all alone without anyone to…," Sabe
was saying.

But she was quickly interrupted by Jaxon finishing her
sentence, his tone sarcastic.

"I know what you're going to say, Sabrianna Williams.
'Love him back to health?' Really! You're acting soooo
desperate, Sabe."

Jaxon shook his head in a gesture of mock, dramatic
disgust.

Sabe, compelled into a hot annoyance, retorted, "I am
not desperate! Presley King is a fine, heart-broken man
suffering over there, Jaxon."

"You don't have to tell me, Sabe, honey. I have two perfectly good eyes. It's just you throwing yourself at him, is so…"

"Jaxon Ivy!" Sabe said slinging herself out of the chair she was sitting in. "You of all people have no room to take a holier-than-thou attitude. I've seen the way Chris treats you."

"He treats me like a princess!" Jaxon hotly exclaimed.

"Enough!" Lana hollered from the back room's doorway. "You two have gotten yourselves all lathered up over nothin'."

Both young people hunkered down in their chairs for a Lana reprimand.

"It's been a terrible shock to this town to lose two of our own. Rosalie King is a dear, dear friend of mine. I know we," she looked sternly at Jaxon and Sabe, her hands on her hips, "want to offer any help we can at this time, but chewing on each other is the worst thing we can do. It's selfish. You're both young. You didn't know any better, but now you do."

Jaxon simpered and returned to folding towels while Sabe sat rigidly in her chair, flipping through her favorite social media site with a scowl on her pretty face.

"Take a seat," Lana said.

Appearing unfazed from managing the histrionics of the young, Lana pointed to the pink leather, rhinestone-encrusted chair she liked to call 'the throne'.

"Climb up."

As Sonya made herself comfortable, she studied Sheriff Walker's mother. Lana was a well-made woman. Tall, with thick auburn hair and green eyes the color of jade, it was easy to see Zeb had inherited her Irish blood.

With Sonya settled and a cape around her neck, Lana put both hands on her hips for a second time and said, "So what'll it be today? I think the lavender strip was a success last time."

Nodding, Sonya replied, "Me too. My hair is so curly, it blended nicely. Let's do it again."

"I'll be right back. Gotta mix the color."

With Lana gone to the back room, Sonya swiveled her chair around to face the two young stylists sitting at the round table.

"You two doing okay?" she asked, her tone kind.

Looking up at the same time, it was Sabe who answered first.

"I'm in shock, Mrs. Caruthers. I went to school with Presley and Wesley. They were both such nice boys. Rosalie, their mom, must be…" Sabe faltered.

"Heartbroken," Sonya offered gently.

Sabe nodded, her lovely, brown eyes beginning to fill with tears.

"If you want my opinion," Jaxon added, "I think he was killed by a jealous boyfriend or husband."

"Why so, Jaxon?" Sonya asked, her mind zeroing in on the idea.

"Because there wasn't a woman within twenty miles of Willow Valley who didn't come within Wesley's radar whom he didn't make a move on. Young or old, he knew how to charm women. Everyone knew it."

"It's true, Mrs. Caruthers," Sabe corroborated. "Wesley was a smooth operator. Not as good looking as Presley, his younger brother, but he made up for it with his charming ways."

"Jaxon did Wesley often have trouble with jealous husbands or boyfriends?" Sonya asked.

"Honey, did you ever *see* Wesley King?" Jaxon asked.

Sonya lightly chuckled.

"No," she answered.

The young man shook his head.

"He could've caused all the trouble he wanted. He stood at least six foot two and had been lifting weights since he was ten. Now, mind you, that's what has the whole town talking. He wasn't shot. He wasn't poisoned. He wasn't hit by a truck. They say he was found with a tiny bump on the side of his head. Incredible!" Jaxon finished.

Sabe gave him a sour side look.

"People hit on the temple, Jaxon, die easily," she said.

From the blue, a vision sprang into Sonya's mind. Her heart beat hard in her chest as a sense of fear settled upon her. Without fail, this kind of unbidden, organic revelations always came to fruition.

Though she'd never laid eyes on Presley King, the brother of the dead man, her instincts told her he was in great danger. But it was the second image of Mrs. Townsend, which horrified her more. The elderly lady was receiving a deadly gift.

"Sabe," she blurted as she opened her eyes, bringing both young people to immediate, stiff attention. "Get my purse. Now!"

Like a woman who's backend was lit on fire, Sabe jumped from her chair and grabbed the purse practically volleying it into Sonya's lap.

"Here, Mrs. Caruthers," she exhaled breathily and flashed a worried look in the direction of a gaping Jaxon.

Digging out her cell phone, Sonya dialed Zeb's number and waited with her heart pounding in her chest for him to answer. Sabe and Jaxon watched her as if she might self-combust at any moment. The terrible anxiety of waiting for the sheriff to answer made each moment feel like a lifetime. His voicemail finally picked up.

"Sheriff, please call me immediately," Sonya pleaded into the phone. "I…I…" her gaze locked on to Sabe's and Jaxon's dual wide-eyed expressions and she reconsidered her next words, "I need you to please call me!"

She tapped 'end' on the phone's glass face and slumped in the chair as Lana came around the corner with the bowl of color in her hand.

Like two young owlets with the return of their mother, both Jaxon and Sabe's heads swiveled in tandem to the left and their mouths made movements before their voices caught up.

"Lana!" Jaxon squeaked out first, "Mrs. Caruthers had one of her visions! Right here in our salon! It was…" he laid his hand where his heart rested. "Amazing!"

A huge smile spread across his face as soon as the words hit the air. He turned to Sabe who nodded, her mouth pulled into a pretty, but taught bow.

Lana regarded her two charges and shifting her weight to the other hip, she slung her gaze over to Sonya.

She asked nonplussed, "What'd ya see, Sonya? Do you know who the killer is?"

No one moved. All eyes were on Sonya and she swallowed hard before answering.

"I did *not* see the killer but," she turned her face to Sabe. The taught muscles at her temples twitched, "I think someone is in terrible danger."

Flinging the cape off of herself, Sonya stood up out of the bejeweled chair.

"I've got to go see the police, Lana. These visions are always right. No time to waste."

She grabbed her wallet and pulling two twenty dollar bills out, she laid them down on Lana's station counter.

"I'm sorry to have to leave like this."

Lana shook her head and picked up the two twenties. Reaching for Sonya's hand, she gently laid the bills back into her palm.

"Sit down, Sonya. Zeb sent a text saying he's gone to Pineville for a meeting. After he's done, he has to handle security for the Pooch Parade beginning at two o'clock this afternoon. His phone is unable to receive calls and he wanted me to stop by at lunch and get Popcorn, his dog-child, and bring her back here. Let me do your hair and," she turned to Sabrianna, "you call the sheriff's office and have them send an officer over. Tell them Lana said so."

Lana's motherly, no-nonsense attitude ruled and Sonya resumed her position in the bejeweled chair. Sabe dialed the sheriff's office.

"Hello? Yes, this is Sabrianna Williams at Lana's Beauty Shoppe. Lana says to send an officer over immediately."

There was a long pause as they waited to hear what Sabe would say next. She put the phone to her well-endowed bosom and said to Lana, "They want to know if it's an emergency?"

Not missing a beat with the application of the color to Sonya's head, Lana replied, "Is that Sarah you're talking to Sabe?"

Sabe put the phone back to her ear.

"Lana wants to know if it's you, Sarah?"

The young woman hearing the answer nodded in the affirmative to Lana who continued applying haircolor. In a bored tone, she gave the next instructions to Sabe.

"Tell them it's a matter of life and death. But tell Sarah to tell the officers to not use any sirens. The last thing I need is half of Willow Valley poking their noses into my shop. Those old men across the street at Tilly's don't need any more reason to gossip either."

Sabe imparted Lana's demands to Sarah and hung up. Within five minutes, two affable officers swung the door open of Lana's shop.

"Hey Mrs. Walker," the taller one said with a grin. "What's the story?"

"Hello, Andrew and Michael," Lana said, again with the hand-on-the-hip nonchalance gesture. "You need to listen to Mrs. Caruthers here. She has something to tell you. Sonya, take the boys back to my office. You can have some privacy there."

Sonya internally cringed. Being taken seriously wasn't going to be easy. Wearing a pink, zebra print cape and her hair lathered up with colorful goo, she gave a whole new definition to the term crackpot. Taking a deep breath, she stepped down from the chair.

"Follow me," she said with a sigh, and led the two uniformed men back to Lana's office.

Once they were sitting down, Sonya offered the officers a weak smile.

"Now take your time Mrs. Caruthers," Andrew said.

"Well," she began, choosing her words carefully, "I saw something and I'm fearful there are two people who may be in danger."

The men exchanged quick, yet serious expressions. Andrew took the lead in the interrogation.

"What did you see?" he asked.

"I saw Presley King and Mrs. Townsend, my neighbor, being hunted but also receiving a deadly gift," she said meekly.

Now, both men crinkled up their eyes in a confused gesture.

"When?" Andrew demanded more than asked.

"A few minutes ago," Sonya replied.

Andrew thumbed in the direction of the front of Lana's shop, "Out in the street?"

Sonya hesitated and clasped her hands together in an anxious way.

"Not exactly. You see I have visions and they're never wrong."

Her words came spilling out of her as she watched their facial expressions turn from confused to disbelief. She knew once the word 'visions' came out of her mouth, she'd lost any hope of the officers believing her.

"I'm sorry to have wasted your time," Sonya said sagging back into Lana's comfortable desk chair. "No one's going to believe me, but you've got to put some sort of extra protection on Presley King and Mrs. Townsend of Pickwick Street. They've seen or heard something regarding these killings and their lives are in great danger."

The men rose from their seats and Andrew again took the lead.

"Mrs. Caruthers, we appreciate your concern and don't worry anymore. There's an officer stationed at the King residence. As for your neighbor, Mrs. Townsend, once the Dog Days Pooch Parade is over, I'll personally go over and check on her. Thank you. Now, we gotta get back to the office. There's a lot to handle with the parade this afternoon."

The officers walked toward the door.

"One last thing," Sonya said to their backs.

They turned around.

"The killer won't use a tire iron next time."

Andrew's face became stone still. Why Sonya instantly knew the murderer's original weapon, she couldn't have answered in a million years, but her words arrested the attention of the two men.

"The next time," she said softly, "it will be poison."

Chapter 30

Zeb had taken the morning to discuss the forensic evidence with the county's lead forensic investigator in Pineville. The wounds on both victims were made by a metal instrument most likely a tire iron or a fireplace poker. The investigator was leaning toward tire iron because they'd found traces of copper in both Roxy's and Wesley's hair.

Another piece of evidence was Wesley King's jacket with dog hair on it. He didn't own a dog. They told Zeb there should be a match for the type of breed within forty-eight hours. As for Roxy Davidson, her corpse gave up nothing as to who her murder might be.

His next stop was to surprise Teddy Davidson at his home. He'd sent one of his deputies to keep an eye on Roxy's widower, so when Zeb was ready, he'd have a bead on where to find him. Fortunately, Teddy stayed put at home all morning, so when Zeb rang the doorbell, he expected him to answer. The surprise was on him.

"Hello, sheriff," Babette Nicols cooed. She offered him a ravishing, unapologetic smile. "Looking for someone?"

Zeb was pretty sure Babette's only clothing she currently had on was the cream-colored, silk kimono tied loosely at her waist. It occurred to him it hadn't taken Teddy long to find comfort and consolation in the arms of a beautiful woman.

"I'd like to talk with Teddy Davidson, Babette. Is he home?" Zeb asked, shifting his stance on the wooden planks of the front porch.

Before she was able to answer, three dogs, Golden Doodles, tried to get in between the woman and the door. Babette, clearly annoyed, let them out. They each gave Zeb a friendly sniff or two and went on their way around the side of the house.

"Well, I wouldn't want to lie to the police, sheriff," she said, opening the door further to reveal an enormous ranch-style room with a wall of windows at the opposite end. Zeb was able to see the hint of a panoramic view of rolling hills out through the massive glass panels. There was also a human-sized photo of Teddy with his stock car hanging on one of the walls.

"Teddy is here all right, but he says to tell you his attorney would like to be present when he talks with you," Babette said, her tone almost childish and teasing, but steely, too. She flashed him another pouty grin. "I'm sorry you came all this way."

"Babette, would you like to tell me where *you* were the night of Roxy Davidson's murder?" he asked, not taking his eyes from her face.

She didn't blink.

"Sure, Zeb," she answered. "I was in bed with Teddy."

"So you're *his* alibi," Zeb said more than asked.

"Ye-e-s-s," Babette said, drawing out the word and nodding. "I'm not his wife, so I can testify we were lovers and we were together the night Roxy died. In fact," she said leaning out through the door in a conspiratorial affectation, "Roxy knew about us and didn't care. She had her own thing on the side. If it's Roxy's killer you want to find, you ought to be looking at who she dated a long, long time ago.

The same guy has never forgotten how she dumped him and stands to make a fortune now she's dead. I'm sure his wife hated Roxy."

Babette leaned back and shifted her weight, causing her kimono to reveal more leg, more décolletage.

"Bye, bye sheriff," she said sweetly. "Hope I've been of some help."

The door closed with only a gentle click of the latch bolt as Zeb turned around and walked easily back to his vehicle. It was true. If Teddy didn't want to talk to him without his lawyer, it was within his right.

Zeb headed to his SUV. He'd hoped to find out more about Teddy's financial situation. Unfortunately, he'd have to wait for any info Harry Sweeny or Teddy's attorney were willing to give on the matter. But, as luck would have it, his visit to the Davidson house produced two freebie nuggets of information.

When Babette swung the front door open, Zeb caught sight of a huge framed photo on the foyer's wall of Teddy Davidson standing beside his stock car holding up a trophy.

In the enlarged photo, Zeb recognized copper lug nuts around the left front tire's wheel hub. Competition vehicles often used copper lug nuts to dissipate the heat coming off the wheel hub. It was a short step from there for the sheriff to remember how the forensic technician found traces of copper in both Roxy's and Wesley's hair.

The second point was the dog hair found on Wesley's coat and pants. The Kings didn't own a dog, but the Davidson owned a kennel full. Everyone knew their favorite dogs were Golden Doodles. What if Roxy was having an affair with Wesley King? Even though Teddy was messing around with Babette, he might have been enraged by his wife's infidelities and like a jealous husband, he killed her and went after her lover.

It was time to get a subpoena to have a look around Teddy's garage and take some samples of their dogs' fur. Next, he'd request a casual conversation with Harry Sweeny. Roxy's brother might be more inclined to talk about Posh Pups, Teddy's finances and what he knew about the Davidsons' extra-marital affairs.

Climbing into the SUV, he turned over the ignition and drove the private blacktop road out through retracting electric cattle gates. Why didn't Teddy come to the door? Why send Babette? Did Roxy Davidson also have a lover? If it wasn't Wesley King, who might it be? Babette hinted at it being Patrick Lilton. She also was pointing the finger at Lilton's wife.

It was time to get back to the office and get his officers in place for the Dog Days Pooch Parade. One thing was for sure, it was looking like Sonya might be right. Money, lust, and greed were definitely at the root of these murders.

Chapter 31

As soon as Lana finished her hair, Sonya hurried home. She needed to contact Fritz to help her keep an eye on Mrs. Townsend and it wasn't a good idea to do so while she was at the beauty shop. He'd be difficult to bring back from Scotland as it was, and when he did show up, he'd be feisty. Best to keep Lana's Beauty Shop and its clients free from too much supernatural drama.

To get home, Sonya maneuvered around the parade route. Taking side streets until she came down the alley behind her house, she finally parked the Vespa in her shed and moving quickly, slung open the gate into her back garden. A happy but muffled barking racket came from inside the house.

"I'm almost there, Willard!" she called, but as her key turned in the door's lock an icy feeling of dread made the tiny hairs on the back of her neck go rigid. Her hand froze in mid-turn. Something wasn't right.

Immediately taking hold of herself before going any further into the house, she concentrated, tapping into the anxious feeling to see if it was truly intuitive or simple anxiety over the earlier premonition at Lana's.

An impression took shape in her mind. It *was* intuitive and it was nothing to do with her own home, but instead revolved around Mrs. Townsend who lived a stone's through across the street.

Not forgetting about the need to contact Fritz, she flung open her back door and called out, "Fritz! I need you to come back. I need your help. Are you here?"

Walking fully into the kitchen, she watched as Willard danced merrily around her feet, doing his 'you are home now and I usually get a treat' capering.

"I see you," Sonya said, taking down the treat jar and handing him his reward. "Where's Marnie?"

Tail wagging, Willard cocked his head to one side as if to imply he didn't speak human.

"Oh I remember," Sonya said. "She's at the parade with Lewis and Clark. Come on Willard. We're going to see Mrs. Townsend. Fritz will show up when he feels like it."

Always up for a gamble, Willard barked excitedly and allowed Sonya to leash him. In less than three minutes they'd made it down the front steps and across the street to Mrs. Townsend's house.

Pickwick was quiet. Most of her neighbors would be at the parade, but Sonya knew Mrs. Townsend preferred the pleasures of her sunroom and all its violets, lacy ferns and a smattering of blooming orchids to the noisy hustle and bustle of an event like Dog Days. Ringing the doorbell, she waited patiently for the tiny lady to appear.

The sheer curtain covering the door's side window rustled and part of one-half of a face with a pair of glasses scanned the front stoop. The eyes behind the round blue-rimmed spectacles were stern and suspicious. But upon seeing it was Sonya, there was a frantic rustling of the many locks and the door swung open.

"Oh, Mrs. Caruthers! How happy I am to see you!" Mrs. Townsend practically cried. "Please, please come inside."

"It's so good to see you, Mrs. Townsend," Sonya replied while internally relieved everything appeared to be fine with the woman. "Do you mind if I bring in Willard? I can also leave him to wait on the porch."

"No, no, no! Bring the little fella inside. He's a good boy, aren't you, Willard."

She stooped over and gave Willard a couple of firm pats on his head.

"I never have any trouble with your Willard, Mrs. Caruthers. Dogs aren't the problem, you see." She paused lowering her voice and giving the room behind her a quick, surreptitious scan. "It's the aliens who are always watching me that cause me the most trouble."

A huge sting of guilt hit Sonya. The poor woman was convinced aliens were somehow monitoring her movements when it was Fritz and his shenanigans to blame. With another self-recriminating realization, Sonya knew it was her fault. *She* was where the buck stopped. Fritz should have been corralled long before now and she was the only person who would be able to do it.

"Mrs. Townsend," she said, as they moved toward the sunroom at the back of the house. "Has anyone from the police department been by regarding the murder investigation? Have you received any visitors since the storm?"

"Well, I have talked with a young deputy on the phone. He wanted to know if I'd seen anything the night of the storm."

"Did you?" Sonya asked as she sat down in the wingback chair Mrs. Townsend motioned for her to take.

Making herself snug in her own fluffy, pink recliner, the diminutive elderly lady sighed and covered herself with a jumbo, multi-colored afghan. Quiet, she appeared to considered the question for a moment or two.

"Honey, I'm not sure what I may have seen. Does that make sense?" she asked looking at Sonya with a measured contemplativeness.

Before rushing the answer, Sonya waited for Mrs. Townsend to reflect for a moment. It was good to do so. The quiet of the room enveloped them both while Willard made himself comfortable in a sunspot on the carpeted floor.

"Yes," the older woman continued, "I know people think I'm batty, Mrs. Caruthers, but when the storm was at its height, I saw something luminescent flying through the hall back there."

She waved her arm up to the side of her head indicating the hallway they'd come through.

"I was so terrified and the storm was beginning to work itself up into such a blow. I grabbed my umbrella and decided to go over to Mr. Poindexter's house. He's such a calming influence. I don't know where I'd be without him."

A warm smile lit up the pale blue eyes and brought a hint of pink into the cool, china toned skin of Mrs. Townsend's cheeks. If the poet John Keats was right about beauty being truth and truth beauty then it occurred to Sonya how an elderly woman's face holds the truest sense of beauty. Nothing, in an aged face can be hidden any longer. All the experiences, hard lessons and every decision of the soul are written across it.

"He is such a dear man," Sonya agreed, but gently turned the conversation back to the first question. "When you went outside did you see someone moving about?"

"Well," Mrs. Townsend said slowly and nodded. "It isn't so much what I saw, but what I heard moving behind me. I thought it might be a limb falling from the wind, but when I turned around to see where the sound came from, I think I saw the hibiscus bush beside the house thrashing about. At the time, I thought it was odd because it moved not like the wind was whipping it, but like something was rustling around *in* it."

She finished with a slight shake of her head as if the uncertainty of what she remembered didn't sit well with her rational mind.

"It would have to be a good-sized animal, you see, or the aliens. Odd, though, because they rarely go outside. I've told you all I remember other than the storm was moving in, and I hurried over to Mr. Poindexter's house."

Mrs. Townsend sighed as she settled herself more deeply into her comforting chair. Sonya glanced down at where Willard lay on the floor with his eyes shut. For a few moments, she let herself be quiet and think.

Somewhere in another part of the house, a clock chimed the hour adding to the room's ambiance of peace. For what seemed like an eternity, but was only perhaps a minute, Sonya let go of regular time to give her mind space to *be* rather than think.

The pause refreshed her spirit. But as she turned her attention back to a now dozing Mrs. Townsend, a minuscule breath of air at Sonya's right ear let her know Fritz was with them. She never flinched. It was his delicate way of announcing himself, especially when he wanted to be gentle and careful.

"Sunny," he breathed softly, "I'm sorry. I forget how fragile the living are sometimes."

She nodded her head to acknowledge his sentiment but didn't dare speak. Mrs. Townsend's eyes were shut as she rocked herself in the recliner-rocker. On the floor, Willard raised his head, alert and aware of Fritz's unseen presence.

"I'll wait for you," his whisper came again to her ear. "At home."

"No, stay, please," she returned with warmth in her voice.

As she uttered the words, Mrs. Townsend's eyes flickered open. A tender smile spread across her face as she awoke from her dozing to see Sonya in front of her.

"You're still here," she said. "How nice. I often think it might be better to go live in a retirement place. It would be better to have more humans around. I don't feel safe here anymore Mrs. Caruthers."

Another stab of self-reproach stung Sonya. She took a quick, deep breath and smiled tenderly at the sweet, earnest face in front of her.

"Call me Sonya. I think we've lived close enough to each other to be on a first-name basis. You might like living in an assisted residence community. If you would like to visit one, I'd be happy to take you."

"Oh, Mrs. Caru…I mean, Sonya, would you?" she asked. "Since the storm and all the hullabaloo with these sneaky aliens all the time, I've been seriously thinking about looking into the one down near the park."

"Pick a day next week and we'll go," Sonya said. "We'll grab some lunch at Tilly's."

Mrs. Townsend sat forward in her chair, wearing an excited expression at the prospect of a day out.

"Oh, that sounds wonderful! If it works for you, let's go on Monday."

Like an eager child at the notion of a play date, the color rose in Mrs. Townsend's cheeks.

"Monday sounds perfect," Sonya said beaming back at her. "But for now, I want you to do me a favor."

"Absolutely!" came the reply.

"If you suspect anything is amiss, call me. I'll be over here in a jiffy. Don't open something sent to you, until you've called me. You will do that for me, won't you? Don't open the door to anyone unless it's the police. Call me first," Sonya asked firmly.

Mrs. Townsend relaxed back into her pink, stuffed protector. A glow infused her face.

"Okay, I will," she conceded and patted the arms of the chair.

Sonya rose to go and Willard regained his four paws.

"I will call you in about two hours," she said bending down to readjust the afghan on Mrs. Townsend's lap. "I think one of the deputies will be coming by later this afternoon after the parade to talk with you."

"Yes, I remember."

Sonya excused herself and promised to turn the lock on the door when she let herself out. Out on Mrs. Townsend's stoop, she knew something wasn't right. Shaking her head, she tried to dismiss it and hurried across to her own house.

"Fritz, Willard," she said, "I've got all sorts of whirly feelings about Mrs. Townsend's safety. I don't like this situation. Not one bit."

"Let me stay, Sonya. I'll keep an eye on her."

"No shenanigans, Fritz. Promise me!" she practically begged.

"Cross my heart and hope to die," he said.

And with a merry chuckle, he was gone.

Chapter 32

The Main Street of Willow Valley leading up to the park was a dog lover's paradise. Anything imaginable for the pampered canine was available within Puptown Alley, the official name for the vendor-lined street. It was the grand opening of Dog Days, people were jostling for places to stand and sit along the street for the Pooch Parade which was gearing up to begin at any moment.

Presley King and his staff had done an amazing job. Dozens of white tents crowded the street and each sporting a brightly colored flag denoting the vendor's name and hometown. As a light breeze danced across the tent-tops, the pendents would flutter and clap noisily for attention.

Grabbing recognition was a tricky business within this circus-like retail village. The shopkeepers' boisterous calls competed with the bandstand musicians who kept the audience delighted with songs spotlighting the charms and antics of man's best friend.

It was a cheerful place to find oneself among the happy hullabaloo of the hundreds, if not thousands, of visitors and their furry companions milling about licking on Pupcicles, shopping for matching sweater sets, and greeting friends of both species.

As for the parade itself, it was always a show worthy of a Hollywood spectacle. Posh Pups, the main sponsor, poured thousands of dollars into it.

This year, Stace D., the famous mystery author, and an ardent dog lover herself, along with her beagle, Maggie, had been selected as the Grand Marshals.

Ensconced in the back of a red 1966 Lincoln Continental convertible bedecked with a banner reading 'Posh Pups Loves Stace D. and Maggie', the author and her beagle would be the lead car of the Pooch Parade.

Maggie, wearing the cap she was known for, a vintage Sherlock Holmes' deerstalker hat with a tiny felt bone on top, was a beloved personality and millions of readers knew the beagle's iconic hat of choice due to Stace D.'s books. One savvy Puptown Alley vendor was cleaning up selling the Maggie Deerstalker cap. Dogs of every breed were seen sporting it proudly, their tails wagging with each delighted human who gushed about how adorable they were.

Directly behind Stace D.'s convertible was the Willow Valley High School marching band. They would be alternating between Elvis', 'You Ain't Nothin But a Hound Dog' and the Baha Men's, 'Who Let the Dogs Out'. In past parades, this last one was always a massive hit. The crowds loved yelling 'woof!' at the right place in the song. It was silly, but if you were at Dog Day's, you were in it for a howl of a good time.

The parade was to begin at two o'clock, and fortunately for Zeb, he had plenty of officers to keep the crowds easily managed. All they were waiting for was Presley King's assistant, Carrie, who was now managing the entire event, to give the signal for Stace D.'s driver to start down the street.

"You look tired, sheriff," Tommy said as the two men stood together near the park's entrance which was also the parade route's finish line.

"You don't look so pink-cheeked yourself, deputy. How are the Kings?" Zeb asked.

"Worst part of this job is telling people their loved ones aren't coming home. Last night was like watching your childhood end. Mrs. King and Presley took it as you'd expect. I think Rosalie's sisters are already here. They drove up last night. Honoria, Rosalie's oldest sister, took charge immediately. Gotta love Honoria. She's a force of nature."

"Good," Zeb came back. "Rosalie will need her sisters for a while. When this parade is over, I'm going over to see Mrs. Townsend on Pickwick Street. You will go see the Sweenys about the lost door key. Remember, Sonya will be coming by, too."

Tommy shot Zeb a quick, curious look.

"Sonya?" he said with a hint of curiosity. "First name basis, sir?"

Zeb didn't dignify the question with a response and fortunately for him, the parade came to life at the same instant with the marching band hitting the first notes of 'Who Let the Dogs Out'. The crowd went wild calling out their 'woofs'.

It was a true celebration of man's best friend. Dogs dressed like clowns jumping through hoops, the local firefighters with their Dalmatian buddies atop a huge float bedecked with a massive red papier-mache fire hydrant, and gigantic inflatable, well-known comic book dogs all made their way down Main Street's Puptown Alley.

A barrage of humane societies with their banners denoting their home towns trooped through with their dogs wearing red ribbons around their necks indicating they were open to being adopted and bringing love to someone's home. Following behind them came the local businesses with their themed Dog Days' floats.

Posh Pups' float, usually a show-stopper, was not to be seen. Roxy and Teddy along with their Golden Doodle girls had always ridden atop a professionally created float throwing candy kisses and pup treats to the crowd. This year, however, it had been discreetly removed from the parade's line-up the day before and unceremoniously parked in a warehouse.

"Well," Tommy said with a sad smile turning up the corners of his mouth, "I'm glad to see Dog Days is such a success. We can use some happiness right now."

Zeb nodded, but his demeanor was in no way touched by the general pleasure of the crowd. A great sense of urgency nagged at his tired brain. Two deaths were two too many.

As a pack of stout Pugs wearing service animal vests went by with their Veterans of Foreign War owners in-tow, Zeb's mind followed the scent of a memory back to the day before. The veterans, wearing their military uniforms and green caps, continued to parade by with their military medals glittering in the sunlight.

The sheriff's mind snagged on something, but before he followed the mental trail, the new cell phone county gave him buzzed in his pocket severing the intuitive connection to some greater pool of knowledge. The readout on the screen was Sonya's number. A sliver of excitement zinged in the pit of his stomach.

"Hello?" he asked a bit too hurriedly into the phone.

"Sheriff? It's Sonya Caruthers. I've spoken with two of your deputies this morning and I've been visiting with Mrs. Townsend. It's my strongest impression she's in danger as well as Presley King and Marnie Scott. I think the person who killed both Roxy Davidson and Wesley King, maybe worried they were seen by these three people."

The initial pleasure of hearing her voice turned over to heightened professional concern.

"Mrs. Townsend stated not seeing anyone during the night of the storm. Same with Marnie Scott when she found Wesley King. Better give me more details, Sonya," he said

"Marnie actually may *have* seen someone. She wasn't sure at the time Tommy questioned her. But as for Presley King, he may not even know he saw or heard something to incriminate the killer. I have the strongest impression these people are in great danger. The feeling came on while I was at your mother's salon and again once I returned home. Mrs. Townsend was fine when I visited her a few minutes ago, but I think it will be poison."

Zeb's stomach constricted at the horror of the idea. He knew he'd better trust Sonya's intuition. She'd been right too many times before. The one thing he didn't want was another body. Whoever the killer was, they weren't likely to leave loose ends. Marnie Scott and Mrs. Townsend were the definitions of loose ends, but Presley King? Was it possible he knew or saw something important but didn't realize it?

"The parade needs another twenty minutes to finish up," he said into the phone. "The contestants will be heading to the competition arena afterward. I'll meet you at your house in twenty minutes and we'll go over to see Mrs. Townsend together. Afterward, I'll take you to see the Sweeny's dog."

He finished the call and tapped Deputy Kirchner on his shoulder. The young man turned to face him.

"You go to the King's residence and stay there until I call you. I know we have an officer already there, but I'll feel better if it's you. Also, I want the entire family especially Presley and Rosalie to have a personal guard with them at all times especially if they go out. Neither of them is to be without protection at any time. Understand?" Zeb said.

"Should I leave now, sir?" the deputy asked looking worried.

"Go, and even if people bring food, throw it out. They're not to eat anything given to them. If it's at all possible, I'd like you to quietly pack them both off to Tulsa to stay with Honoria. No one is to know where they've gone. Understand? The funeral will have to wait anyway until the investigation is complete."

Tommy looked like someone had just sucker-punched him, but he nodded his acquiescence and hurried off through the crowd. Zeb watched him weave through the mass of humanity and disappear. Scanning the congested streets full of people, his trained eye noted his deputies' positions.

Soon the parade was finished and a large majority of the onlookers moved toward the massive tents where the dog competitions were to take place.

Somewhere in the sea of humanity, Zeb mused, Marnie Scott and her two beagles were probably munching on corndogs. As if the mere thought of her conjured her into being, he saw her familiar face separate and pull free from the swarming crowd. She made her way in his direction after she gave him a wave of acknowledgment.

"Sheriff, I've got something I need to tell you," Marnie said while trying to bring Lewis and Clark to heal. "I may have remembered something about yesterday…you know at the place…where we found…Wesley."

Her sentence fragmented. It was as if she was trying to keep the image of the dead man from looming with fresh zeal back up into her mind. Zeb nodded his head but didn't speak as a way to encourage her to continue.

"Lewis must have picked up the scent of a raccoon or squirrel as we came down into the woods yesterday because he shot off. Clark followed right behind him. When I turned my head to see where they were going, I saw a person standing off in the distance. The boys started barking, diverting my attention for the moment. When I looked back, the figure was gone."

"Anything you can tell me about the person you saw?" Zeb asked.

"Nothing really," Marnie said and sighed. With her head slightly lowered, she was silent for a brief moment. The cloud of uncertainty finally cleared and she looked up with bright eyes and a quick smile.

"Wait!" Marnie practically cried. "The color of the hoodie blended in with the colors of the Sycamore foliage. It was bright orange."

"Was it the bright orange of a hunter's vest?" Zeb asked.

"Nooo…" Marnie answered, "not neon, more like a soft carrot color."

For a moment neither one spoke, both caught in the imagery of Marnie's memory.

"Do you think it was a woman or a man, Marnie? First impression?" Zeb asked quickly.

Where she'd been examining again the concrete beneath her feet for the last few moments, she now turned her face up to look him square in the eyes.

"Honestly, Zeb, I think it may have been a woman or a thin man. The color of the tie-dyed hoody was something either would have worn."

Zeb nodded with a slow smile pulling at the corner of his mouth.

"Thank you, Marnie. Come along with me. I want you to ride back to Sonya's house with me and I'm gonna put you on a plane to Atlanta tomorrow."

Marnie's expression showed her befuddlement.

"I'm taking no chances, Marnie. You may have seen our killer. Whoever it is, they mean to leave no one behind who has the slightest hint of who they are."

He saw her grip tighten on her dogs' leashes. As they walked together down the crowded street, he heard her let out a sigh before she spoke.

"Sheriff?"

"Yes?"

"I feel like I'm gonna faint," Marnie said softly.

"Three deep breaths, girl," he came back, his voice reassuring and strong. "You're with me now and soon you'll be in Atlanta. Safe and sound."

Chapter 33

The smell of fresh brewed coffee met Sonya's visitors as they came through her front door. Zeb and Marnie went into the kitchen to talk with Sonya leaving Lewis and Clark to wait in the parlor.

Lifting their beagle noses, they picked up a different scent, something unusual causing their hackles to rise on the backs of their necks. Trotting in, Willard gave them a welcoming wag, but neither Lewis or Clark returned the greeting.

"I know, you can smell him," Willard said, "and, yep, he's a ghost, but this time, believe it or not, it's a dog."

"Dog?" Lewis, the bolder of the two beagles brothers asked.

"Dog," Willard confirmed. "You'll see. He's good."

A small, rubber ball rolled toward the two beagles. Their eyes followed its course as it made its way to their front paws and stopped. Lewis nosed the ball back in the direction from where it came. A bodiless yap to their right made both beagles jerk and recoil in the direction of the front door.

"Nothing to worry about, guys. This is Beast and he's trying to be friendly," Willard explained. "He's enjoying the new ball I gave him."

The two brother beagles exchanged uncertain glances. With noses searching the air for information on the unseen canine presence, they followed Willard into the dining room.

Taking the red ball with his mouth, Clark made the first effort to show he welcomed Beast's hospitality and lay down with the rubber toy between his front two legs. He gave a little whine and nosed the ball in the original direction.

Another bright, excited yap and the edges of a wheaten colored terrier materialized. With an upright tail wagging in playful greeting, Beast stayed put waiting for Lewis and Clark's response.

The new arrivals stood up on all four legs and wagged their tails. And once there was comfortable pleasantness among the group, Willard got down to business.

"We need to go see Pickles, the Sweeny's dog. He told Lou, the Chihuahua, he's got an unusual scent to show us. It showed up the night the woman was killed at his house and it's not normal for his people and his territory. I thought you guys, with your good noses, might be able to pick it up."

"We are leaving," Clark said. "I don't like it. Marnie mentioned something about a plane to that man in there. Can't be good."

Clark looked over at his brother for reassurance.

Lewis sat back on his haunches, his tail limp on the ground and added, "Yeah, we only flew once and it was terrible. Marnie wasn't with us. We were down in some loud place and locked in separate crates. Our heads felt funny and Clark threw up a lot. I wish we could get out of it."

"You may be able to," Willard said with a mischievous smile about his muzzle.

The two beagles' ears pricked up as they waited to hear what advice Willard was willing to impart.

"We go over to Pickles, have him show us this scent he's got and then trot out to the place in the woods where you found the body. If your noses can work their magic, we should have something to show Sonya. That might keep Marnie from going on a plane."

"I like it," Clark said with enthusiasm. "Beats waiting around here for the crates to show up."

"Well, it can't hurt to go see Pickles, but I'm not guaranteeing anything," Lewis added, his tone sounding unconvinced.

Willard thumped his tail.

"Good, let's go right now."

The three dogs along with Beast headed toward the kitchen and the pet door exit when they heard the front garden gate swinging open and someone walking up the steps to the main door.

"You've got company," Clark said. "Should we check it out?"

Willard paused to see if Sonya would go to the door. None of the humans acted like they were aware of the visitor. They continued their conversation around the kitchen table. Giving a loud bark, which Lewis and Clark easily joined in on, the three dogs announced to the people someone was about to arrive.

No knock, no doorbell rang. Willard knew this wasn't the normal protocol for humans. Only the mailman never announced himself and he'd already been here today.

"Come on guys. Let's see who's out there," he said and trotted to the bench seat overlooking the front garden and porch area.

With Lewis and Clark in tow, he jumped up on the cushioned seating area and nudged his nose through the lace curtains only to see the back of a slim person wearing a hoodie walking hurriedly away.

"Quick, guys," Willard said. "Can you catch any scent from the person?"

The boys both put their noses to the air coming in through the open screened window.

"Yep, we got it," Clark answered. "Smells like the stuff Marnie puts on her feet."

"Yeah, and did you catch a whiff of those things we like to eat from Puggly's?" Lewis chimed in.

"Oh yes, I do!" Clark said excitedly. "They're still out there on the front step. The person left them."

"Come on let's go out through my door in the kitchen. We can run around to the front porch and see what you're smelling," Willard said and hopped down from the window seat.

In quick succession, all three dogs tramped through the kitchen, squeezed through the doggie door and ran around the house to where something delicious was sending off waves of yummy scent molecules into the air.

Lewis was first on the scene. He pressed his nose to the top of the paper box bending and crumpling the lid.

"Whoa! Wait a minute!" he said. "Something bad is in here."

Clark, with more hesitancy, approached and with his nose, sniffed the box. Inside twelve beautifully arranged donuts of every shape and type were slowly being mashed into one single mass.

"Ewww!" Clark said bringing his nose abruptly up and away from the box. "Same stuff we smelled the day we found the dead rat. Remember Lewis? It was over in the house we used to visit when we lived by Grandma."

"What are you talking about?" Willard asked.

"Grandma. You know, Marnie's mom. We used to live right next to her before we moved here. There was a farm and we found this dead rat. Marnie took it away from us. She was upset and said it would make us sick if we ate it."

"We better get rid of this thing in case Sonya finds it. People don't have our noses. They might eat it," Willard said and nudged the box.

"What are you three doing?" Sonya asked behind them. "Looks like someone left something for Marnie. Has her name on it."

Willard heard the sarcasm and fear in Sonya's voice.

Bending down, she picked up the crumpled box and headed through the front door. Willard growled at the box and tried to pull it out of Sonya's hands.

"Don't worry, Willard," she said. "I've got a feeling about these donuts."

The dogs followed her inside.

"We've gotta get the box away from her," Lewis said, as all three dogs trailed the woman into where the other two humans were sitting.

"I don't think you need to worry," Willard said to his friends. "Sonya sounds upset the donuts are here."

"Look what someone left at my front door," Sonya said putting the box down in the middle of the kitchen table.

Zeb opened the box.

"Might be a bit mashed." He looked down at the dogs. "Think these guys were about to have a mid-afternoon snack?"

"I hope not," Sonya answered.

Selecting one of the cream puffs, Zeb gave it an appreciable smile.

"I don't know. Looks free of dog slobber. Might still be pretty good."

"I wouldn't eat any of them, sheriff," Sonya said taking the delicate pastry out of his hand and laying it back down in the box. "Instead, you should take this over to your forensic people. This might be your first real evidence, and it might also prove I'm not a lunatic to your deputies, Andrew and Michael."

Chapter 34

As all three humans and all three dogs stared at the box of unholy donuts, Sonya heard Fritz at her ear.

"I've been watching over Mrs. Townsend, Sonya. There's a box for her, too. I've been bating it around the room so she doesn't touch it. She's keeping to her sunroom. Better get over there."

"Wait!" Sonya exclaimed and grabbed the still seated Zeb by the shoulders. "Mrs. Townsend! She's had something delivered to her, too!"

Zeb and Marnie looked like lightning had struck in the middle of the room.

"How do you know?" the sheriff cried.

In a frantic gesture of confusion, Sonya waved her hands about her and said, "Fritz told me! Come on we've got to stop her from touching the box."

Running to her kitchen phone, Sonya took down the receiver and dialed the number for Mrs. Townsend. Everyone, including the dogs, waited with expectant faces to hear Sonya make contact. No one answered.

"Come on," Sonya said putting the receiver back in its cradle. "We need to go check on her now!"

A posse of humans and dogs made the distance between the two houses in less time it takes to swat a fly. At a good jog, Sonya hit Mrs. Townsend's front steps first and rang the doorbell.

An eternity of seconds passed, but finally, a slight ruffling of the side window curtain and the emergence of one bespectacled magnified eye made all who stood on Mrs. Townsend's stoop sigh with relief.

"Mrs. Townsend," Sonya called, "it's me, Sonya. Please let me in. I want to check on you."

Locks jangled and clanged and eventually, the heavy door crept gingerly open.

"Hello, Sonya," the bird-of-a-woman said, blinking with wonder at the menagerie of people and dogs waiting on her doorstep. "Is there something the matter? The aliens have been making such a racket, I've stayed in my sunroom. I must have fallen asleep in my chair."

"No one has visited today except me?" Sonya asked, her tone anxious.

"Noooo, though the postman did drop off a package or two," came the reply.

"Please, Mrs. Townsend," Zeb interjected, "may I see the two packages."

"Well, of course, sheriff," she answered and turned to walk down the hall giving a wave of her hand indicating for them to follow.

"Sonya," Marnie said, "I'll wait out here with the dogs."

Into the study, Zeb, Sonya and Mrs. Townsend crowded around a walnut desk bearing the hallmarks of the Eastlake period in furniture design. Two brown paper-wrapped packages sat innocently there with only twine, postage markings, and recipient addresses to give any indication of what might lie within.

"Mrs. Townsend would you please bring me a plastic trash bag," Zeb asked.

"Of course, I'll be right back."

Sonya waited for the older woman to be out of earshot and said, "Neither package has a return address."

"I know. This may be our lucky day if your *feeling* was right," he said with a mischievous grin.

"Sheriff," Sonya said, her response tinged with annoyance and her color rising. "Fritz told me there was a package here. He's been watching over Mrs. Townsend. As for my instincts or *feelings*, as you put it, they are always right. It's just not always clear how they'll play out."

He turned to her and their eyes met. Tapping one of the boxes, he answered, "Sonya, if even one of these packages or your box of donuts has proof of poison, I'll never question your feelings again and I'll owe you BIG."

He paused, not shifting his gaze from hers and continued. His voice dropped to a softer tone.

"Maybe, you'd let me take you to dinner to show my gratitude."

While Sonya's face was showing signs of blushing, a gust of wind originating from the corner of the study, blew directly at the two humans with such force it knocked everything not tied down in the room about including Sonya right into Zeb's arms.

"Keep ye filthy hands off my lass!" boomed an unseen voice.

Both Zeb and Sonya froze and blinked as papers whipped about them and feathers from a stuffed pheasant trophy attached to the wall filtered through the whirling tempest.

"Aliens! They're here!" Mrs. Townsend cried from the doorway. "See! See! I told you. This is proof they exist!"

Sonya gently pushed herself free of Zeb's arms as the storm died completely away leaving the three humans to watch feathers and whirling dust particles wafting quietly back to rest on the chair, desktop, and floor.

Swallowing hard, Sonya returned her gaze upward to see Zeb with an expression of total befuddlement. It was a good time for some sort of explanation.

"I think, yes, I think we might have experienced one of those freaky earthquakes we have here in Missouri. Yes, Most definitely an earthquake," Sonya offered.

Both Mrs. Townsend's and Zeb's faces were manifestations of utter disbelief, but to his credit, the sheriff grabbed the proffered if not the ridiculous interpretation of events and went with it.

"Earthquake?" Zeb asked. He was slow to catch on to Sonya's suggestion, but it finally took. "Yes! That must be what happened. I want all of you to go to Mrs. Caruthers for now. It'll be safer there."

Looking back and forth between Sonya and Zeb, the older lady's shoulders sagged and she shook her head.

"If you don't want to believe your own eyes and ears, that's your business, but what happened just now was *not* of this world. I'll go with you over to Sonya's only if you'll explain why you're so interested in those packages," she said.

Zeb took a deep breath and appeared to be weighing his words.

"To not put too fine a point on it, Mrs. Townsend," he replied, "We think someone may have put something harmful in these packages to…" he paused.

"To shut me up permanently?" she finished his sentence with a twinkle in her eye and a knowing smile on her face.

"Perhaps," he said with a tilt of his head.

"You may have heard or seen something the night of the storm when Roxy Davidson was killed. The murderer doesn't want to give you the chance to remember."

Drawing herself up straight, Mrs. Townsend said, "Not to worry, sheriff. I'm perfectly happy to relinquish the packages. And as to the point about something being locked away in my memory, I think I may be able to give you a real *key*."

"A key?" he asked, sounding unsure of her meaning.

Slipping her hand down into her sweater's pocket, she fished something out and displayed it with an outstretched palm.

"The key!" Zeb exclaimed. "This may be the missing key from the Sweeny's house."

"Thought it might be important," Mrs. Townsend said, her face bright with satisfaction. "After Sonya left today I started thinking about the night of the storm and the hibiscus bushes. I didn't touch it. I've watched a lot of those police shows on TV. I picked it up with the plastic baggy, so should have fingerprints if the killer didn't wear gloves."

She continued to study the key in her hand but offered no further explanation. Zeb and Sonya exchanged puzzled glances.

"The hibiscus bushes?" the sheriff pressed.

"Yes, of course, the hibiscus bushes. They moved oddly like something was inside them the night of the storm. After Sonya left, I got to thinking I ought to go out to the bushes and sniff around a bit. I found the key and I saw where someone had indeed been messing about in there."

Zeb's facial expression morphed instantly from confusion to pure delight.

"Sonya, I mean, Mrs. Caruthers would you please take Marnie and Mrs. Townsend to your home. I'm going to call for one of my deputies to come and sit with you ladies for the remainder of the evening and through the night. Sonya, do you mind if they stay with you?"

Sonya nodded, "With pleasure! It'll be fun to have some guests. I think we will all feel better if we are together. One, thing, though, I still need to go over to see the Sweenys and their dog. Remember?"

"That's right. I'll take you over before I go to Pineville. Thank you, Sonya. Also, I'd greatly appreciate it, Mrs. Townsend," Zeb went on, "if you would please put the key you're holding down on the desk here. I'd also be extremely grateful if you would show me this hibiscus bush, this wonderful hibiscus bush you're talking about."

The women smiled at the sheriff's obvious excitement.

"Come on Mrs. Townsend," Sonya said. "Let's get out of his hair. I think it's best if we all stay together. Safety in numbers, you know."

Chapter 35

"Don't you think this means there is hope now for finding the killer?" Marnie asked Sonya.

All three women, including a true pack of dogs, were sitting on Sonya's back porch listening to the regular din of human, insect, and bird noises early autumn afternoons were famous for in small-town America. They watched as Officer Laura Pope performed her security patrol along the perimeter of Sonya's back garden wall. She was to be their protection for the next twenty-four hours.

"The key must be the Sweeny's and if poison turns up in those donuts or in whatever was in those packages, our sheriff might have multiple points of evidence to develop his case," Sonya said, as she nudged the wooden floor with her toe to keep the porch swing moving gently.

"If they were deadly donuts, they were meant for me, Sonya," Marnie said, taking a sip of her diet drink which she'd chosen to offset the brownie she'd consumed. "And I've been given the okay to leave for Atlanta. I'll stay tonight, but tomorrow, I have every intention of being on a plane."

"You're safe for now. Officer Pope is with us all night for protection. We need to celebrate the good luck we've had today," Sonya said.

"I like your attitude," Marnie said with a smile. "It gives me hope."

"Well, this is lovely for me," Mrs. Townsend said, her enthusiasm for the evening ahead showing in her voice. "I don't remember the last time I had a sleepover with friends. It's like I'm a school girl again."

"Good! This is going to be fun," Sonya said. "It's us girls plus one probably very bored police officer."

"Hey, don't count me out," Laura interjected as she came around the back of the house with a smile. "I've heard lots of good things Mrs. Caruthers about your hospitality from Deputy Kirchner."

"Excellent!" Sonya said clapping her hands with pleasure. "We'll make dinner, put on some pj's, and watch a good movie with popcorn. First, I've got to go visit the Sweenys. Zeb will be here in a minute to take me over."

"I'll keep things safe here," Laura said, unconsciously resting her hand on her gun holster.

They all looked at the gun and nodded in sober agreement.

"As for the movie, Sonya, I don't want to watch anything scary," Marnie said with a nervous laugh. "I've had enough creepy stuff already this week."

"No aliens!" Mrs. Townsend said with a bright smile. "Please call me Lillian, my given name. We are certainly all friends here."

"Of course, Lillian, and no ghost stories tonight either!" Sonya chimed in.

No sooner was the word 'ghost' out of her mouth, she crossed her fingers behind her back and surreptitiously knocked three times softly on the porch railing for good luck.

Sonya was not above using whatever folklore, superstition or mythology to manage the grey zone surrounding the reality of ghosts, spirits, and entities. All the rapping and finger-crossing was probably ineffectual, but it couldn't hurt. Besides, she needed luck on her side and Fritz *anywhere,* but at home tonight whipping himself up into a 'boo' fest.

They heard the front gate latch click and the hinges long whine as someone pushed through the gate. Officer Laura held up her hand indicating the women's conversation should cease. Marnie got up.

"Let's go inside, shall we, Lillian?" she asked.

"Look, it's only the sheriff," Sonya said. "Hello!"

"Are you ready to go?" he asked with a smile.

"Absolutely."

"My truck is out front," Zeb said, "I'll drive."

Soon they were pulling up in front of the uninhabited Victorian and finding their way around the back to the garage apartment. Alfonso met them and showed them up the stairs. Both Sweenys were hard at work on laptops as Zeb and Sonya were brought inside.

Once pleasantries were exchanged, Zeb pulled out the key Mrs. Townsend found in her hibiscus bush and presented it for the Sweeny's consideration.

"That's it," Deidra acknowledged. "So, whoever used it to get into our house must have thrown it as they ran away from the storm? It gives me the shivers to think the killer was slithering around out here."

She wrapped her arms tighter around herself.

"If they could have returned the key to the fern pot, I think they would have. But the key being thrown indicates the killer was about to be interrupted and they made a run for it. My guess is you pulled up in the driveway and they bolted."

Deidra and Harry looked horrified.

"You're saying, you think I was going in one door and the killer was leaving by another?" Deidra asked.

"They probably heard or saw you arriving and couldn't leave the house by the front door which is closest to the fern pot. We've asked this before, but have you had enough time to think more about who knew the key was in the fern pot?"

They both shrugged.

"Honestly, sheriff, we've told you everyone we can think of. We rarely used that key. It was for our family who helped with Pickles or dropped something off. The lady who cleans for us had her own key, but she knew about it."

"We've taken her statement. She claims to not have told anyone about it."

Zeb paused briefly and pushed on. Sonya knew he was choosing his words carefully.

"Would it be okay if Mrs. Caruthers took a look around your main house? She may have special insight into the events surrounding Roxy's death."

The two Sweenys nodded.

"Please do Mrs. Caruthers. We would greatly appreciate your help. Should Deidra and I come with you?"

"Your welcome to come," Sonya said. "It may be therapeutic for you and the house."

Harry stared at her like butterflies had flown out of her ears and Deidra choked back a laugh.

"The house? Therapeutic for the house?" Harry repeated. "What do you mean?"

"Simple. Your house was abandoned after an awful crime was committed there. It had nothing to do with the murder of your sister. Roxy passed over peacefully and though I can feel the residue left from the violence done in the house, I can tell you these negative energies can be cleared away and protective energies put in place. I would highly recommend doing so soon."

The other three people in the room looked like stricken children. It was Deidra who spoke up first.

"Sonya, I want to go into the house with you. I love my house and I miss it."

Sonya smiled.

"That's the right attitude. Time to go home. Just one question for you both?"

"Yes?" they asked in unison.

"What is your belief system?"

They exchanged uncertain looks, but Harry answered, "Do you mean are we religious?"

Sonya, her tone business-like, said, "What I'm asking is do you believe in good and evil? Do you believe in a protective force of good?"

"I do," Deidra said. "After what's happened in my house, I can also say I believe in evil, too."

Sonya nodded.

"Dark deeds shouldn't win. Let's go get your house back."

Chapter 36

The Dog Days' afternoon events were underway and the enormous tented arena was brimming with serious contestants and their prized pooches. Tonight was the first round of judging, but a major glitch in the proceedings had tongues and tails wagging.

Harry Sweeny had stepped down as judge due to Roxie's murder. Teddy Davidson, however, had kept his judge title along with two new judges to replace the two lost ones. This sudden and unexpected change meant most Golden Paw contestants were on new, shaky ground. Up until this year, the advantage had usually gone to either a poodle, a German Shepherd, or a beagle, but with two of the regular judges gone, the next big winner was anybody's guess.

"It's going to be a real dog fight, now," Tamara Lilton, murmured through clenched teeth as she waited on the arena floor with her favorite Lhasa Apsos, Sugar, who'd been brushed and fluffed to perfection.

"Worried, chica? You do look down in the mouth or is it time for another trip to the Botox lady," came a voice so soft, it almost hissed.

Tamara slowly turned around, having recognized Babette Nicols' voice. There was no missing the sarcasm in her friend's tone.

"See you replaced your dead lover pretty fast, Babsy," she returned, both her well-crafted eyebrows raised in a taunting stare. "I guess since you're obviously sleeping with Teddy, this competition should be a shoo-in for you."

"If you're referring to Wesley King, he wasn't *my* lover Tams," came the cool reply dripping with insinuations.

Affecting indifference, Tamara Lilton shrugged and returned her gaze to the arena's dais where two women and two men dressed in evening attire were being introduced as the new judges.

"Ladies, gentlemen and our canine friends," rang out the announcer's words to the crowd of at least a thousand people. "Tonight begins our first round of judging and allow me to introduce the four individuals responsible for selecting this year's Golden Paw recipient."

"Where's Harry Sweeny?" Babette asked.

"I guess he's not going to show," Tamara answered and sighed. "It's been such a terrible two days. My heart goes out to that family."

"Strange," Babette replied focusing her attention on the four judges.

"What is?"

"Hmmm?" Babs coyly returned.

"What is *strange*?" Tamara asked, thinking Babs knew something special about the judges giving her a leg-up on the competition.

"Your last comment inferring you have a heart. I know all about you and Patrick trying to steal Posh Pups for a song. I also know Teddy is going to sell his shares to another company if your precious Patrick doesn't pay through the nose. You both would screw anybody over to be King and Queen of Willow Valley, so don't pretend to be sad, Tamara, about Roxy's death. Hell, I wouldn't be surprised if you didn't engineer it yourself."

Taking her dog's lead more firmly in hand, Tamara
twitched the line and started to go. She'd had enough of
Babette's inferiority complex.

"Good luck, Babs," she called over her shoulder.
"You're going to need it!"

"Oh, Tamara!" the blonde called after her. "I saw you
the other day leaving Wesley King's house so don't pretend
you weren't seeing him as well. You think you're so much
better than me, but I know you must have been sleeping
with him."

Like a viper who's been surprised by an equally vicious
mongoose, Tamara Lilton swung around to face her
frenemy and retraced the distance she'd gained.

"You bitch!" she sneered. "Don't you dare try and lay
that on me. I've never had anything to do with Wesley
King." Putting her hand on her extremely trim hip and
cocking her body to one side, she added, "If anyone was
dallying around with Wesley, it was *you*!"

"You can say what you want Tams, but I saw you. Hair
mussed, clothes slightly askew. It was you and, if I'm not
mistaken, you were driving your Sammy's car. Nice piece
of camouflage. No one would ever guess. Granted
Samantha is closer to his age than you, but you know what
I mean."

Tamara's face went white.

"You saw Samantha's car at Wesley King's house?
When? Tell me this instant!"

The predatory expression drained from Bab's face. Her
teeth and claws retracted. The tone of her voice went from
poison to one of uncertainty.

"The same day they found him. I thought it was you,
Tamara. I'm…I'm so sorry."

Both women, eyes locked, didn't move. Men may be fair game, but even they didn't play the kid card.

"I've got to go," Tamara said. "I've got to call Samantha."

Pushing through the crowd, Tamara Lilton's frenzied mind tried to manifest images of her baby, Samantha, being caught up in Wesley King's arms as his lover. She shivered at the thought. The man was usually more into experienced women. Strange of him to change his modus operandi. He would have known Samantha was underage.

Rattling her head to free it of the distressing pictures bubbling up from her frightened mind, Tamara put her hands to her temples and tried to pry a more benign truth from Bab's possibly vicious fiction.

Sam was only seventeen. She'd shown no signs of having a boyfriend, well not since the last one anyway and he'd been a gangly teenager who didn't even drive yet. Wesley was a man. How in the world would Samantha have gotten involved with him?

It hit her. A fear so intense causing Tamara Lilton to come to a dead stop in the middle of the thousand spectators waiting for the first dog and its handler to come out into the arena. What if Sam had *seen* the killer? Or worse. What if she knew something about Wesley's death?

"Oh God, please, please don't let my baby have gotten messed up in this horror story!" she prayed to herself.

A mother's instinct is the closest thing to mortal omniscience on the planet. Tamara could feel Samantha was in some kind of danger. Taking out her phone, she quickly used the family locator app to find her daughter.

With a heart beating like a hammer in her chest she waited for the avatar to appear. Sam's cartoon head with a ponytail soon showed she was at home. Tamara tapped her daughter's name and the phone dialed.

"Hey, mom," came the girl's voice sounding every bit the indifferent teen.

"Sammy, tell me you were *not* seeing Wesley King," Tamara practically pleaded.

"Who?" Samantha asked, sounding even more bored. "I kinda like Joshua Cadman right now, but his mom won't let him drive yet even though he's seventeen. By the way mom I need to buy a t-shirt for the tennis team's trip to KC next weekend. Coach says we all need one."

Her daughter's oblivious tone rang true to Tamara's critical mother-ear, but she pressed on to be certain.

"Your car was seen over at Meadowmere Place a couple of days ago. Do you know why it was there?"

A palpable, extended silence came back to Tamara this time and her stomach twisted with renewed heightened anxiety.

"Sammy, why was *your* car at Meadowmere Place and do you know Wesley King? He was killed two days ago. Tell me right now!"

Finally, the teenager's voice cried, "Mama, I swear it wasn't me. I loaned my car to a friend. She wanted to go see her boyfriend. I was at tennis practice so I told her she could use it. I know I'm not supposed to loan it out, but it was only a few blocks…"

"Who used your car, Samantha?"

"Marcy Hollingsworth. She's a tall brunette. She's a senior. Kinda looks a lot like you," came the answer. "Mom? Is Marcy in trouble?"

"For God's sake, Samantha, do not call the Hollingsworth kid or text her about this. Let me take care of it. Do you understand me?" Tamara enunciated the last four words with force.

"I won't call her," Sam promised, sounding sullen, but also scared.

"Also, stay home and don't leave the house. Is daddy there?"

"Yes."

"Put him on the phone," Tamara demanded.

While waiting for her husband to pick up, Tamara scanned the arena to see Babette wearing a form-fitting jumpsuit do her first trot through the arena with her own dog. The male judges were having a hard time paying attention to her poodle.

"Yes. What's up Tamara?" Patrick said. "I've only got a minute before I have to get on a conference call."

Rolling her eyes at Babette's audaciousness, Tamara's mouth pulled into a grim line. She plunged forward with her agenda.

"I've asked Sammy to stay home. She loaned her car to Marcy Hollingsworth who promptly drove it to see her lover, Wesley King, on the same day he was found dead. Any ideas about what we do next?" Tamara asked, her tone blunt.

Quiet for a few moments, her husband answered, his tone sounding every bit the hardened corporate raider.

"Let me handle it."

Tamara Lilton unceremoniously tapped 'end' on her phone's glass surface and replayed the last ten minutes of conversations in her mind. Handing messy problems over to Patrick usually meant she dropped them from her mind entirely. However tonight, the knot in her stomach was tenaciously staying put.

"Something's wrong. I can feel it," she thought to herself.

Tamara did something uncharacteristic. She put love before victory and left the arena tent to find her car.

"We've got to get home, Sugar," she said out loud as if the dog understood human conversation. "I've got a bad feeling about Sammy's car being in the neighborhood where both Wesley King and Roxy Davidson were murdered. Something doesn't add up."

Chapter 37

Willard, Clark, and Lewis, had slipped the bonds of Marnie's control to follow up their lead on the unusual scent Pickles wanted them to investigate. They were on their way to the Sweeny's home when the tantalizing perfume of hamburgers being grilled brought the dogs to an abrupt stop in the middle of the alley between Sonya's house and Meadowmere Place.

"That's almost as good as chicken," Lewis said. "I think Pickles can wait, but those hamburgers might not last long."

"There's turkey, too," Clark added, his nose tipped upward and twitching to catch every available molecule of air saturated with cooking meat.

"Nope, we must talk to Pickles today," Willard said as he restarted his trot toward the Sweeny's house. "He told Lou the Chihuahua he smelled something strange the night the woman died in his house. Scents can be washed away with rain and we need to get some answers soon. Don't forget you guys might be on a plane tomorrow if we don't."

Clark and Lewis with eyes half shut in a delirium of olfactory overload shook themselves. The reminder of the hated, impending air travel broke the meat temptress's hold and they resumed their hike behind Willard.

The afternoon wind was calm with the occasional whisper of a breeze making for a perfect autumn afternoon. And though the cicadas were already humming only falling quiet en masse after long symphonic crescendos, the sun promised another four hours of daylight. Plenty of time to gather any information before heading home to Sonya's.

Willard and the beagles, upon coming to Pickle's back yard gate, sniffed the air for signs of the old lab.

"Lookin' for me?"

All three visitors jumped with hackles raised at the suddenness and closeness of Pickle's greeting.

"Bath!" Clark barked.

"Hey, watch your language," Lewis said reprimanding his younger brother for using a dog's curse word.

Clark sitting back on his haunches gave the others a steady, hard look.

"Sorry boys. I'm having a rough night," he said. "I'm not looking forward to a plane ride tomorrow."

Willard and Pickles, in the universal sign of dog forgiveness, wagged their tales and panted congenially.

"Lou the Chihuahua, said you'd be by sometime," the old lab said, his tone easy. "I guess you're here to check out the weird smell. I'll be honest with you, Willard, I've been staying out here in the yard because I need to protect my people. Something, I don't know what it is, has been sitting on the front porch for the last two days. It's making the hair on my back stand up. Haven't had a chance to go recheck that smell."

He gave a little shake causing the fur and skin to roll one way and the ears the other.

"I think I can help you out, Pickles," Willard said. "It's a ghost, but it's a ghost *dog*. I'm gonna introduce you. You'll like him. It took Lewis and Clark a few minutes to get used to him, but he's a good sort."

Pickles sat back on his hunches while Willard called Beast to show himself. The Cairn terrier yapped a greeting and slowly materialized.

"I'll be dogged! First time for everything," Pickles said. "Seems a friendly enough fellow."

"He is and he's probably not going anywhere until we help Sonya find out who killed the woman here at your house. We saw her, Pickles. She was redheaded," Willard said.

"You saw her?" Pickles asked. He breathed a sigh. "I knew her well. She was always so good about the treat jar and never asked for the usual 'sit down' or 'rollover' nonsense."

All four canines swallowed hard at the mention of the hallowed treat jar. A human, generous with the hand-outs, especially if you didn't have to perform tricks for one, was always beloved by dogs.

"Well, we don't want to have to get on an airplane, Pickles," Lewis finally said, "so do you remember anything, anything at all about the night the redheaded lady was killed in your house? Lou said something about you smelled an unusual scent."

The older dog looked at Lewis with a sage expression on his face but continued to sit quietly for a few moments as the other three dogs assumed similarly relaxed positions around him. It wasn't long before the Lab's tail started to softly beat the ground as an idea must have begun to stir in his head.

"You know," he said, "when I came down the hall and found her lying on the ground, I smelled something not on her before. You know the stuff people put on their chests when they're sick? Stinks! It was in the air, and later I found traces of it on the garden gate, the door handle and the pot on the porch."

"I know what you're talking about," Willard said and snorted disgustedly. "Last winter, it was all over Sonya. She was sick with something she called the flu. The flu smells bad!"

"Come over here, boys," Pickles said as he trotted toward the front of the yard. "You can still smell it."

The sun was touching the tops of the old oaks along Meadowmere Place. Out on the shady sidewalk, a few walkers meandered down the street chatting softly about their day, the weather, and their lives. The four dogs took turns sniffing at the various places Pickles pointed out.

"It's not exactly the same as Sonya's flu smell," Willard said.

"No," chimed in Lewis. "It *has* another smell, too."

He turned to his brother, Clark.

"You know the stuff Marnie uses when she coughs a lot."

Clark brightened up with his tail beginning to wag from left to right like a windshield wiper.

"I know the stuff you mean, Lewis."

"Well, boys," Willard said. "We need to trot over to the place where you found your body, in Meyer Woods. If the same smell is over there, I can show Sonya."

"Can I go along?" Pickles asked. "It'd be nice to get out of here for a while. I feel better having met Beast. Is he gonna stay here and watch over things?"

Having dematerialized again, Beast gave a sharp yap in the affirmative.

"Sounds like he's staying put, Willard said. Come on and go with us, Pickles. The more noses the merrier."

"That's a long trip, Willard," Clark said. "Marnie will be worried if we aren't home soon."

"I got an idea, boys!" Willard barked. "Ever been on the bus? Lou and I have used it in the past."

The other three stayed mute. It was common knowledge among the dog community about Willard and Lou's trips to visit their girlfriends

"Well, come with me. I'll show you how to use four wheels instead of four paws to get you where you want to go. We can be in Meyer Woods in two shakes of a dog's tail!"

Chapter 38

Deputy Tommy Kirchner stood in the middle of the driveway and waved goodbye, a weak smile plucking at one corner of his mouth. The elegant, black Cadillac Escalade with Rosalie King, Presley and the two aunts from Tulsa, Honoria, and Althea, pulled away from the curb, its departure almost noiseless except for the crunch of the gravel under the tires.

The Kings decided it was best to go home to be closer to their family until answers were found in Wesley's murder. Also, Zeb's suggestion they would be out of harm's way five hours west of Willow Valley was strongly supported by Rosalie's older and alpha-female sister, Honoria. No one else in town, except Zeb and Tommy, was privy to where the Kings were going.

Knowing Rosalie and Presley were in safe hands, relief tentatively trickled down Tommy's spine making him feel like a slowly deflating balloon. He'd worked over twenty-four hours straight without sleep. Seductive thoughts of curling up in a fetal position in the back of his police vehicle swept through his mind.

Heading to his police vehicle, he climbed inside, shut the door, and slumped into the seat. Laying his head back against the padded rest, he let his eyelids slip down over dry, burning eyes.

Exhaustion like he'd never known rolled over him. Sleep would be deep and dreamless. Every fiber of his body was spent and within seconds, he fell asleep.

The sound of his phone ringing jerked him awake. Fumbling for it, his mind trying to process how long he'd been out, Tommy tapped the green dot on the phone's screen.

"Hello," he said, his voice cracking with sudden use.

"You sound beat, boy," Lana said on the other end of the line.

"I am. I feel like mush, Lana. Might only be my bulletproof vest holding me together right now."

"I'll keep Sheba another night for you. Better get some good sleep, kid."

The line went dead. Lana was a woman of few words, but she was the kind you wanted for a friend. She'd do anything for you, even keep your dog for days and treat her like a princess to boot.

He reached forward and turned the key on the ignition. With the car in drive, he steered it out through the back entry gates of Rosalie and Presley's home. His mind started pulling unrelentingly again at the weeds surrounding Wesley's murder. The negligible bit of evidence the forensic team found in Wesley's room wasn't enough to assist the police much in their investigation.

Presley told them the last time he'd talked to his brother, a woman had been in his room. Unfortunately, he had no idea who she might be except her name was probably Sam and she played tennis because of the sticker she had on her back window.

To find out who the mystery woman was, there would have to be a long line of past loves, past one-night-stands and all the other female players in Wesley's love life rounded up and interviewed. Not exactly a fun job. It would be a three-ring circus. Half the women in the county and even the surrounding areas would have to be hauled in for a statement. How Wesley hadn't been killed before now was a miracle.

Arriving home, Tommy climbed the stairs to his empty apartment. Inside, he stripped to boxers, opened his windows in his bedroom and looked out. Even though it was only six o'clock with the sun still up, he was determined to go to bed. The weather had begun to cool in the evenings making for a nice option over air conditioning.

Why is it, he thought to himself studying the red-leaved maple tree outside his window, when you are at your lowest the lightest touch of nature is so therapeutic? He turned and flopped down on his mattress, face planting into a pillow.

The late afternoon air wafted like a lullaby through the bedroom. It was tinged with the smell of honeysuckle, dampness and a whiff of cut grass. Instead of letting his mind wander down the dark, nightmarish avenues of the last twenty-four hours, he forced himself to think about something light, something to nourish his grief-stained mind and soul. It was slow to take hold, but eventually, a memory creaked into play like the way old films flitter and flash their first frames until the images start to roll seamlessly. Soon he was deep asleep.

Indian Creek with its water still fresh from the spring rains glittered into view. He saw each pebble of the creek's shallow bed, as well as darting silver minnows, crawdads and a brightly colored perch swimming below the rippling water's cool surface.

The memory narrowed further. Two twelve-year old boys labored blissfully at tugging an old, fallen tree across a hot gravel beach to the water's edge. They were readying their favorite camping site, and under a clear, star-filled night sky they would build a roaring fire, roast a package of hotdogs using found sticks, drink cans of root beer kept cold in the running water and sleep in hammocks tied up among the birch trees bowed out over the murmuring creek.

Later, crickets would chirp a timeless, but always enchanting bedtime story while cicadas in the branches above the boys would hum their age-old tune about love, life and loss sending them to sleep under a star-filled nighttime sky.

A soft summer wind rustling the trees would rock the hammocks as gently as any mother might have done at a baby's cradle. The world was good and true in that childhood place. More importantly, it made sense.

In a safe place constructed from comforting memories, Tommy's spirit lapped up the regenerative peace. It didn't last though. His brain too wired for problem-solving took over. Twisting and turning, it whipped up the dark waters of his unconscious until a nightmare loomed and bobbed like a predatory man-of-war honing in on its prey. Was there any kind of meaning, his mind asked, to be found in the last twenty-four hours?

The hellish dream took hold, dishing up images of Rosalie crying, begging him to bring her son home. Wesley caught under fiery limbs and Tommy fighting unseen demons. It was the last scene, though, with Presley screaming at him to help him free his brother from the branches that Tommy's mind begged him to claw his way up out of the dark bowels of his nightmare and break through into the light.

Lurching upright in his bed, his heart pounding and his body covered in a cold sweat, Tommy looked at the alarm clock. He'd only been asleep two hours before the nightmare kicked in.

It hit. The epiphany came with such force it caused him to grab the bed sheets with both hands, yanking them up towards his abdomen.

"The hot dog sticks!" he yelled. "I thought it was strange at the time!"

He jumped out of his bed and went in search of his cell phone which he found laying on the back of the toilet. Frantically dialing Zeb's number, he went around his bedroom collecting clothing and trying to put them on using only one hand.

"Hey," Zeb answered finally. "Did you get the Kings off to Tulsa?"

"I did. They should be halfway there by now."

He paused to draw breath and focus his words.

"I remembered something, sheriff. When we found Wesley in the brush pile, I saw a couple of long, slender sticks like the ones we used to whittle when we were kids to roast hot dogs. At the time, I must have dismissed it thinking it wasn't important, but I'm going back out there right now to see if I can find those sticks. If I'm right, and my tired imagination isn't playing tricks on me, the way those sticks were shaped might lead us to why Wesley was out there in the first place."

"Okay, Kirchner," Zeb said, drawing each syllable. "Tell me what you're thinking."

"When Presley and I were kids, we'd go to Indian Creek and camp out. Presley always loved to whittle our hot dog sticks. His dad gave him a buck knife and it meant the world to him. He would shape the sticks to a fine point and do this kind of notching on the edge. He always said it was how his dad taught him and his brother so the hot dog wouldn't fall into the fire. I've got to check the brush pile, sheriff. If I'm right, Wesley was alive when he went out to Meyer Woods and most likely was there with someone for a picnic."

Zeb's answer didn't come immediately.

"I've got another deputy out there. We can't take any chances someone will come back and burn the pile. If you find anything, call me and let me know. We've had a good break in the case. Found the key to the Sweeny's house, but also there's been a threat against Mrs. Townsend's and Marnie Scott's life. I've got another officer watching over Sonya's house where both women are staying. After you check out the brush pile, call me. Got it?"

With renewed energy and hope, Tommy Kirchner's mouth broke into a smile.

"Absolutely. Thank you, sheriff. I should have an answer for you soon."

Chapter 39

Tamara Lilton made the twenty-minute trip from downtown Willow Valley to her house's entrance in less than ten minutes. Tapping a preprogrammed button on her dashboard, the massive metal gate guarding her home's driveway retracted making way for the Volvo to enter her fifty-acre estate.

She would have to traverse another quarter-mile of curving asphalt and perfectly manicured grounds stretching out on either side before arriving at what Tamara, Patrick, Samantha, and their three Lhasa Apsos called home. It was a palatial brick and stone, six-thousand square foot Tudor-style megalith overlooking Willow Valley in the distance.

Tamara steered her vehicle around the cobblestone circle in front of the house and into one of the opening garage bays. Overhead fluorescent lights turned on as the car crossed some unseen laser beam bringing the entire garage into brilliant illumination.

With the press of another button, the door lowered again into place. In this well-lit area surrounded by the familiar, Tamara's heightened tension lowered a few notches. Quickly opening Sugar's carrier door on the seat beside her, she helped the dog to the ground, and the two of them made their way into the house.

"Samantha!" she called at the top of her lungs, her tone tinged with uncertainty. "Honey! Come here! I want to talk to you!"

What she wanted, first, was to see Sam's face. She needed to have a visual on her daughter so she could relax completely.

Tamara didn't get to where she was by being anything less than calculating, manipulative, fearless, and focused, but her handling of Samantha was the exact opposite. Loving, instinctive and fiercely protective, Tamara was the epitome of a mother bear. Only a fool would have crossed her when it came to her child.

She flung her Hermès bag on the mudroom's counter and started in the direction of Sam's room, but the sound of a young person's bare feet running along the marble floor hallway stopped her progress in the kitchen.

"I swear, mom," the waif-like teen said as she entered, "I didn't know Marcy was going to see some dead guy."

Samantha popped herself up on the top of the expansive granite covered kitchen island and picked at the corner crust of a blackberry cobbler sitting there probably made by Terrence.

An intense desire to hug the girl welled up in Tamara's heart. She reached her arms out and took hold of Sam's pretty, delicate hands and pulled her toward her into a warm, tight embrace.

"Mom?" Sam said, her words muffled against her mother's chest. "Are you okay? You're acting weird."

Tamara kissed the top of the pony-tailed head and laughed softly as she released her.

"He hopefully wasn't dead, Sammy, when Marcy saw him or, for that matter, after she left him."

She paused to release the girl.

"I guess I was scared. I'm glad you're safe and at home."

Samantha smiled and treated her mother to another warm, unexpected hug.

"It's okay, Mama. I didn't know the man who was killed. It's awful it happened though. Do you think Marcy is in trouble?"

Tamara pulled opened a drawer full of silverware and took out two spoons, handing one to Sam. Mother and daughter exchanged sheepish grins. With earnest, they tore into Terrence's enticing berry dessert.

"I hope Marcy's not in any real trouble," Tamara said after swallowing. "I do think we need to tell her parents tonight. Have you said anything to Marcy about what I told you?"

Tamara watched Sam's face for any subtle signs of truth fudging.

"No, I didn't. Besides, I haven't had time to even do homework. Daddy came up to my room after you called and said he wanted to know if I was making it a regular practice to loan my car out to people. He was grumpy and all control-like."

Samantha rolled her eyes as if to say she found her father's interrogation tiresome and irrational.

"I told him I loaned my car only the one time because Marcy was desperate for some reason to see Wesley and practically begged me for the car. She said Babette told her to ask me. Daddy made me feel like I'm some kind of accessory to murder. I'm scared. I promise, Mom, I didn't know anything."

Tamara knew Patrick's cross-examination of his daughter's decision to loan out her car was necessary. The one thing she and her husband were on the same page about was how they raised Samantha and, in this case, the teenager needed to be brought back in line about lending her car to people.

"Daddy's right, baby. No one is to be driving that car but you, unless you are sick or incapable of driving. Promise?" Tamara said, one eyebrow arched for serious effect.

This elicited an overly dramatic sigh, but also an acquiescence from the girl.

"Okay! Gosh, you guys act like I wasn't trying to do something *nice* for Marcy."

"Samantha, these kinds of things will always happen in life. Loaning your car, as I'm sure your father has explained, can sometimes have unexpected and unpleasant consequences. Unfortunately, you're about to live through one of those now. We need to go to the police and explain things. We, Marcy, along with her parents are going to be smack-dab in the middle of a murder investigation. Do you understand?"

Samantha's slight shoulders drooped with the weight of the situation and her eyes widened into large, frightened orbs.

"Mom! This is going to be horrible! Marcy is going to be so mad at me!"

"Honestly, Samantha, that is the least of our problems right now."

"Wait!" Tamara said, remembering her daughter's mention of Babette. "What did you say about Babette telling Marcy to ask to borrow your car?"

Sam looked at her mother with an expression of slight befuddlement.

"Oh yeah, Marcy said Babette had called her because she had proof her boyfriend was cheating on her. Of course, you know Marcy wrecked her car and her parents haven't bought her another one. She has to raise half the money herself."

"Sam," Tamara interrupted, "tell me the part about Babette."

"She told Marcy since we both play tennis, maybe I'd loan her my car to go over there. Honestly, mom, I didn't know Marcy's boyfriend was some old guy. Her parents are going to kill her!"

Deep in Tamara's brain, a hot-burning poker of hate seared along the edges of her last conversation with Babette. If she could have gotten her hands around Babette's neck at that moment, she would have probably killed her.

"Samantha, I want you to listen to me," her tone low and serious. "Do not go anywhere near Babette Nichols. She's a cold, calculating witch. I want to see your car. Come with me."

Two minutes later, mother and daughter were going through Sam's Subaru.

"I guess there's nothing here," Tamara said tossing a tennis bag back into the rear seat. "I just wanted to make sure your car was okay."

"What did you think, mom? Marcy would use it to make out with her boyfriend or something?" Sam asked.

Sam's comment reminded Tamara of her own youth and how she kept all sorts of necessary items like a blanket or even a cooler in her trunk.

"Open the trunk, Sam," she commanded.

With a shrug, the teen did as she was asked. The place where the tire and tools were kept under a sturdy plastic mat had been lifted and left askew.

"Have you been in here, Sam?" Tamara asked.

"No, I never use my trunk."

Tamara's stomach tightened again into a knot. Pulling the mat up again, she saw a bloody rag wrapped around what looked like a tire iron. Shocked, she dropped the plastic cover.

"Go get your father," she practically whispered.

Sam's face registered fear and went running off into the house yelling, "Daddy! Come here!"

Patrick came running down the hall.

"Patrick, look at this in Sam's trunk!" Tamara cried.

She pulled up the mat again to show her husband.

"We need to call the police," he said. "Girls step away from the car, we can't touch it anymore. Come on, everyone back inside the main part of the house."

Once they'd all returned to the living room, Patrick Lilton did something rare. He went over to the wall-mounted iPad and tapped in a code. A soft, modulated female voice announced all security systems were now activated.

Turning to face his wife and daughter, he smiled with warmth in his eyes.

"I love my girls," he said and walked over and took both of them into a strong hug. "I don't know what I'd do without you."

Wrapped in his arms, Tamara experienced two extremely conflicting emotions. An unusual burst of love for her husband quickly followed by a sickening feeling. Something evil, something predatory had brushed up against her family. If she wasn't careful, she could lose everything, no, — *everyone*, important in her life.

Chapter 40

"I'm going back to Willow Valley. I want to help find my brother's murderer," Presley said as he, his mother, and his two aunts were an hour into the drive toward Tulsa. The statement hit the group like a slap in the face causing Aunt Honoria to nearly wreck her precious Escalade.

Instantly, his horrified aunts threw at him a quick-fire round of rebuttals to his announcement. They claimed it was madness to go back to Willow Valley. Didn't he remember the police wanted to be sure of his safety? His friend, Tommy, explained he and Rosalie were to be in Tulsa. And surely he agreed, the investigation shouldn't be hampered in any way?

When Presley shrugged off these truths, Aunt Honoria, watching him like a hawk through the rear-view mirror, played her masterstroke.

"Your mother, Presley, needs you right now. Putting yourself in danger? How can you do that to her? This is no time to be a hero."

"I'm not trying to be a hero, Aunt Honoria. I'm going for Wesley. I can't shake off the feeling he wants me there."

Rosalie remained quiet throughout the debate. When she must have realized her sisters weren't making much headway with her only surviving child, she roused herself from the fog of loss and shock.

Threatening every kind of motherly retribution and applying hot compresses of guilt, she gave a valiant try to dissuade him, but to no avail. Taking the last, feeble option left to her; she extracted his promise to answer the phone each time she called.

A quick search of the internet on his smartphone revealed the closest car rental agency. Fifteen minutes later in the Rent-A-Car parking lot, he said goodbye allowing Rosalie to kiss him at least ten times and hug him twice much to the amusement of the two teenage lot attendants.

Finally, he contracted his tall frame into the rented compact car, pulled out onto the freeway, and focused on the road leading him home.

The evening traffic was beginning to intensify when Presley turned his car down the last highway to Willow Valley. An increasing desire to see *where* his brother was killed had taken hold of him as if Wesley was beside him on the drive home urging him to stand and witness the physical spot where he'd died.

It was crazy stuff, and Presley was beginning to doubt his sanity with every mile he traveled. He couldn't explain, though, the definite weighty presence of his brother in the car. Presley knew he couldn't rest until he saw where his brother had drawn his last breath.

Not unexpectedly, he made the drive in much less time than it had taken Aunt Honoria to travel the same stretch. As he pulled into the turn-off to Meyer Woods, he stopped the car and turned off the motor.

The weight of the last twenty-four hours rolled over him. Exhaustion and grief were taking their toll. Putting his forehead down on the steering wheel, he shut his weary eyes.

"What the Hell am I doing?" he mumbled out loud. "I drove all this way and I've got no idea what I'm supposed to find."

A comforting silence filled the car's interior. Long rays of sunlight flickered through the tree canopy settling in round patches upon the top of his head, his arms and his arched back. Nothing stirred, that is until something did.

"Brother," he said, taking a deep breath, holding it and letting it out.

Tears burned in his eyes and a lump rose in his throat.

"Why am I here? How can I go on in this life without you? You were my big brother! You are supposed to be here always!"

Like a dam breaking, the sobs poured out. The release of his emotions was the truest thing he'd felt since Tommy told him Wesley was dead.

The waves crashed again and again, but they finally receded and Presley lifted his face to the warm rays of sunlight coming through the windshield of the car. With his eyes shut, the tension in his body completely gone, he sat back and relaxed in his seat.

A soft tapping on the window brought him abruptly upright, his heart hammering in his chest.

"My God!" he yelled.

Stooping over and looking in at him with a half sheepish, half worried look was Sabrianna Williams.

"Hey," she said, her words flat sounding through the glass. "You okay, Presley? Sorry if I scared you."

Even with his heart still pounding hard from the aftershock of surprise, a part of his brain managed to relay a new emotion, embarrassment. He instantly knew she'd heard him crying. Turning the car's engine back on, he lowered the driver's side window.

"Sabrianna Williams? What are you doing out here? This isn't any place for you to be."

"Well, Presley King," she returned, "considering the circumstances, the same thing could be asked of you."

Chapter 41

The evening sun was about an hour from touching the
horizon when Zeb, Sonya, and the Sweenys stepped
through the front door of the sleeping Victorian.

Sunlight filtered through the diamond-shaped, beveled
glass living room windows bedazzling the polished wooden
parquet floors. A hushed heaviness infused the space except
for a faraway, almost imperceptible hum emanating from
some sort of appliance in the kitchen.

At the windows, long, cream-colored sheers quivered
into life from unseen air conditioning currents. It was as if
the house had gone on living, keeping itself whole in hopes
its people would return.

Moving down the hall following Zeb, Sonya came to
the place where Roxy had died. No one spoke and the
house's stillness enhanced the feeling that it was holding its
breath awaiting its sentence.

Finally, Sonya turned around and said to Harry and
Deidra, "This home of yours has known many transitions
and what I mean by that, is life as we know it, has come
and gone within its walls and in its gardens hundreds of
times."

Deidra blurted out, "Hundreds of times? How in the
world did over a hundred *people* die in this house?"

"Not only people and not all of them adults, Deidra,"
Sonya returned. "Two children and one infant, dogs, cats,
more birds than can be counted, other animals and even

trees and bushes have called this place home at one time. They all passed on to another place. All those energies leave traces behind. Kind of like ripples from when a stone is thrown into the water. I only feel good passings. Some were sad, even tragic like Roxy's, but far too many happened, to let a single one keep you from re-embracing your home."

Harry sighed putting both hands on his hips in a gesture of befuddlement.

"When you put it that way, I feel like this house is more of a cemetery than a home."

Sonya laughed.

"Oh, Harry! There's not a two-foot by two-foot section of habitable land on this planet that couldn't be described the same way. We live in a soup of always morphing energy. Most people never know it's going on around them. Some, like me, can to tune in, so to speak, to the static of life."

"Well, to us, it feels like what happened here is a horrible wound," Deidra said and sighed.

"The key is to ask for what you want," Sonya replied. "Ask. Use your words. Say them out loud. If you want to feel content again in this house and free the house of the tragedy of your sister's brutal murder, ask and you shall receive. Redemption is free for the asking. Believe in divine intervention, protection, and goodness. It's real and it only works when you ask."

No one said anything. Zeb's phone rang. He excused himself and walked back into the living area and out onto the front porch.

"Sonya," Harry asked, "I want to make peace with what happened here. I don't want to walk down this hall every time and think about Roxy being murdered. What can we do?"

"Change your perspective, your attitude about it. Have a ceremony to expiate the sin committed here. Pray for Roxy. Pray for her killer, too. Let go, I know it will take time and work on your part, but when you let go of your fear and anger, ask for only goodness and light to be in your home, you'll be at peace with what happened here. Always keep a candle burning to bring light to this place. When you walk past this spot, make a conscious decision to remember how Roxy's life was a gift and how much you loved her. Forgive the person who took her life. That is the legacy…love."

"Will you help us, Sonya?" Harry asked.

"I'd be delighted. For now, though, you need to ask for divine support and healing."

Sonya reached inside her purse and pulled out a candle in a tall jar. Taking a permanent marker and handing it to Harry, she said, "Write your sister's name on the glass."

He did as she asked.

"Now, write one word of healing to Roxy beside her name."

Harry was quiet for a moment. Sonya sensed his emotion rising, and soon a tear made its way down his cheek. He wrote 'love'.

Taking the jar candle from Harry, Sonya handed it to Deidra.

"Deidra, when you think about this house, what is the one word that comes to your mind first? Once you have it, write it on the jar, too."

Without hesitation, Deidra wrote 'home'.

"Good!" Sonya said with joy. "Now, add one word to the jar asking for what you want for your home."

Deidra smiled broadly and wrote 'blessed'.

"Excellent choice," Sonya said.

Taking the candle back, Sonya took out a matchbox from her pocket and sitting the candle down on a hall table, she struck a match and lit the candle's wick.

"Okay, let's hold hands and say a prayer."

Like well-behaved children, Harry and Deidra clasped hands and joined with Sonya in a soft prayer to let Roxy know they loved her, and as a testimony to her life, they would keep a candle lit to her memory as long as they lived in their home. Sonya asked for constant protection for the home.

Grace flooded the space and Sonya gave them both hugs and whispered in the ears a simple truth.

"God is good. Grace is always a prayer away."

Chapter 42

"Okay, get Pineville over there," Zeb said. "But I want Michael to go over to the Lilton's tonight and talk with their daughter. We need to know if the girl saw or heard anything. Send Andrew to get a statement from Marcy Hollingsworth."

Sonya and the Sweenys walked out of the house.

"I was hoping to see your dog, Pickles," Sonya said to the Sweenys.

"It's strange," Deidra replied, "but he's been hiding this afternoon. I haven't seen him. Sometimes he likes to go over to our neighbor's house and play with their dog. I'm sorry, Mrs. Caruthers. He's not here."

"Not to worry, I'll check back tomorrow."

"We've got to go into the office to clean up some paperwork, but I think tomorrow night we'll move our things back into the house and sleep here," Deidra said.

"We'd better be going. I've received a call from dispatch," Zeb said.

Waving goodbye, Sonya and Zeb got in his car and headed to her house.

"Did you feel anything Sonya about who the murderer might be?" he asked.

"I don't know the person, Zeb," she answered, shaking her head, but not turning to look at him. "Whoever killed Roxy was there to steal something."

"Are you saying it was a thief?" Zeb asked, his tone incredulous. "They may have found the murder weapon, Sonya, and I believe it was used to kill both Wesley and Roxy."

"No, I'm saying, Roxy was killed for gain. The murderer wanted money or power, possibly both. They may have killed to hold on to power or gain more wealth. This was also premeditated. Honestly, Zeb, it's tied up some way with money. Lots of it."

"It always boils down to either greed, love or reputation," Zeb replied. "Here we are."

They'd pulled up to Sonya's house and Zeb got out and opened her car door.

"Thank you for your help," he said.

Sonya smiled up at him.

"My pleasure. I'll let you know if I think of anything."

"You owe me a dinner," he said.

Their gaze, mutual, hung uninterrupted, verging on the intimate. Sonya broke first, blushing and turning away as she answered.

"You pick the restaurant, Zeb, and I'll wear a blue dress. Sound fair?"

There it was again, a twinge of excitement at the idea of having her alone. He found his voice and when he used it, even he heard the excitement in his answer.

"I guess you knew my favorite color was blue."

She never turned back but threw her answer over her shoulder.

"I've already told you before, Zeb. I never guess."

After making sure she got in all right, he headed for his office. Fifteen minutes later he was dialing the Liltons with his pen tapping on a mountain of files laying on his desk.

"Guess you got my call," Patrick Lilton said when he answered the phone.

"Guess you've got something to tell me," Zeb came back.

"My daughter's car was borrowed by Marcy Hollingsworth the day before Wesley King was found dead in Meyer Woods. Sam says Marcy wanted it to see her boyfriend."

"How did all of this come out, Patrick?" Zeb asked.

"At the Posh Pups competition tonight, Tamara was talking with Babette Nichols who told her she'd seen Samantha's car at the King's residence."

"Who found the bloody rag and tire iron?"

"My wife."

"What made her look for it?" Zeb pushed on.

There was a short stint of quiet before Patrick answered.

"She had a feeling. I…I don't know why she went to look, but when I asked her why she said she had a feeling something wasn't right."

In Zeb's mind, he'd come, in the last forty-eight hours, to appreciate the instinct of women.

"I tell you what, Patrick," Zeb said slowly, "I'm going to talk with the Hollingsworth family tomorrow morning. In the meantime, if I were you, I'd keep a tight hold on your daughter. My forensic team will be out there in about an hour and the officer in charge is going to be Deputy Michael Davies. We'll need to take casts of the tires to see if they match the ones we found in Meyer Woods and do a complete sweep of the car's inside."

"Are you thinking Sam's car might have been used to…" Patrick started to say.

"Take Wesley King to Meyer Woods?" Zeb finished for him.

"Oh my God!" Patrick, he blurted out. "Do you think the killer knew it was Sam's car?"

"One thing I can be pretty certain of Patrick," Zeb said. "These murders have one thing in common."

"What?" Patrick almost demanded.

"Rich people," Zeb replied. "And my guess is, out of the three families involved, yours is not only the richest but has the most to gain."

Chapter 43

Sabe continued to look at Presley through the driver's window like it was he who shouldn't be in Meyer Woods.

"Presley, open the door and let me in," she finally said.

He hit the unlock button and the girl walked around the front of the car and opened the door. She easily slipped into the passenger side.

"Are you okay, Presley?" she said. "I never expected to see you out here."

Either it was her gentle tone or it was the unexpected appearance of someone from his childhood, but Presley, much to his immediate horror began to well-up again with tears. He couldn't answer her. Instead, he dug in the empty glove compartment for something to wipe his face.

Laying a soft hand on his arm, Sabe pulled out some tissues from her purse and offered them to him.

"Here," she said.

"Thanks," he managed to choke out. "What are you doing out here Sabrianna?"

"I came out here because, well,…" Sabe hesitated, but finished with, "I've had the weirdest feeling all day. I needed to see where…he died."

She flashed him another worried look and continued.

"It's like somethings been pulling at me and wouldn't let go until I came out here."

Presley looked at her now like she'd slapped him. She started to say more, but he held up his hand to make her stop.

"Me too! I've been driving like a madman to get her today. I'm supposed to be in Tulsa. I know this sounds as if I'm crazy, but I had to see this place."

Sabe nodded her head up and down

"Come on," she said. "Let's go together."

The ruts of the road were beyond what the Civic was up to traversing and Presley mentally chastised himself for not thinking to rent something with four-wheel drive.

"We're going to have to walk," he said to her.

"That's fine, but I want you to know, I came prepared," she said.

Pulling a handgun from her purse, she let him see.

"Holy Hell!" Presley blurted. "Why'd you bring *that* thing along, Sabe? You could kill someone."

She slipped the gun back in her purse.

"Damn straight, it can. I've got my conceal carry license so don't think I'm some hooligan who doesn't know how to use this thing properly. Stick with me, Presley. If the lunatic who killed Wesley is out there tonight and tries any crazy crap, they'll be messing with the wrong woman. I'll protect you."

Her words stunned him. What if she was right and the murderer was stalking around the woods waiting for his next victim? Speechless, he continued to stare at her. It was the first time he'd seriously looked at Sabe. Another slap of truth hit Presley. Sabrianna Williams was gorgeous.

She stepped out of the car and he quickly followed.

"You know how to handle a gun?" he asked, running up behind her.

He noticed the curve of her body in the jeans she wore and how her intricately long braided hair was swinging with each step she took.

She turned around and flashed him a beautiful smile.

"Honey, I'm an amazing shot. Daddy taught each of his girls how to handle a gun. Being the daughter of an army drill sergeant has its perks."

Here was this woman half his size who was signing herself up to be *his* bodyguard. He found it laughable, but as he let it sink in, it was also kinda nice. He double-timed his steps to catch up with her.

"Sabe, don't you think it's a man's job to protect a woman?" he asked, his grin more playful than macho.

"Oh, I don't know, Presley King," she answered, one enticing dimple, he noted, revealing itself on her left cheek, "it's the female that's the more deadly of the sexes. Besides, I came prepared. Are you?"

The last rays of sunlight illuminated the pretty woman's head like a halo. She stood there waiting for his answer, her expression serene, confident and genuine. The coil of tension in Presley unraveled and something else, something warm took its place.

Sabe shifted from one foot to the other, watching him.

His answer came in the form of action.

"Glad you thought to bring the gun, Sabe. We'd better go before it gets too dark."

She smiled.

"Let's walk together."

The September evening was warm and enough sunlight filtered in through the canopy to make it easy for them to see the path. Leaves of red, orange and yellow were sprinkled about the wood's floor. Walking beside her, he quietly marveled at the extremes of emotion he'd experienced in one day. Somehow her presence was like a balm and yet, at the same time, powerfully exciting.

Neither spoke until Sabe said, "I'm so sorry about Wesley. We're all going to miss him. I know for sure there's going to be a lot of broken hearts with him gone."

He couldn't help it. He shook his head and laughed at her last words.

"Oh yeah," he said. "Wesley definitely will be missed by the women of Willow Valley and beyond. I've wondered on more than one occasion how he managed them all."

His own words triggered his memory again of the day Wesley died and the woman who'd been in his brother's bedroom.

He looked down at Sabe and started to tell her what he'd remembered, but before he answered, something running and rustling through the leaves brought his head up. With his instinct jumping into overdrive, he scanned the wood and at the same time reaching out for Sabe, pushed her behind him.

Four dogs of differing sizes came romping down a low hillside off to Presley and Sabrianna's left. Tails high and tongues lolling, the happy menagerie of canines appeared to be oblivious to the presence of the two humans.

"Where are those dogs going?" Sabe said and laughed. "They sure look like they're having fun."

"Come on. They're headed for the middle of the woods. That's where I think we need to go. Let's follow them."

He reached for her hand and she didn't pull away. For a few minutes, they plunged through the woods like children at a game in pursuit of the dogs.

As the path broke into the clearing, Presley and Sabe, came to a dead stop. Their joie de vivre drained out like water through a sieve, for standing with both hands on his hips, mouth in a hard, grim line and staring at them with a look of sheer, unadulterated anger was the one man Presley had hoped not to run into: Deputy Presley Kirchner.

Chapter 44

"Harry, I feel so much better about things," Deidra was saying as she handed her husband a cup of tea. "I think we should go with Titan's offer."

After their visit with Sonya, they'd gone back to the office. They'd been going over Titan's proposal and awaiting the arrival of Teddy to talk with him about selling the company.

"If Titan will pay us thirty-million dollars for a business in this economy of booms and busts, we'd be crazy not to take the money and run," Deidra continued.

"Deidra," Harry said, his voice measured and firm, "Our problems are two-fold. Patrick Lilton *says* he'll do right by Posh Pups and the community. Words are cheap. I want it in writing. He doesn't spell any of those conditions out in this contract. Any anyway, I don't have a leg to stand on because Teddy is threatening to sell his shares to the highest bidder. I don't know who he's talking to. He's our second problem, and frankly, our biggest at the moment."

Deidra slumped back in her chair with a resigned sigh.

"I'll tell you one thing's for sure, darling. Tamara Lilton would never turn Willow Valley into a ghost town. Her greatest dream is to be the queen of it. Patrick wouldn't dare take away the pretty, little kingdom she rules over."

Harry watched his wife as she sat propped up on the edge of his desk. She was as lovely as the day he'd met her, but in recent years they'd grown apart. It was only since

Roxy's death, a renewed closeness had resurged in their marriage.

"Only when I know he intends to keep his promise in writing as a condition of the sale, will I ever sign the contract. That is if we can get Teddy to sell us his shares."

"That's a pity for you, brother," Teddy Davidson said from the doorway causing the startled Sweeny duo to turn in his direction. "You know, from the first time old Charlie Sweeny told me to call him dad on my wedding day with Roxy, I've always thought of you as a brother."

Teddy's tone was sarcastic. He leaned up against the door jamb in a relaxed, cowboy manner and taking out his penknife, started cleaning his nails.

"I'd hoped as family," he said, "we'd all see eye-to-eye about selling the company. To tell you the truth, Harry, I've grown to hate Posh Pups. It was a sore spot in my marriage. You've always been so tight-fisted, Harry, but now that's all changed. My wife's death means I own Roxy's shares. You're cheap ways, brother, are of no concern for me now. I'm in the driver's seat and I'd be an idiot to sell my shares to the lowest bidder—you."

Teddy gave his sister-in-law an easy smile and wink. She in return rolled her eyes and compressed her lips in an expression of irritation.

"If Deidra throws her lot in with me, we don't need *you* to sell this business. We have a majority and you know it," Teddy said looking at Harry dead on. "Roxy is gone and I want out."

"Go to Hell, Teddy," Deidra said, her tone dry.

Harry jumped in quickly, saying, "I'll buy your shares tonight. You'll get market value for them."

"That *is* a fair offer, but I might want to see what a few others who've come sniffing around, would give me for them. Once its announced Titan is interested in buying us out, those stocks will be worth twice as much, much more than what you'd pay me for them tonight."

"Teddy," Harry said rising from his seat, his face beginning to flush with rage, "you sell your shares to some company and it gives me no bargaining power to make sure they don't strip Posh Pups of its value and do exactly what I know they might do…toss it on a tax heap and burn it alive!"

Harry slammed his fist down on his desk and continued.

"Why in the hell would you want to see this town go down the toilet and everyone in it so you can go off with your whore, Babette Nichols, and live off the lifeblood of my family's hard work?"

"Who told you about Babette?" Teddy asked, his voice rising with each word.

"Tamara Lilton!" Harry came back, his face warming with color. "She saw you and Babette together."

"So what?" Teddy hissed, his tone thick with menace.

Looking the other man up and down, a sneer tinged Harry's next statement.

"I wouldn't be surprised if you killed my sister. You're a son-of-a-bitch and I'll see you in hell before I let you ruin this company like you ruined my sister's life!"

Like a bull stung by the lance of a matador, Teddy lunged across the room at Harry.

Diedra rushed from her seat and jumped in between the two men barely escaping her own husband's first punch landing square on Teddy's left jaw.

"Stop it! Stop it right now!" she screamed.

But it was too late. Harry pushed her out of the way with such force, she was barely able to keep her footing as she plunged into the couch.

Both men, fully in the heat of battle, continued pummeling each other with Teddy throwing the most punches. It was only when Teddy knocked his brother-in-law up against the desk causing Harry to land flat upon its top, that Deidra scampered over to where her purse sat and dug within its prodigious girth.

Scrambling off the desk's top, Harry headed back into the fray as Teddy reached for the tactical knife attached to his belt. But before he unsheathed it, a loud noise electrified the room. Teddy's body shuddered, convulsed, and fell forward revealing Deidra holding the present Harry had given her last year for Christmas—a still crackling taser gun.

Chapter 45

"Trust me. The butler didn't do it. It's always the *last* person you'd expect who's the murderer," Marnie mumbled through a mouth full of popcorn. "I've watched all the Agatha Christie movies ever made, Lillian. I know my way around a murder mystery."

Mrs. Townsend, now on a first-name basis as Lillian, laughed. The three women were enjoying a fun movie about two intrepid, not particularly bright but fearless lady sleuths who'd been chased by a killer into an old lime kiln.

"I thought you didn't want to watch something scary?" Lillian teased.

"Beats the movie Sonya wanted to watch," Marnie came back. "A love story. Interesting choice don't you think, Lillian? Is SOMEbody's getting a soft spot for a certain good looking sheriff."

"I heard that and I am not getting any soft spot for anybody!" Sonya exclaimed from the kitchen.

Walking into the living room with a tray full of cups, a teapot, and some shortbread cookies, she sat her load down on the coffee table and squeezed in between the other two women. Pajama-clad Marnie and robe-wrapped Lillian were already cozily ensconced on the couch and sharing an enormous afghan. Sonya started pouring steaming camomile tea into the chintz patterned teacups.

"Oh get real," Marnie replied while reaching for a cookie. "There is some kind of chemistry between the two of you."

"I have to agree with Marnie," Lillian said. "You blushed Sonya in my study today when you fell into the sheriff's arms. Neither of you, in that instant, was aware of the mini cyclone of papers taking place or the loud voice hollering something about lasses and filthy hands."

Pausing for an instant and taking Sonya's proffered cup of tea, Lillian continued, "You know, I hear that voice all the time in my house. People think I'm an old luny woman, but you can't tell me you didn't hear it today. I won't believe you."

She sipped her tea while giving the other two women a steely stare.

Sonya and Marnie both sat on the couch looking straight ahead, one with a cup of tea hovering below her lips and the other with her mouth full of shortbread cookie. Sonya took a tiny sip while Marnie swallowed hard.

"Okay," Sonya said, "it's like this, Lillian. Time for me to come clean about a few things."

She put the cup in its saucer and lay it back on the table. Turning her body to face Lillian, she took a deep, measured breath.

To her left, Marnie mumbled, "This should be good."

"You've no doubt seen the sign on my front porch. The one that says *Spirit Therapist*?"

Lillian nodded.

"Well, I do have a knack for helping people with spirit issues. It's something I've been doing for fifteen years, but I've seen ghosts since I was a child. There is something about me that brings them in, increases their strength and allows me and others to see them, even talk with them."

Lillian smiled sympathetically and took a second dainty sip of the sweet-smelling chamomile tea.

"Sonya, I've seen the sign and if you're willing to accept I've got an alien issue, I'll accept you are able to wrangle ghosts."

"You don't have an *alien* issue, Lillian," Sonya said gently. "You've got a *Fritz* issue."

Marnie burst out laughing, snorting through her nose some of the tea she'd been drinking.

"A *Fritz* issue?" Lillian came back. "Explain."

"Yeah, *explain*, Sonya," Marnie said still chortling while reaching for another cookie.

With a good, strong elbowing of Marnie's ribs, Sonya pushed on.

"You see, a few years ago while on a trip to Canada, I sort of ran into a ghost who for whatever reason decided to take a shine to me. His name was Laird Fitswilliam of Dunbar and at the time, he'd been enjoying his retirement from living for at least two hundred years. The problem with Fritz," Sonya paused to add, "oh by the way I don't call him Fits. It sounded so rude so I call him Fritz, is he can be extremely high spirited and prone to pranks. He likes to come and go as he pleases. On any given week, he likes to pop in here for a visit at least two or three times. I've warned him repeatedly to leave my neighbors alone, but, well, unfortunately, he rarely listens to me. He was a Laird when he was alive in Scotland and still has a strong sense of his rights and privileges."

Lillian held up her hand for Sonya to stop.

"So, what you're trying to say is you believe you've got a ghost who lives here on an irregular basis and you think he might be my alien problem," she said.

Sonya nodded, her expression clearly saying this was, as always, a hard sell.

"Yes, that is what I'm asking you to believe. When I heard Fritz today in your house, I knew he was there and for the most part he's such a dear, but lately, I've had to reprimand him because I'm terrified he might cause someone real trouble. But to his credit, he was the one today who told me you might be in danger with the box of candy. That's why he was batting it around, so you wouldn't go near it."

Sonya looked at her upturned palms laying in her lap.

"I'm so sorry Lillian. I've owed this apology to you for some time, but I've been a coward. I didn't know how to tell you about Fritz. You would think in my line of work, explaining ghosts would become easier and easier, but the truth of it is it's always difficult. People think I'm, well for lack of a better word, crazy."

Mrs. Townsend reached over and patted Sonya's arm.

"Not to worry, dear. You're in good company."

The three women laughed out loud together, a new feeling of real friendship warming their hearts.

"But," Lillian said once they were all quiet again, "I've got a favor to ask of you, Sonya."

"I'll do my best," Sonya replied.

"Would you please show Fritz to me?"

It was the last request, Sonya, The Ghost Wrangler, was expecting from the delicate and genteel lady of more than eighty years. Marnie broke into a fit of laughter and curled herself up more snuggly into her corner of the couch.

"I like your style, Lillian. You've got a lot of moxie!"

The request hung in the air.

"Okay," Sonya said slowly. "Are you sure?"

She turned to Marnie.

"What about you? Are you up for this?"

Marnie giving her best Cheshire cat smile said, "I was here for the seance last spring, Sonya, and I heard the racket from Mr. Pepper's camper. Bring it on. I figure you know how to manage this Fritz pretty well. Let's see what happens. This is a way better thrill than the movie we started."

Sonya shrugged her acquiescence and called out, "Fritz! Fritz? Would you please come home? I need to talk to you!"

She didn't offer him a reason for why she wanted him. He might not show up if he knew. Fritz was a wild card. This was a command performance of sorts, and in true Fritz fashion, he might want to play hard to get. Likewise, if he thought it was a trap where he might be put on the spot to apologize, he wouldn't show for weeks. The best way for Sonya to handle the high-spirited spirit was to stack the deck in her favor.

She tried again.

"Fritz! I need to talk to you!"

It was quiet for more than a few minutes, but slowly like how a radio station crackles with static and finds its perfect reception, the room's air filled with the rollicking singing of two male voices.

"I came home on Saturday night,
As drunk as I could be.
And there was a hat upon the rack,
Where my hat ought to be.

So I said to my wife, the curse of my life,
"Explain this thing to me,
Whose is that hat upon the rack,
Where my hat ought to be?"

Followed by mocking, but silly female voices:

Oh, you drunken old fool,
You silly old fool,
You're as drunk as a fool can be,
That's not a hat upon the rack,
But a chamberpot you see!"

Raucous male laughter exploded as Fritz and his disheveled, whiskered-faced singing partner materialized before the three speechless women.

Chapter 46

"You're supposed to be in Tulsa!" Tommy exclaimed. "It wasn't a suggestion, Presley. It was an order."

"I don't take orders from you, Kirchner. I'm here because of my brother. I…I… believe he wants me here," Presley stammered.

"And you!" Tommy went on, turning his heated gaze on Sabrianna. "This place may be dangerous. We've got a twenty-four-hour watch on it. The person who killed Wesley tried to burn this brush pile once. They might wanna come back here and burn the entire wood down. Why are you out here?"

"I can't explain it, Tommy," Sabe said, looking perplexed. "All day I've wanted to come out here. It's been a nagging thought and impossible to get out of my head. I've been worried about…"

Sabrianna hesitation was brief as her eyes flitted between Presley to her left and Tommy to her right, but she quickly added, "How Wesley died."

Tommy shook his head. These two people were his friends. He couldn't blame them. The place had triggered a strong desire in him to revisit it as well.

Though he'd just arrived, he hadn't had time to look for the hot dog sticks. He'd taken a few minutes to be alone. The place felt sad and sacred at the same time.

"Presley, do you remember when we were kids and we'd go camping on Indian Creek?" he asked.

A smile lit up the other man's tired face.

"I do. Why do you ask?"

"You had a pocket knife and you always sharpened the sticks making sure to put a notch near the end. You said your dad taught you to do it that way so the hot dogs wouldn't fall off."

Presley nodded his head up and down slowly, a faint blush of happiness warming his expression at the memory of his father.

"I do remember. What's this all about Tom?"

The deputy pointed toward the ground. There beside his right foot were two sharpened sticks and near their tips, notches identical to the ones the King boys had always carved when a marshmallow or a hot dog needed cooking over an open fire.

Presley walked over like he was going to pick them up.

"Don't touch it, buddy," Tommy said, his tone gentle. "They need to be examined. I saw them last night, but I think with the shock of Wesley's death, the importance of the notches on the stick didn't register with me. I came back out tonight when I remembered. They're right where I saw them, laying up against the side of the brush pile. Wesley must have come out here with someone who he was friendly with because he made two."

Those carved notches, tiny almost negligible markings, held the priceless last moments of Wesley's life. All three people's gazes were riveted to the place where the sticks lay. The lump grew in Tom's throat. Tears burned as they slowly filled his eyes. As a way to shut the grief down, he took a deep breath and let it out.

Bending over to see in the fading light, Presley studied the sticks closely.

"There are bite marks on them," he said. "Do you see them?"

Tommy knelt to get a better look. Indeed there were marks, almost like an animal had chewed on one end.

"Maybe a dog?" Presley added.

"Yeah, but a small one," Tommy replied.

"These need to be handled with care and gone over by the forensic examiner."

The deputy's ear picked up a rustling sound.

The four dogs who'd been sniffing about the back part of the area unseen by the three people, and not close enough to be in view yet, made their way around the brush pile. One trotted amiably up to them. With the sun almost down, Tommy recognized it as Sonya's dog.

"Willard?" he asked. He looked over at another set of dogs, two beagles, busily sniffing around the edges of the pile. "Is that Lewis and Clark, Marnie's boys?"

A third dog lumbered around the back of the brush pile.

"And Pickles! What are all of you doing out here?"

Willard came up and greeted Tommy, and let him give his head a good pet. He watched the dogs return to the brush pile and begin sniffing as they would have watched four children play on monkey bars in a playground. But when Lewis let out a commanding bark, he noticed how the dogs trotted professionally over to where the beagle was whining and digging.

With four dogs all zeroing in on a spot, it was hard for Tommy not to follow. Clark and Lewis got down. Their noses twitching with the strong scent they'd found, they both sneezed and snorted as if the smell was too much.

"What is it, boys?" Tommy asked.

Lewis, his attention riveted to something he wasn't able to retrieve himself from under the mess of twigs, whined and continued to dig.

"Let me have a try," the deputy said, gently moving the two beagles out of his way.

Reaching in and clearing away the leaves, he touched a bit of cloth and pulled it free from the hiding place. It was an extremely dirty, tiny dog jacket, blue and smelling of lavender, eucalyptus, and camphor.

The dogs, Lewis and Clark, barked again, a crisp, firmness in their tone. Willard and Pickles nosed-in to catch a whiff as well. All four dogs went into snorting and sneezing fits.

Holding the coat up to his nose, Tommy took in the strong fragrance.

"Does it smell bad?" Presley asked.

"No, it smells good. Well, to me anyway, but not so much to our friends here," Tommy replied. Lifting the jacket for the others to smell, he asked, "Here, tell me what you think?"

"I know that scent," Sabe said at once. "It's lavender and eucalyptus. We have some lineament at the shop. Lana's always mixing up stuff for our clients. This is one she uses for people who have anxiety or have nasal congestion."

"Certainly worked for those guys," Presley said pointing at the four canines sitting calmly in a row in front of them. "They're relaxed and they each sneezed enough to clear out anyone's head."

The people laughed as they looked down at the dogs who were indeed all panting languidly.

"I bet Lana has records of who buys her salve, Sabe. I'll have her email me a list tonight. Thank you for that information."

He paused still studying the four dogs, adding, "Funny isn't it?"

"What is?" the other two asked in unison, quickly exchanging shy smiles between them.

It flashed across his mind they were probably attracted to each other, but he went ahead and finished his first thought.

"If we hadn't come out here tonight, we wouldn't have found the jacket, recognized the scent on it or realized there were bite marks on the sticks.These are clues we wouldn't have found. How do you explain it?"

Sabe and Presley were quiet, but they nodded.

"It may be a coincidence," Sabe suggested.

"What made you remember the sticks?" Presley asked Tommy.

"I fell asleep, exhausted, and I wanted something happy to think about. The first thing that came into my mind was our camping trips as kids. Fishing, hanging our hammocks up in the trees and cooking hot dogs. It was like a bolt from the blue remembering how you always notched the sticks. I realized Wesley must have known the trick, too."

The night had completely fallen and the forest was full of the sounds typical for the time of year like rustlings of nocturnal animals starting their day. A feeling of tranquility descended on the group of humans and canines.

"I want to have a memorial put here for my brother," Presley said, his voice rough with emotion. "He was a good man and he loved his family."

For a moment no one spoke. Presley continued.

"For what happened here, this is still a beautiful place and I don't want Wesley to be ever alone out here. What do you both think about getting Meyer Wood designated as a nature reserve? It would be kept safe, free of people ever dumping trash. We could develop trails for walkers and bikers."

Tommy and Sabe nodded and smiled.

"It's a good idea, Presley," Sabe said. "I'm sure the whole town would do whatever they can to make it happen."

"I'll help, too," Tommy added putting one hand on Presley's shoulder. "It's time we get everyone home though."

The four dogs got up from their sitting and resting positions as Tommy walked over to his vehicle and opened the back car door.

"Come on, all of you. In the car! I'm gonna take you home and get these sticks over to Pineville. You guys deserve some ice cream for your help out here tonight."

All dogs know the words 'ice cream' and without any further commands, they each jumped delightedly into Deputy Kirchner's SUV.

"Sabe, you and Presley are gonna have to share the same seat," Tommy said smiling inwardly to himself. "I've got too many passengers tonight so Sabe can ride on your lap, Presley. I'll drop you both where ever your cars are parked, but Presley, you're gonna follow me back to the office."

"You mean the police station?" Presley asked. "What for?"

Tommy chuckled as he pulled his car door shut. He took a head-count of his passengers, and tapped the car's door locking mechanism.

"Because, old buddy," he said putting the car in motion. "Behind bars is the perfect place to keep you safe tonight."

Chapter 47

"Is he alive, Deidra?" Harry asked, his words sounding breathless and scared.

"Oh, yeah. He's as healthy as a horse, I didn't give him a full charge," his wife answered, her expression bright and her eyes twinkling. "I didn't see his face, but he sure flailed around like a jumping jack toy."

They both stopped dead, looked at each other and broke out in full body gut laughing. Once they'd regained some sort of composer, Harry, gave his wife a look of pure admiration, walked over, picked her up and kissed her.

"He was going for his knife, Deidra. Can you believe that? What kind of dope uses a knife in a good fistfight? Especially, my own brother-in-law?" he asked, putting her down.

"Says a lot about Teddy's character," Deidra said, giving the man on the floor the second annoyed look of the night. "I didn't know he was messing around on Roxy. What a pig! And with Babette! I take pilates with her."

She paused for a moment, adding, "You know, I've never used the taser before. I've been carrying it in my purse, occasionally recharging it. Hey, look! He's beginning to move."

"Teddy?" she said bending over him. "You wanna sit up? We need to come to some sort of understanding about this business situation tonight."

Harry, leaned against his desk, crossed his arms over his chest.

"You know Deidra, we made a good team in that fight."

"Well, we got to stick together, baby," she answered. "I'd never sell you out. Besides, Teddy is an idiot. Those corporate piranhas will eat him alive in contract negotiations and they won't give him one penny more for his stocks than he'd get from us. We need to remind Teddy which side his bread is buttered on."

Deidra leaned over her reviving brother-in-law and said loudly, "Teddy, can you hear me?"

He groaned.

"You're not going to sell your shares to anyone but us, Teddy. Do you understand?"

Another groan, but a definite shaking back and forth of the head.

"You're being obstinate, Theodore," Deidra said sweetly. "I think you'll want to either hold on to your shares or sell them to us. Wanna know why?"

One of Teddy's eyes opened slowly and indicated the rest of Teddy was paying attention.

"Listen closely. You're being greedy, Teddy. Harry will give you tomorrow's market price for your shares, but if you sell Posh Pups out, I'll be forced to go to your mother and daddy and tell them how you cheated on Roxy and don't give a damn if the Posh Pups' factory is closed down. Half of your relatives work there, and some of them are pretty mean critters."

Teddy tried to rally, but though the spirit was willing, the flesh was still a perfect mush pile. He did manage a whimper. Deidra pushed forward with her explanation.

"Your daddy, his brothers and most of those wild cousins of your up near Lanagan would hunt you down and beat you senseless. My tiny taser experience would feel like being kissed by an angel compared to what they'd do to you. So who's it gonna be, Teddy?"

She fell quiet but nudged him with the tip of her shoe to encourage an answer. The cowboy stayed quiet. Looking up, she flashed her husband a brilliant smile.

Finally, the man on the floor, nodded and managed a weak, but definite, "You."

"Good! I'm glad we understand one another."

Turning to her husband, she said, "Baby, better get out your checkbook. This is gonna cost you."

Harry, shaking his head right to left, but with a look of complete admiration on his face for his wife, said, "He's not going to back out of this is he?"

"No, he won't have time to," she answered, picking up her cell phone and tapping in a number. "That's why we pay our attorneys so much money, darling. So, they'll be here when we need them most."

It was quiet while she waited for Jared Turner of Kime, Carston, Turner & Watson to answer.

"Jared, this is Deidra Sweeny. Yes, I know it's eight o'clock. Sorry, to interrupt your tennis game. How quick can you meet us here at our offices? We need you to draw up some papers."

There was a pause while she listened.

"See you in twenty minutes."

Chapter 48

"A.u luu luu hhhhhuuu!" Fritz howled with merriment, clapping the other man hard upon the shoulder. "You always were a good man, Fergus! That reminds me of the time we found ourselves up against the last shehag of Loch Lomand."

"I take you to mean your wife, Dunbar," the shorter, round-bodied man said playfully. "A beautiful, but fearful creature, she was, who ran me off many a time from your own front door!"

Fritz's new companion and an obvious past partner in crime appeared delighted by the recalled memory of a good fight with Fritz's wife, Mary. He feigned a shiver. Both men again laughed heartily at Fergus' antics.

"The only thing that would save me, Dunbar, was to grab her by the hand, twirl her prettily about and begin a jig while singing."

Beginning to carp about the room, the newly arrived Fergus started another tune.

"Tho' women's minds, like winter winds,
The noblest breast adores them maist-
A consequence I draw that.
For a' that, an' a 'that,
And twice as meikle's a' that;
The bonnie lass that I love best
She'll be my own for a' that!"

The little man was a sight to behold as he danced about the room. A full head shorter than the tall, well-groomed Laird of Dunbar, this Fergus was more like a shaggy, unkempt man of the mountains. His face was covered by a curly, unruly red beard that took delight in growing every which way except downward. Piercing blue eyes shined brightly, if not twinkled, from deep inside wrinkled crevices on either side of his bulbous, red nose.

His attire was a mixture of an old coat, torn leggings pulled up to his knees made from some sort of faded, brown cloth and a ragged kilt being held up by a slender belt. Atop his head, at a rakish angle, sat a green Highlander's bonnet. A frazzled looking feather still clung to the headpiece with the same comedic tenacity infused in the entire being of the charming person known as Fergus.

His singing and dancing done, he hugged Fritz roughly around his shoulders and the two men again broke out into another round of cheerful laughter. Fergus held his comfortable paunch (most likely formed from one too many evenings spent at The Howling Hound) as it moved up and down with each boisterous guffaw that sprang from the center of his being.

"Your Mary was a lovely woman, Fitswilliam. Black, shining hair and blue eyes like a winter's sky, but not a wife to put up with the rebel natures of two scallywags such as us."

With one long arm, Fritz wrapped Fergus' shoulders in a brotherly hold. They stood there together unaware of their current place and time but staring at the floor considering their past sins.

"There are days, Fergus, I regret my handling of her. She will not let me near the old family pile, but on spring nights, I hide up in one of the old rooms near the top of the house and listen to her sing. A tune so sad it'd tear your heart to pieces."

"Ya need to go to her, Fitswilliam! On your knees begging for your forgiveness. You're a stubborn man and your pride broke her heart the day you headed out to hunt grouse knowing you were sick. They say she begged you to not go, but you drank down the whiskey to warm your blood and left her with two wee lasses to care for once you were gone. I know what loss of one you love can do to your soul. I will search forever for my dear old bonnie Beast."

Fergus was either indifferent or oblivious to his new surroundings and it was only when a sharp, high-pitched bark came from the empty air in the room, did he look up with astonishment lighting up his face.

"What is that?" he bellowed. "I know that yip like I know the back of me hand!"

He was quiet for a moment. Again, two loud yips pierced the silence. Fritz stood regally beside his friend. A smile playing at the corner of his mouth.

"It must be him," Fergus said slowly, his eyes wide with uncertainty and his body beginning to tremble. "I say, show yourself, my bonnie boy, my Beast!"

The women, like dominoes dropping, plopped down one-by-one back into the safety of the couch. The cadence and rhythm of their movement brought Fritz's attention back to the current century and he turned to Sonya with a smile.

"I've brought Fergus, my old friend and compatriot, to you, Sonya! The Laird of Lochbar may I introduce to you my lovely Sunny."

The Laird of Lochbar drew his attention from searching the corners of the room to face the three women sitting on the couch. With a deep bow, he doffed his bonnet and swept it across the floor in front of him.

"It is my greatest pleasure dear ladies to make your acquaintance."

He replaced the droopy headgear and smiled broadly in the way of a good-natured, cheerful old soul. Returning his gallantry, three women still in wonderment at the visitation in front of them managed weak, "Hellos," and, "nice to meet you, toos."

It was Mrs. Townsend surprisingly, and not Sonya, who embraced the extraordinary moment. Standing to her feet, she stretched out her hand in an expression of greeting to the amicable spirits. Fergus, in a reciprocating effort, accepted her hand and lifting it to his mouth, kissed the back of it delicately. The woman, clearly charmed by his old-world manners, smiled brightly.

"It is a great pleasure to meet you, Laird."

"Have you seen a wee dog, my Lady?" he asked her. "I've spent many a weary time hunting my Beastie, but to no avail. I sometimes believe I hear his yap, but I've yet to find him. It is torture to my heart."

But before Mrs. Townsend could reply, there exploded in the room another sharp, excited bark. In less time than it takes a dog to wag its tail to and fro, the Cairn terrier, Beast, appeared on the floor between the Laird of Lochbar and Mrs. Townsend.

With a cry like it came from a deep, lonely place in his soul, Fergus dropped to his knees and scooped up into his arms the now wiggling and joyful dog. Man and Beast took turns showering affection on each other. There were many kisses both human and canine shared between the two.

"I've missed ye, my dear dog. Why did ye never come to me? What happened to ye out in the unholy storm?" the Laird of Lochbar asked.

The happy, panting dog had no answer, but to continue wagging his tail.

"May I call you Fergus. Your Lordship?" Sonya asked.

He stood to his feet, still holding Beast in his arms, and turning to her, he said, "Please, dear lady. This is the happiest day of my afterlife. You may call me by my Christian name, Fergus."

Sonya pointed to Beast, and said, "Fergus, you find yourself now in the New Word, or what it was called in your time, the American Colonies. Your dog's spirit has been attached to another family who's lived here in this town for at least two centuries. I think he may have been buried near their home and this week one of their members died a terrible death. Beast may be a protector for them and re-awoke when the woman's spirit was waiting for the transition. He won't go back with you, Fergus, until his job here is done. I believe he's staying to protect the family from someone who means them harm. He goes to the house where the woman was killed and guards the door."

"He must have been taken by someone the night I lost him in the mountains," Fergus said, his tone sad. "I've missed him terribly, but Beast knows his mind. I'll wait 'til he's ready to go."

"The family's name is Sweeny," Sonya said. "Did you know anyone by that name in Scotland?"

Fergus screwed up his forehead as if he was thinking hard on the name.

"Knew many a Mac Sween," he said, "but some of the family over the centuries moved off to Ireland and called themselves Sweeny. Might have been a sailor who took

Beast. Many of them came to Scotland and worked the canals during the time Telford was building the Caledonian. Made the Highlanders mad because the jobs were meant for them not the Irish. My Beast must have taken up with a sailor who crossed the sea to America."

Fergus and Fritz both shook their heads as they continued to study the terrier. It was in this quiet moment Mrs. Townsend rejoined the conversation by first clearing her throat in a delicate manner of catching the group's attention.

"Fritz?" she asked with a mischievous tone in her voice. "I think we might know one another."

Sonya stiffened as Fritz's gaze locked on the floor in front of him, but Mrs. Townsend pushed on.

"I live across the street and keep African violets. Haven't we met before? Oh YES! I remember now! You occasionally like to drop by to make sure my heart is in working order."

Chapter 49

An unusually cool wind scattered paper cups, confetti and some free-wheeling leaves about the lonely, quiet vendor-lined street. The sun had set hours ago and Puptown Alley was a ghost town. Everyone associated with Dog Days was either wrapping up the first evening of competition or comfortably relaxing in homes or RVs awaiting the second day of events.

Zeb stood in a pool of light cast by an overhead street lamp waiting for one of the borrowed county deputies to arrive and take over the security duty of the vendor tents. The department was stretched thin. Even he had to pitch in and help. For a moment he shut his eyes and asked for a tiny bit of enlightenment regarding the case. Any help would be sorely appreciated.

Only an hour ago he'd received news from the head forensic officer. Arsenic was in both Mrs. Townsend's candy and the donuts found at Sonya's door. Who'd ever laced the foods, had been exceedingly thorough and careful. Not a shred of DNA, a fingerprint or a witness had been found who'd seen the donuts delivered. It was official. They had a serial killer on the loose.

Michael had called and the forensic people were done at the Liltons. No trace of Wesley King was found in Samantha's car.

If he didn't get some traction with his investigation soon, it would be out of his hands and the state would take over. His officers had collected statements from over fifteen women known to be involved with Wesley King.

Teddy Davidson, Harry, and Deidra Sweeny had alibis for the night Roxy Davidson was killed. Babette and Teddy swore they were together during the time his wife was being hit over the head with a tire iron.

Lana, his mother, confirmed what Babette had said about who Roxy's possible paramour might have been. When Zeb had talked with Patrick, he chose not to discuss it over the phone. Best to wait until he came in tomorrow morning. This meant they'd also need to look into Lilton's wife's whereabouts at the time of Roxy's death. She may have known and wanted Roxy out of the way, too.

If things kept going like this, he'd have a statement from every female, every boyfriend and every husband in the four-state area. It had been an investigation needing lots of manpower and unfortunately, all available human resources were being drained off by Dog Days.

The phone rang. Looking down to see who it was, he saw it was Deputy Kirchner.

"Walker," he answered.

"Found something at the brush pile. Two sticks carved in the way both Wesley and Presley were taught by their father. Both have dog teeth marks. Has to be a small breed. Also, weirdly enough Mrs. Caruther's, Marnie's, and the Sweeny's dog showed up at the site and dug out a small dog vest from the pile. It has a scent on it Lana might recognize. I think we've got a real break in this case."

Zeb's heart had started pounding with excitement the moment he heard Tommy finish his third sentence.

"Get the sticks and the dog vest to Pineville. We've got a busy night ahead of us, Kirchner. I want every woman ever known to have had anything to do with Wesley King *and* who has a dog…"

"Has to be a small dog, sheriff," Tommy interjected, "with white fur."

"Thank you, God!" Zeb exclaimed.

"Definitely providential," Tommy replied. "Got a problem though, sir."

"What?"

"Presley got it into his bullhead to come back to Willow Valley. Says he needed to see the place where his brother was killed. I've got him in a safe place."

"Holy hell," Zeb said. "That boy needs his head examined. He's a potential victim. Put him under lock and key, Kirchner. That's an order."

"Already ahead of you, sir. He's got a free night in the pokey."

"Good!" Zeb replied. "How did you learn about the scent?"

"Sabrianna Williams was also with Presley when I ran into them in Meyer Woods. They said they were both independently drawn to the place. She recognized the scent from some concoction your mom makes to sell at the salon."

"Sabrianna Williams?" Zeb asked, sounding suspicious. "Was she ever involved with Wesley King? Did she do Roxy Davidson's hair? What did you find out?"

"Honestly, sir, I think she's all about Presley, not Wesley. Your mother would know the dirt on the love lives of her stylists."

"True," Zeb answered. "I'll give her a call when we're finished. Those sticks, I don't remember seeing them. Where were they?"

"Laying up against the back of the brush pile. They blended perfectly with all the other debris but earlier when we were going over the entire scene, my mind was so distracted when I saw them the importance of them didn't register, until two hours ago."

Zeb didn't say anything for a moment. He was thinking about the implications of those hot dog sticks, the dog vest, and the bite marks.

"I think Wesley crawled in under that brush pile to retrieve a dog and, on his way back out, the killer bashed him in the head covering up the body with whatever sticks, brush, and leaves were available around the pile. This murder may have been preplanned."

Quiet again, Zeb worked the reasoning out in his mind before continuing.

"You know what this could mean?" he finally asked.

"Yeah, I've been thinking through it, too, sheriff. Our murderer might be a woman," Tommy replied.

Nodding his head, Zeb agreed.

"I'd bet my badge on it, Kirchner."

Chapter 50

Fritz never flinched, but instead, shifted his gaze slowly over to Mrs. Townsend. As he did so, his eyes widened and his eyebrows lifted for he must have realized his prankster-goose self was about to be cooked. With typical Fritz poise, he went with the role he loved best: the charming Laird of Dunbar whose memory isn't quite what it used to be since his death two hundred years ago. The living, he liked to tell Sonya on occasion, were easy dupes for the departed.

Smiling brilliantly, he took Lillian's hand and said, "Dear lady, I've spent many an evening keeping watch over you. Consider me your constant protector."

He gave her a lovely bow, and when once upright again, he shot Sonya a dirty look.

"I'm so pleased to meet you, Fritz," Mrs. Townsend replied. "Sonya mentioned something about you enjoying trout and salmon fishing…when you were alive. You must be an excellent fly fisherman having lived in the unspoiled beauty of the Highlands?"

The cast was made and the hook found its target. The unexpected shift to a topic Fritz loved but buried two centuries since, cunningly baited the Laird of Dunbar and he joyfully bit.

"Why yes! I know my way around a Spey rod and enjoyed the pleasures of a drift boat on the River Leven. Fergus and I would skate flies for grilse and sea trout at sunrise, throw dry flies at wild browns on the Clyde and close out our day dapping on Loch Hope. Not all in one day, you understand, but we've wooed many a Scottish fish."

He sighed deeply from the unexpected resurgence of such pleasurable old memories.

"Are you a devotee of the angling art as well, Mrs. Townsend?"

"I, too, have tickled the trout in your bonnie home of Scotland along the River Dee," Mrs. Townsend said with a happy smile. "My husband told me when we married, if I wasn't to be a fishing widow, it would be best if I learned how to fly fish. I've caught rainbow trout in Argentina, steelhead in British Columbia and, of course, good old brown trout in the White River of Arkansas. Good waters, all."

Fritz was delighted. For a brief moment, he'd forgotten about Sonya's double-cross and even Fergus' reunion with Beast. Mrs. Townsend had serendipitously plucked at a long unremembered but powerful spiritual string that warped and weaved through his previous human life.

A resurgence of youthful memories surrounding lovely days spent along wild, rushing mountain streams angling for the elusive trout resurfaced in his mind and Fritz found himself reflective and, as a response, beginning to dematerialize.

"You're going already?" Mrs. Townsend asked, causing a slight rejuvenation in the Laird of Dunbar's image. "I hope I haven't said something upsetting?"

"No, no, dear lady, you have not," he said softly. "This conversation holds a deep truth for me. Lately, I've thought about my reality here and how I've clung to it from uncertainty for what waits for me in the beyond. It's been great fun, this life between here and there, but something more is waiting for me, and I've known this all along. Many a time as a boy and later as a man, I've cast a fragile concoction of feather, fur, and twine in hopes I'd find a piece of myself, a reflection of my soul, below the water's surface."

"Ahh, Fritz," Mrs. Townsend agreed, "I understand. This place, this life is like a stepping stone among many within a wild, beautiful river. Each well-worn point a starting place with millions of options to choose from going in any direction you wish to go. To stand forever still on any single one is a waste of the adventure that may be waiting for you out there. You're the dreamer. What will you dream for yourself?"

No one in the room spoke. Eloquence and wisdom may be purchased by age and experience, but these two gifts are less dependent on numbers of years and more so on a natural tendency of gentleness, sensitivity, and a strong inclination towards empathy for all things. Mrs. Townsend had collected and nurtured all three throughout her life.

But the delicate, life-affirming spell she'd cast was broken by a loud, commanding knock on Sonya's front door. As everyone's heads swiveled in the direction of the sound, a second interruption quickly divided their attention.

A calvary of dog paws, rustling through the kitchen along with panting and barking announced the arrival of Willard, Lewis, and Clark, all happily scrabbling into the living room. With their paws and legs showing signs of mud and leaf debris and their muzzles and noses still sticky from the ice creams they'd inhaled, the humans all talked at once.

"Where have you been?" Marnie exclaimed more than asked.

All the pups, their tails wagging in greeting, sat on the floor while offering their people relaxed doggy smiles.

"They've been eating ice cream I think," Lillian added. "That beagle has cone crumbs stuck to his left ear."

"Ice cream! Who would've bought them that? Better see who's at the door, Sonya," Marnie said, her voice showing signs of nervousness. "Be careful, it might not be Laura."

"I'll check before I open it," Sonya answered and headed for the foyer.

Fritz and Fergus evaporated as the three dogs went into another round of bark-greetings. Out on the front porch waiting patiently were Tommy and Laura. Sonya threw the door open and motioned for them to come through.

"Please come in," she said.

With the two officers, Sonya and their canine escorts returned to the living room. Tommy explained his visit.

"Mrs. Caruthers I found your dog Willard and Marnie's boys, Lewis and Clark, along with the Sweeny's dog, Pickles, out in Meyer's Wood this evening. Thought it was odd they were all out there, so I loaded them all up in my car, got them a pup cup at the Dairy Lane and brought them home. Hope that's okay."

Marnie and Sonya, both with furrowed brows, turned to look at their pooches who all sat contentedly thumping their tails on the floor.

"Meyer Woods? What on Earth would they have gone out there for?" Sonya asked.

"There's a maniac probably running around out there," Marnie interjected. "They could have been hurt!"

"The weird thing is," Kirchner said, "without them, we wouldn't have had two major breaks in our investigation tonight."

"What do you mean?" Sonya asked.

"Well, it was strange. Lewis and Clark were sniffing around the place where we found Wesley King and one of them burrowed under the brush pile and pulled out a dog vest. It was almost like they knew what they were looking for. Each dog, in turn, sniffed the vest and sneezed."

"Sneezed?" Sonya, Lillian, and Marnie asked in unison.

"Yes, sneezed. That's when I realized there was something on the dog coat. One of the two other people who were out there with me recognized the scent. Do you know Sabrianna Williams?"

Sonya and Marnie nodded.

"She said the scent may be one Lana Walker puts in the lotions she makes and sells at her shop. I'm driving the dog vest over to Pineville for forensics to check it out for dog hairs and to have the scent checked out. Lana is at her salon going through her sales receipts. She's getting together a list of clients who purchased lotions with that scent. We're narrowing it down, finally."

"You've almost got the killer, Tommy. I know it," Sonya said with a huge grin across her face. "Thank you, thank you for all you do as police officers. We are so fortunate to have men and women willing to work so hard to keep our communities safe."

"Yes! Thank you," the other two women chimed in giving the two young officers maternal-like, proud smiles.

The two blushed at the praise.

"Laura is going to stay the rest of the night here, Mrs. Caruthers. We'd like to ask because of the weather if she can stay inside in your living room. We're supposed to get another storm tonight."

"Absolutely, she can. I'll fix her up a nice bed on the couch."

"Good. You ladies are all set. I'm going to Pineville after I drop off Pickles at the Sweeny's."

Kirchner said his good-byes and left. Fritz, Fergus, and Beast also appeared to be gone. After making Laura her bed on the couch, Sonya along with Marnie and Lillian retired to their bedrooms upstairs to find refuge in soft, warm beds and good books.

Slender veins of lightning looking like faint, gossamer tendrils etched across the nighttime sky. Far away in the distance, rumblings of thunder whispered a curious lullaby over the nestled valley promising another evening storm to help brighten the chance of a beautiful autumn morning.

Before long, everyone was asleep including Laura who was snoring briskly in her cocoon of blankets and lavender smelling pillows. Outside, as the night progressed, the wind picked up making the three wind chimes on Sonya's porch tinkle and jingle.

Willard's ears, always alert, even as he slept in his cozy bed at the foot of Sonya's, twitched at the sound of the floorboards on the house's porch groaning under the weight of something or someone moving across them. The dog, tired from his unusually exhausting day, only shifted and rearranged himself more comfortably in his snug bed, falling deeper into sleep and blissfully unaware of what moved in the darkness in the garden below.

Chapter 51

The Sweeny's attorney, Jared Turner, had Teddy's signature on the contract and was heading for the front door in less than twenty minutes from arriving. He'd been annoyed at being called off the tennis court, but since he also liked his monthly retainer paid on time, he did most of his grumbling in the privacy of his car.

Deidra and Harry watched their brother-in-law's jacked-up, expensively tricked-out truck follow their lawyer's new Porsche 911 out of the Posh Pups' parking lot. Realizing that in some way they'd paid for both men's high-priced man-toys, they shared a heavy sigh in the same way parents do when they write exorbitant tuition checks to their children's colleges.

Teddy had spent some time whining at Turner about how he'd been attacked and didn't like being forced to sign an unfair contract. He pointed at Deidra saying she threatened him with blackmail and had physically attacked him. No one appeared particularly moved by his plight.

"It's your funeral, Theodore," Deidra languidly replied to his accusations. "Remember your mama, daddy and those cousins from Lanagan. I'll personally pay their plane fare to any place on the planet you might run if you don't sign. You've got a fat check in your pocket, Teddy, to help with the sting of signing away your ownership rights to Posh Pups. You're spoiled and greedy, Teddy, and the only reason you want to hold on to this company is to make Harry and I squirm."

Turner only shrugged and tapped the contract impatiently with the end of his pen.

"I need to get back to my team, Teddy. We win this match and we go to the state tournament. If you've been blackmailed, call the police."

Getting no sympathy from the sweaty, anxious attorney, Teddy finally scratched his signature in three places within the contract.

Posh Pups was safe, for a while anyway, from corporate raiders and a treacherous brother-in-law, but it had a way to go before Harry would feel right about turning it over to Titan.

With both the high-priced, high-maintenance people gone, the exhaustion of their day settled upon Deidra and Harry.

"Let's get home, baby," Harry said pulling his wife into his chest in a tight hug. "You were amazing tonight. I owe you a treat. Name the destination, and I will book tickets tonight. Paris? Rio? You've always wanted to go to Austria."

He kissed her.

"Hmmm," Deidra replied, once she came up for breath, her eyes still shut, "I liked that kiss. You kinda hit first base with that one, slugger. Got any other dirtballs, tough guys or lazy employees you need me to rough up?"

"I say we go home and sleep for two days. What do ya think?" he asked.

Deidra nodded and they both laughed.

"Let's roll, Harry. Lock up the building. I'll be in the car."

They'd left Alfonso, their bodyguard to watch their home. It was an annoyance always having an outsider with them. Privacy had become a rare commodity since they signed Alfonso on.

The car ride home was quiet. Raindrops hit the windshield as they pulled into the driveway. Pickles, sitting on the old Victorian's front porch, jumped off and ran to them.

"Come on, Pickles!" Deidra called. "Upstairs before it rains!"

The old dog bounded down the side steps and trotted toward them, his tail wagging. Above all three, and the sleeping town, a streak of lightning cracked. Harry grabbed his wife's hand, and they ran to the door of their back yard retreat over the garage. Alfonso met them and said he'd park the car. For the last couple of days, he always slept in a made-up room beneath the apartment.

Another lightning strike lit up the sky somewhere to the West and the thunder rolled heavily over the town of Willow Valley.

"It's gonna be another good one," Harry said as they reached the top of the flight of enclosed stairs and threw open the door to the apartment.

Deidra made straight for the sash windows and pushed them up letting in the sweet-smelling air laced with the scents of rain, honeysuckle, and roses from the garden below.

"Let's open the windows, Harry. Alfonso will be mad, but the air is wonderful tonight."

He came up behind her and wrapped his arms around her waist. A gust of wind rushed into the bedroom causing the curtains to flap and billow.

"Come to bed, Deidra," Harry murmured close to her ear.

A series of sharp, punctuated yaps as if made from a small dog somewhere within the room, startled Deidra causing her to quickly turn away from the window. As if on cue, window glass shattered through the room making Deidra scream.

Pickles, sounding the alarm by barking, ran for the open door of the apartment and disappeared down the steps. Harry grabbed Deidra to himself and ran for the back of the room away from the windows.

"What happened?" he cried.

"Harry…Harry," she said, her voice rough with pain, "I think the glass pierced my back. It's burning. I can feel blood going down…," she went limp in his arms.

"Deidra?" he asked, trying to see her face in the dark. "Honey?"

A sticky, warm wetness oozed down the back of her shirt and onto his hands where he still held her. His brain burned with fear, but like a man in a nightmare, he had no power to stop his movements. Pulling one hand free from the back of his wife, Harry's arm muscles trembled as he held his palm up in front of his face.

Even in the darkness, he saw it was covered with blood.

Chapter 52

Rushing down the garage apartment's steps, Pickles passed Alfonso running the opposite direction. The lab let his nose do the work as he met the ground. Even in the rain, he found the scent.

The same smell as when Roxy died and at the brush pile today in the forest. Focusing his entire attention on hunting the scent, the Lab tried to trace the direction of the trespasser's exit from the yard.

A sharp yap brought his attention upward to the main house's front porch. Sitting, as he'd been doing for days, in the comfortable wicker sofa was Beast. He had a new companion, Fergus. Both appeared indifferent to the storm's bluster and fuss. Beast's tail wagged like a windshield wiper at seeing Pickles.

"How did you know to bark up there? Did you see someone come through here?" he asked Beast and the man sitting beside him.

"We saw a person come into this place and point a pistol up at the window," Fergus said. "It was my good, faithful Beast who knew to warn ye like he did so many years ago up in Weem Woods."

"Did you see which way the person went?" Pickles asked Beast.

The terrier leaped down from his place and gave an affirmative yap. With an intense rigidity in his stance, he turned and pointed his muzzle at the back garden gate. As

Pickles followed Beast's direction, he found footprints in the soft, mushy grass.

"I'm going to follow the scent. Stay here and keep watch over our people."

Another sharp yap from Beast meant he understood and both ghosts resumed their place on the porch. Pickles jumped the short, rock wall at the back of the Sweeny's property and followed the scent down the alleyway.

The rain was letting up and the wind died enough for him to hear the sound of sirens coming closer. They always hurt his ears, but he couldn't let his people down. Keeping his nose tuned to the ground, he continued his search for the smell.

Up ahead, a possum or some sort of nighttime creature rustled in the hedgerows to his right, or was it? His hair bristled. Instinct told him to stop and hide. Hunkering down, almost into a crawl, the Lab tucked himself into a weedy spot, and not too soon, either.

A human, slender and wearing a hooded raincoat was hurrying back along the alley. In their hand, something metal caught the light.

He watched the person go past him looking for something on the ground or in the hedgerows. Taking out a cell phone, they turned on a flashlight and zeroed in finally on his hiding spot.

"I see you," he heard the person say. "Shouldn't have followed me. Go home! I don't want to have to use this thing especially on a dog."

The figure raised the metal thing, pointing it at him, but hesitated. As he looked into the shadowy face within the hooded raincoat, he trembled and wanted to bark. Pulling himself up onto his four legs, his hackles raised to their greatest height, he let loose with all his ability the loudest barking he'd ever managed in his lifetime.

Sirens, initially sounding far away, honed in on Meadowmear Place. Flashing red lights appeared at the end of the alley and Pickles heard a vehicle rapidly coming down the gravel alley road. The person hesitated, dropped their aim and took off running.

This was no time to quit now. Pickles allowing for a good distance between himself and the figure, followed quietly while keeping to the dark parts of the alley. Human voices both male and female called to each other behind him. Flashlights flipped back and forth across the road.

Now at the end of the alley, Pickles hesitated. He watched the killer open one of the gates and slip into a back yard. Should he go to the people he knew were here to help or should he continue to follow the person?

The choice came easy. Pickles realized where he was… at the garden gate of Willard's house.

With his friends in danger, Pickles turned and ran with all the speed left in his old rheumatism-filled legs back to the good people, barking with all his might.

Chapter 53

Zeb arrived at the Sweeny's house only minutes after the ambulance. The call from dispatch about the incident came through as he was leaving the park. Within three minutes, he was pulling up in front of their house. From the street, he saw the emergency medical technicians rolling a gurney with a female on it. Harry Sweeny was walking beside it, holding the woman's hand and talking in a frantic tone.

"Is she going to be okay? Can I ride with her?" he asked as Zeb came running up behind the group.

Recognizing one of the paramedics, a man named Sanders who worked for one of the county ambulance services, he asked, "Sanders, how is she?"

"Extremely lucky," Sanders replied. "The bullet only grazed the flesh between her back and arm. A top marksman couldn't make that shot in the dark and up through a window. It was one of those flukes of nature or a miracle. The bullet passed through the area below her armpit. She'll be fine, but she's in shock. If you're going with us Mr. Sweeny, get in. We're shutting the doors."

"One moment," Zeb called, "Mr. Sweeny we'll need a statement from you and your wife. I'll send an officer over to the hospital."

"Fine, but I've got an idea that might help you find the gunman. Our dog, a chocolate Lab, ran down the steps and after the person. He's still gone and Mark Alfonso, our hired security person, went to look for him."

Harry pointed toward the alley.

"Follow the dog. With the rain, you might see prints."

The doors shut and soon the ambulance pulled away from the curb as three other Willow Valley police vehicles were in the process of arriving. Suddenly, a loud barking was heard from the back of the property where Zeb saw one of his county cars must be parked from the flashing of the emergency lights.

"Sheriff!" he heard Michael, one of his officers, yell. "It's a Lab and it's back here in the alley! Come quick!"

Zeb ran through the garden to where Michael and Mark Alfonso were standing. Sure enough, the Sweeny's dog stood in the alley barking and running back and forth. He quickly looked down at the alleyway's muddy ground.

"Give me your flashlight Mike," he said. "I want you to go back and secure the scene. You," he pointed to Alfonso, "Come with me. We're gonna follow the dog."

The two men started running at Pickles, who immediately turned and lopped down the alley away from them. Every few seconds, Pickles would turn around to check if they were still coming.

"Do you have a feel for our location? I'm not completely familiar with the layout of this town yet," Alfonso asked Zeb.

Still running, trying to avoid potholes full of water, Zeb tried to lay out a map of Willow Valley in his mind. It was complicated. Meadomere was developed in the early nineteenth century with additional neighborhoods tacking on to it as decades passed. The entire area was more like a rabbit warren when it came to roads and back alleys. Only the later subdivisions built after the 1920s were more grid-like in their design.

Up ahead Pickles rounded a corner and barked. The two men stopped, watching the dog, who became almost animated in his efforts of barking and agitated pacing to get the men's attention.

"Honestly, I'm not sure. Some of these alleys are dead ends. It's been years since I've driven them. We're going to have to trust providence and take a chance on Pickles," Zeb said to Alfonso.

The dog took off again into the darkness.

"Leap of faith, huh?" Alfonso said more than asked. "What the hell, let's go!"

Chapter 54

"What do you hear?" Sonya whispered.

She'd awaken to a low, menacing growl and Willard sitting upright in his bed looking intently at the window that overlooked her back garden. Since she'd owned him, he'd only done this once and it was when a man tried to break into her house.

Getting out of bed, Sonya crept to her bedroom door and listened. If it was a burglar it was a good night for one, what with Officer Laura staying here.

A soft whisper of air brushed across her cheek, Fritz's way of letting her know he was present.

"I'm here," he said.

"Thank goodness. It isn't like Willard to growl unless he feels threatened. Is someone trying to get in?"

"No. It's someone in your alleyway. I watched as they came up onto your porch earlier tonight, but left by the back gate. By the way, Fergus is here. He's on the roof. I'm not sure why he likes being on the roof. I think he misses his mountains back home. Anyway, he tells me a person used a pistol at a house down the street. Someone was hurt but left in an ambulance. Beast is with them."

"What if it's our killer, Fritz? I'm scared," Sonya said, her tone hushed. "We need to wake Laura."

"Let her sleep. A lot of movement will cause the person to run. I think they're hiding from all the police who've surrounded our neighborhood. We don't want to let him get away, my dear," Fritz said. "We've got to help catch him."

Sonya's jaw dropped. "Really? An armed killer, Fritz? Someone might get hurt."

Fritz appeared unconcerned and made a shrugging gesture.

"Fergus and I will rout the villain to a trap. That's the easy part. This cowboy with his pistol can't hurt me, Sonya. What a surprise it'll be for him!" he exclaimed.

"Listen!" Sonya said. "Do you hear the emergency sirens?"

The Laird of Dunbar wore an expression of contempt.

"Foolish caterwauling! That'll only make our cowboy with his pistol flee the faster."

"Okay," Sonya said, "what do you want to do?"

Fritz screwed up his mouth in a deep-thinking side pucker. He did a bit of soft-shoe jigging which he claimed always helped with the generation of great ideas.

"I've got it!" he declared. "If you want to catch a fish or in this case a cowboy, you need some bait. Cowboys like horses to run away from tin-badge wearing lawmen. They'll want a horse of sorts. You've got the perfect contraption."

"What kind of contraption are you thinking?"

"Your motorized conveyance."

Sonya wrestled with his phraseology.

"My Vespa?" she asked, uncertain if she'd caught his meaning.

"If that is its name, yes. Vespa will be our horse. The shed you keep it in will be this ruffian's prison."

"How do we let them know there's a scooter back there?" she asked, thumbing in the direction of her shed.

"Easy, Fergus will slip down from his shingle-covered mountain, open the door to the shed and illuminate the interior so our criminal can see Vespa. Naturally, they will try to steal her because they know they're cornered by the law who are on every side. Once this hooligan goes through the door, I will be waiting to slam it, throw the bolt and catch our killer!"

"That's fine and dandy, Fritz, but what if they don't want a scooter, or don't go for the shed, What do we do?"

Fritz sighed and threw up his hands in a melodramatic gesture of an annoyed genius.

"Oh for the love of peace, woman! If I have to lower myself to a common ghosty, fine! I'll do the old chain-rattling rigamarole and chase the ruffian into the shed myself. Does that please you?"

Sonya couldn't help a giggle at Fritz's expense especially when he was exasperated. She reached up and gave him a comforting pat on his arm.

"Your idea is a good one, Fritz. What do you want me to do?"

Appearing to be mollified by her compliment, he said, "Once we've chased our cowboy into the shed, you wake the policewoman. She will do the rest. Best to keep your house guests and their fellow canines quiet for now. Also, slip down and make sure you have your doors secure. If you hear gunshots, don't be afraid. Fergus and I are, well, you know, already dead."

Sonya sighed.

"Let's pray it goes according to your plan."

"Not to worry. I'm off, Sonya. Keep watch through your window."

In an instant he was gone, leaving Sonya to ask herself why she'd ever let Fritz run a ground campaign against a possible murderous lunatic.

Chapter 55

"Who knows, it might work," she said with a sigh. "Fritz, in a pickle, can be resourceful."

Hoping she wouldn't be seen or heard as she crept downstairs, she was grateful for the few nightlights along the hall and stairs to safely guide her steps, but not so bright as to give away her movements to anyone looking in the windows.

Tiptoeing through the living area, she heard the soft breathing of Laura asleep on the couch. The desire to wake her was almost too overpowering, but she remembered Fritz's admonition to not do so until they had the cat in the bag, so to speak.

The front door was locked with its bolt secured. The only other door was the one leading from the back kitchen to the yard. This would be trickier. At night, Sonya always left the light on over her sink, and since she didn't shut her curtains in the kitchen, it would be possible for the interloper in her yard to see her.

"Guess I'll have to crawl, Willard," she whispered as she got down on all fours in the dining room. "Ouch!" she cried in a low groan, "my old knees."

Finally, after ten torturous feet of bare wood floors, she arrived at the kitchen door. Reaching up, she checked the deadbolt and it was indeed latched. Willard's ears pricked up. His throat quivered with a low rumble.

"Shhhh! Willard." Sonya said. "We must be so quiet. Understand?"

The terrier only cocked his head in the way dogs do when they don't understand, but are trying. Looking at Willard and sitting so close to the door, she had a tiny epiphany. Why not use the doggy door to see what was happening in the back yard. It was the perfect window without the worry of being seen.

With feline quietness, Sonya slowly flipped the door up and peeked through. Her timing was perfect. She saw the shed door was open and the Vespa illuminated by the single overhead bulb. Fergus and Fritz's trap was already set.

Red and blue lights from police vehicles flashed about the hedgerows but faded away. The officers were looking for someone who had to be hiding within Pickwick's pretty yards.

Something moved along Sonya's garden wall where a mature Southern Magnolia tree stood. The tree's fallen leaves from the earlier storm crackled as they were stepped upon. Whoever it was, was heading for the shed!

"Do you hear that Willard?"

Willard's ears stood straight up. A dog, a large one from the sound of its bark, was coming rapidly down the alleyway and giving it everything it had to make as much noise as possible. The silhouetted figure dashed into the shed. Fritz's idea was working.

All of a sudden there was a huge commotion in the shed. Lights blinked. The sound of old paint cans tumbling over each other, and a new dog's yapping told her things might not be going as smoothly as Fritz had hoped. Through the din of commotion, she heard her scooter's engine roar into life.

"Oh, no! Tell me I didn't leave those keys again in the ignition!"

She got to her feet, but quickly fell to the ground as three gunshots exploded and Fritz bellowed, "You rum-running rascal! Take your buttocks off my Sonya's Vespa!"

Too late though, out like a red rocket from the shed's door whizzed her beautiful Vespa with a tall thin person atop it. Laura came running through the kitchen and Sonya heard the rest of her guests, both beagles and women, making their way down the stairs. No longer restrained by Sonya, Willard bolted through the dog door.

"Wait!" she yelled, but it was too late.

As she threw open the door, she saw a hooded figure trying to drive the scooter but being buffeted by both Fergus or Fritz who galloped over and around the miscreant like ectoplasmic tornadoes.

"You mangy, horse thieving cowboy!" Fritz yelled, as Willard barked and bit at the tires of the scooter. "I'll have your head on a pike! That's how we Scots deal out justice to low-living, pistol-packing villains!"

Sonya out of the corner of her eye saw what appeared to be light beams from flashlights whipping back and forth in the dark coming quickly down the back alleyway.

"I've got him, Fritswilliam! He's a wily devil, but nothing compared to reeling in a hooked-jaw arctic char!"

Fergus was now wrapped around the rider's head causing the driver to navigate the Vespa about the garden wobbling and weaving. With each turn, sod was torn up from the ground and sprayed in all directions. Sonya's heart flopped over and landed square in the pit of her stomach. Her beautiful garden was being destroyed.

As the scooter took a decisive turn toward the front gate, Marnie, Lillian, and Laura all ran out to join Sonya on the back porch.

"What in Heaven's sake is going on out here?" Laura demanded.

But as she cried out her question, Pickles galloped through the back gate followed in quick succession by Zeb and Alfonso. The women on the porch and the men standing in the yard stood as dumb witnesses to the crazy bedlam of four barking dogs, one out-of-control scooter and two fairly visible Scottish ghosts clinging to one disheveled Babette Nichols who at that moment lurched through Sonya's front gate and headed wildly down Pickwick Street and straight toward Puptown Alley.

Chapter 56

Willow Valley's Police Department was cram-packed with people, officers, dogs of every breed, and three invisible ghosts comfily perched atop the long row of vending machines watching the pandemonium with glee.

Once Zeb was able to mentally process what he was seeing in Sonya's back yard, he called for backup from his deputies. As the impromptu parade of Vespa, canines, Alfonso, Zeb, Sonya, and Laura went running down Pickwick, the two police cars called by Zeb got into the act and turned on their sirens causing several inhabitants of the surrounding neighborhoods to come out of their homes.

Typical to small towns, these people got caught up in the spectacle out of curiosity and soon the cavalcade made its way to the park and Puptown Alley. The vendors cozily ensconced in their RVs came out to see what all the hullabaloo was about and they, too, joined the procession.

It was sheer luck Babette, who had Fergus still attached to her head and Fritz riding the handlebars, finally crashed into a vendor tent full of dog beds and was taken into custody by Deputy Kirchner.

"I need all of you to please go back to your homes, RV's or whatever you use as a domicile right now!" Zeb was saying through an electric megaphone. It was the only way to be heard over the outrageously loud babel of human voices. "We have everything under control."

It was Earl Higginbotham who managed to vault his voice over the others and asked, "Sheriff, did Babette kill Roxy Davidson and Wesley King? We have a right to know

Zeb! This town's been under a cloud of fear and suspicion for three days!"

Recognizing he might have a free-for-all on his hands, Zeb decided it was time to use a strong hand on his townspeople. He put the megaphone again up to his mouth.

"Earl," he said long and slow into the speaker, "No one's been convicted of any crime but I want every one of you to take your backends out of my building and go home. I'm gonna start passing out tickets of two hundred dollars each for disorderly conduct and interfering with police business. I feel like starting with you Earl!"

Like water buffalo who don't tempt fate by harassing irritable, powerful lions, the crowd made a collective sigh and funneled out of the Willow Valley Police Department, dispersing into the night. Only Sonya waited.

As soon as the place was clear, she tentatively smiled at Zeb who came over to where she was sitting.

"Do you have her in a cell?" she asked.

"Yes and I'm having her hands checked for gunpowder residue. The gun found was the one the bullets were fired from at Deidra Sweeny. I'm afraid, she's most likely our killer. We'll know more by tomorrow. I'll let you know everything once I have more information. Do you need a ride home?"

Sonya smiled and shrugged.

"No, well unless you're gonna keep my scooter for evidence."

Zeb laughed.

"I'll bring it to you in a few days, but for now, Tommy!" he called. "Take Mrs. Caruthers home please and make sure she and her guests are all tucked in safely."

Tommy came over and offered his arm to Sonya.

"It's been a big night, young lady. Let's get you home."

Chapter 57

Days later, Sonya, Lillian, and Marnie were enjoying a mid-morning breakfast on the front porch. They'd been evaluating the carnage of Sonya's back yard and talking about the events of the last few days. As for the garden, things looked dismal, but as for the capture of the possible killer of Roxy and Wesley, things looked hopeful.

"If all of us put in some elbow grease, Sonya, I think we can have it looking ship-shape before the end of autumn," Lillian said, looking younger by ten years due to the excitement and camaraderie of her stay at Sonya's.

"You know who would be wonderful for this kind of work," Marnie mused, "with the added benefit of getting him out of my hair for a few days? Dale, my handyman. How about I ask him to come over and help you out? He's a charmer, Sonya. Never a dull moment when Dale's around. Such an amazing landscaper."

Marnie finished with enthusiasm and a pleading, hopeful look on her face.

"Okay, okay," Sonya laughed, putting an end to any more Dale endorsements. "Ask him if he'll please come by and take a look at this wreckage. It's going to need a strong back and an even temperament. Why look at that entire section of flower beds where my peonies have been mashed? Ruined! Mounds of dirt will have to be moved to get things back in order."

The three women each sighed as they must have realized the enormity of the project and went back to nibbling bacon or drinking coffee.

"Even though it's a fine mess out there, I think Fritz and Fergus were truly courageous," Lillian said, her eyes bright. "What a night! I've lived over eighty years, girls, and never have I witnessed such a sight."

Marnie burst out laughing causing her to go into a snorting and coughing fit.

"That expression on Zeb's face when he came through the back gate. He looked like someone who'd seen a ghost. Made a believer out of him! So glad I didn't miss it by running off to Atlanta."

The sound of a horn honking brought their attention to the street. Zeb and Tommy were getting out of the police car. They had Sheba, Tommy's shepherd with them.

"Glad to see you both looking so rested," Sonya said to her new arrivals. "Mind the mess, gentlemen and come on up for a cup of coffee. Sheba, I haven't seen you in a while. Would you like a treat?"

Upon the uttering of the most hallowed word in dog language being spoken, the entire pack of Lewis, Clark, and Willard immediately materialized back on the porch. Ears up and tails wagging, they went through the proper canine protocol to receive the beloved treat.

"Okay, okay," Sonya said, bringing out four Posh Pups organic dog bones. "You each get one. Deidra Sweeny sent Marnie and I the most wonderful gift baskets full of goodies for our boys. She even included a deerstalker hat. Can't wait to use it this winter on Willard."

Once the dogs were happily chewing in random places about the yard and the humans were situated with cups of hot coffee and plates of something tasty, Zeb filled the women in on the news.

"We wanted to come by and give you an update," Zeb said with a huge grin. "Last night Babette Nichols confessed to both murders. It took a good deal of forensic evidence, but we got extremely lucky. She didn't wear gloves the day she took gasoline from Teddy Davidson's garage to use on the brush pile at Meyer Woods. Also, Teddy admitted a tire iron had gone missing as well and acknowledged the one found in Samantha Lilton's trunk was his. The brass shavings found in Roxy and Wesley's hair came from the lug nuts of Teddy's race car. Once we'd gotten access to the Davidson's house, things started falling into place."

"Did this Teddy Davidson person help kill his wife?" Lillian asked.

"We weren't sure at first, but Babette's fingerprints on the gasoline handles at the Davidson garage made no sense. Why would he use gas he knew had special additives easily linked to him to burn the brush pile and why would he use his own tire iron? Only Babette's and Teddy's head mechanic's fingerprints were on the gas tank handles. When she claimed she only borrowed gas from Teddy's tanks, we told her about the additives in the race car gasoline and they weren't present in her own car's tank. She knew she was caught."

"Oh, how horrible!" Marnie said, shaking her head. "Did Teddy encourage her to kill his wife?"

Zeb replied, "Teddy definitely wanted out of his marriage, but his love of fast food and fast women, actually saved him. At the time Roxy was being murdered, we have him on a surveillance video at Big Brother's Burger. That night, the drive-thru line was pretty long and he was there for twenty minutes. After he got his food, he was caught again on video at a place out on fifty-nine highway buying an adult video. Once Babette admitted she'd been the one to kill Roxy, we asked her if Teddy Davidson was involved."

"Well, was he?" Marnie asked, her eyes wide as saucers.

"She was adamant about his innocence, but trying to understand why she killed Wesley King was a bit harder. The night she murdered Roxy, she'd planned to kill her at the Sweeny's hoping to implicate Harry. She thought Teddy would inherit more of Posh Pups if Harry was out of the picture. Roxy, herself, had mentioned at the pilates class how she was at odds with her brother over the sell of their company."

"So, Babette wanted to frame Harry Sweeny for his sister's death?" Sonya asked.

"Absolutely. Babette overheard in the restaurant an argument between Harry and Teddy over the business. As Teddy's lover, he told her he was going to clean them out. Something must have clicked in her brain. She was tired of being the lowest woman on the totem pole of wealthy, powerful women in Willow Valley. Being already involved with Teddy, she must have hoped if she got rid of Roxy and framed Harry, Teddy would marry her and she'd have the lifestyle she'd dreamed of plus the added benefit of helping Teddy to get rid of his oppressive in-laws."

"How did she get Roxy to the Sweeny's house?" Marnie asked. "That would have been difficult."

"It was tricky, but once she'd formulated the idea at the restaurant, it was as if fate threw her a bone. When Harry Sweeny got up to go to the restroom, he left his phone on the table. She took it and sent a text to Roxy asking her to please come over to his house for some important papers she needed to sign. It was the perfect bait. Once Babette sent it, she immediately deleted it from his phone so he'd look like he'd deliberately removed the text. It took some doing, but we finally got the phone company to give us the phone texts."

"The Sweeny's, then, are cleared of any involvement?" Sonya asked.

"Harry's alibis that he was in a rainstorm between St. Louis and Willow Valley ended up also being confirmed by two truckers. We contacted regional trucking companies known to run that section of interstate weekly. It paid off. Two drivers remembered seeing a black Suburban pulled over during the worst part of the storm and a man fitting Harry's description walking along the highway."

Sonya said, "So, Babette Nichols must have thought Harry Sweeny would be in town instead of on his way home from St. Louis."

"Babette thought he *was* in town, not meeting with a vendor in St. Louis based on something Deidra Sweeny had told her at pilates class that morning. Deidra said Harry would be busy that evening meeting with a vendor for Posh Pups. Babette assumed Deidra must mean a Dog Days vendor already set up along the park, not one in St. Louis. That mistake put Babette's patsy for the murder too far from the crime scene. Harry was where he claimed, caught in a torrential downpour thirty miles away when his sister was killed."

"How did Babette do it?"

"The night of Roxy's murder. She'd met Teddy after his work. They did their thing and he dropped her off at her pilates studio. She didn't want her car to be seen near Meadowmere Place, so she'd setup a rendezvous with Wesley King, another one of her lovers, at his house, which isn't far from the Sweenys. She parked her car in the alley and let herself into the Sweeny's house with the key in the fern pot."

"Okay," Lillian interrupted, "how did she know about the key in the fern pot?"

Zeb smiled and answered, "The Sweenys had a maid, who was also a part-time pilates teacher at Babette's studio. We questioned the woman and she admitted having mentioned to Babette how she'd lost her original key and was using the one in the fern pot to get inside when she cleaned their house."

"She took a chance hoping the key would be there," Sonya said.

"I don't think she left much to chance. Babette must have parked her car in the alley and checked to see if the key was there. Let herself in, returned the key, and waited for Roxy to show. When she did, she killed her and let herself out. The problem was Roxy and the storm."

"How so?" Marnie asked.

"Roxie didn't return the key to the pot. If she had the key on her, then it meant she wasn't met by Harry to let her into the house. Because the storm was probably at its peak when it was time to leave, Babette waited as long as possible. She most likely didn't want to go out and put the key back in the fern pot, but Deidra Sweeny came home and so Babette had to make a run for it. She took the easiest route, down the front steps and across the street into your yard, Mrs. Townsend, and hid in your hibiscus bush. That's when she lost the key."

"My goodness! How chilling to know she was right beside me when I left my house to go over to Mr. Poindexter's," Lillian said with a shiver.

"Well," Zeb continued, "At first she wasn't admitting to killing Wesley King, but the common link of the tiny brass shavings in both victim's head, was a strong case for Babette performing both murders. Plus, finding the picnic sticks with the bite marks and the dog coat at Meyer Woods put her at the spot. The Kings don't have dogs and when we tested Babette's dog's hair and mouth impressions, both were a perfect fit. In the end, she killed Wesley because he found her clothes she'd worn at Roxy's murder in the trash can probably when he took out the trash the next day. He called her and asked her about them. He must have wondered why she wanted to meet at his house when from our investigation, we found out they only ever met at a local motel. A change so out of their normal routine must have occurred to Wesley as unusual especially after finding the clothing. Too many questions, so she arranged to meet him at Meyer Woods telling him it was all a weird mistake she could explain and wouldn't it be fun to have a picnic."

"How did she get him in the brush pile?" Marnie asked softly.

"Babette's little poodle was highly trained. Anyone at the Dog Days competition would have told us of its ability to crouch down and run easily through small round tubes. Dog competitions have these agility courses, so she sent the dog into the brush pile, probably while Wesley was bringing things from the car for their picnic and claimed the dog was stuck. He tried to crawl in under the bush pile to retrieve the dog and on his way out, she clubbed him with the same tire iron she used to kill Roxy. The dog's coat was a potential connection to her, and she didn't want to leave Wesley there for someone to find, so she went home and came back the next day with the gasoline from Teddy's garage to burn the evidence."

"It's crazy how we'd never have had those pieces of evidence without Willard, Pickles, and your dogs, Marnie," Tommy pointed out.

Zeb agreed.

"It was those dogs who tipped the scales. Babette, being a pilates instructor, was always using a salve to relax her muscles. The same ingredients are sometimes in menthol rubs for people who have congestion. Traces of the salve found on the Sweeny's lost house key was also on Babette's dog's coat, her personal items, the picnic sticks, and Teddy Davidson's truck. The salve's chemical makeup is the same as the stuff mom is concocting for sale at her hair salon. Only three women have ever bought the same blend of lavender, eucalyptus, camphor, and menthol."

"Who?" Marnie demanded. "Who were the other two women?"

With a mock look of surprise on his face, Zeb shifted his weight in his chair and said, "Well, weirdly enough, I'm surprised you've *both* forgotten."

His eyes, with a hint of a twinkle in them, shifted back and forth between Sonya and Marnie, who wore expressions of confusion.

"Oh my gosh!" the both exploded in unison. "I bought that lotion!"

"I bought it when I had the flu last winter," Sonya said.

"I use it for my sore muscles from working on the RV park," Marnie added.

"You both bought the salve from mom," Zeb said, "and neither of you have alibis for the night or the day of the two murders."

"Zeb!" Marnie exclaimed. "You've already said Babette Nichols confessed. You don't think either Sonya or I would kill someone? We didn't even know Roxy or Wesley."

Tommy burst our laughing.

"Now Marnie," he said consolingly, "Don't worry. Zeb's pulling your leg."

Lillian joined in and asked, "Why did Babette Nichols try to kill Marnie and me?"

"Marnie happened to be an unintentional witness when she interrupted Babette who'd come back to torch the brush pile. As for Lillian, I think she was afraid you saw her the night of the storm."

"Why did she shoot at Deidra and Harry Sweeny last night?" Sonya asked next.

"Shooting Deidra Sweeny was her only act which was not premeditated. Teddy called her on his way home from a meeting with Harry and Deidra Sweeny that they'd strong-armed him into selling his shares to them. She told us she was sick of rich people always getting their way and making others pay for their greed."

"So, Roxy was right," Sonya said softly.

"Right?" Lillian asked.

"Yes, Roxy said she felt greed and lust on her killer. In some way, it's as if all the people involved were caught up in money's dirty grip."

No one spoke for a moment. Somewhere a lawn mower's motor hummed into life. Two yellow butterflies danced within a ray of sunshine over by the water fountain in the middle of Sonya's yard and a woodpecker was working tirelessly at finding hidden insects within a Sweet Gum tree.

"I guess life goes on," Sonya said softly.

"Well, Sonya," Zeb spoke up finally, "you said the central motivation of these crimes was about greed for money. Babette Nichols wanted to not only move into what she hoped would be a rich woman's shoes but to also ruin her own friend's life. One of the perks of killing Wesley King was to implicate Tamara Lilton."

"Who is Tamara Lilton?" Sonya asked.

"She's Patrick Lilton's wife, the CEO of Titan, the company who had a bid in on buying Posh Pups. From what we understand from talking to Teddy Davidson, Babette and Tamara enjoyed a strange friendship. Babette was tired of Tamara rubbing her nose in her wealth, so framing her for Wesley's murder was a bonus."

"This is all about money, lust, and greed," Marnie said, putting down her second muffin. "I've lost my appetite."

"Well, there's more," Zeb said. "The day Wesley called Babette to ask her about the clothes he found, she knew she needed to find some other woman to take the fall for his murder. Marcy Hollingsworth, a dead ringer for Tamara, was also currently sleeping with Wesley. So, Babette called the girl and told her Wesley was sleeping around on her. The kid took the bait. Marcy asked for advice from Babette who told her to confront Wesley. Babette knew the girl didn't have a car but was on the same tennis team as Samantha Lilton. It was Babette who suggested she ask to borrow Samantha's car."

"Oh, how evil. That child could have been in real danger!" Lillian exclaimed.

Zeb nodded.

"Babette had managed to incriminate two people, but her hopes were on the evidence going against Tamara. The horrifying last piece of evidence was found deep in Samantha Lilton's trunk: the bloodied tire iron used to kill both Roxy and Wesley. Babette must have slipped it in there after she killed Wesley."

"Oh, dear God!" Sonya exclaimed. "How utterly horrible!"

"Her attempt wasn't well planned and even though Marcy Hollingsworth was with Wesley King the day after the storm, she was playing a tennis tournament at the high school at the time of Wesley's death. Same for Samantha Lilton who played in the tournament, as well as, Tamara Lilton who was watching her daughter's match and sitting by two other women who confirmed her whereabouts."

"Thank you, Zeb," Sonya said, her smile a sad one, "for sharing with us the whole story. What is going to happen to Roxy's Golden Doodles, Bea, Rue, and Betty? I made a promise to Roxy they'd be taken care of."

Tommy spoke up.

"I know you've been worried about them, Sonya," he said. "Roxy had a kennel full of dogs Teddy isn't interested in caring for, so Deidra Sweeny has offered to keep Roxy's Golden Doodle Girls and find homes for the rest. If you know anybody who needs a lap dog, there's some nice Lhasa Apsos for adoption, too."

"Hmmm," Lillian said thoughtfully, "I'd like to see those dogs. It would be nice to have some company at home. If you can, Tommy, bring two for me to see, okay?"

"Sure will, Mrs. Townsend. Name your time and I'll bring them over for a visit."

Marnie stood up and asked Lillian and Tommy to help her carry the dishes inside. The two complied, and as soon as Zeb and Sonya were alone, he reached over and tenderly took her hand.

"Would you let me take you out to dinner tonight to thank you for all your help?" he asked, his words tinged with hopefulness. "I also have a check for you. We often pay for outside experts in their field to help with investigations. You deserve this money. The Sweeny's also mentioned they would be sending something over as well."

He handed her a check.

Sonya smiled, her cheeks showing a hint of color.

"First, I would love to go to dinner with you. Also, thank you for acknowledging my help. It means more coming from you than from anyone I know," she responded.

"I'm looking forward to taking you out for dinner. I've mooched enough meals from you, lately," he said with a laugh, but his expression turned suddenly dark.

"Umm, what about your ghost friend? Is he going to be…around…on our date?"

Sonya burst out laughing.

"You don't hit me as the type to let a ghost scare you off, Zeb," she asked, her eyes bright with mischief.

He sat back in his chair and regarded her for a short moment. As a big grin spread slowly across his face, he laughed.

"You're a spooky, little woman, Sonya Caruthers," he said leaning over close to her, causing Sonya to blush even deeper. "But even if Fritz does come along on our date, I wouldn't miss taking you out for the world."

"It may be a fine mess, Zeb," she whispered.

He kissed her softly on the cheek.

"Totally worth it," he whispered back. "Seven o'clock okay?"

Sonya smiled and answered, "Seven is perfect."

Chapter 58

"See you've got a date," Fritz said.

He'd been listening to Sonya and Zeb's conversation but waited until Zeb was gone before talking to her.

"You heard all that, did you?" she asked him. "You'll be good about this, Fritz, won't you?"

"I can see you like him," he responded. "I've always known, you would find someone again, Sonya. You know I want you to be happy. I've been thinking about Mary since I met up with Fergus. My conversation with Lillian the other night was a reminder of something I'd forgotten."

"Are you thinking about going home, Fritz, and making up with Mary?" Sonya asked.

The Laird of Dunbar forced himself to materialize in the chair opposite the table from her. Sonya was his best living friend. Though he loved to flirt with her, their relationship was about being with someone good and kind, someone who cared. He would miss her.

"Yes, Sonya. I want to go home. I want to make my peace with Mary and take her with me. I was a selfish husband and an indifferent father. I owe her and my children an apology. If I'm lucky, they'll forgive me."

"I'm sure they already have, Fritz. I've never heard you speak of seeing your children's ghosts. They've surely gone on to where they belong."

Fritz was silent. She was right. His children hadn't clung to their old lives. Only Mary had waited for him.

Whether out of anger or love, he wasn't sure, but she'd waited for him.

"I'm taking Fergus and Beast with me, too. We will all go together. I wish you could be there, Sonya, when Mary and I cross over. I'd like to wave good-bye and see your face as I go," he said, his voice strained with the emotion.

"Oh, my dear, sweet Fitswilliam," Sonya said gently. "When it happens, I'll know, and if I'm asleep, I'll see you go. Either way, you have my love and blessing that you'll find what you're looking for. We'll meet again. I know we will."

He stood to go.

"It's a new beginning, Sonya," Fritz said. 'I wish you well, my bonnie lass."

She, too, stood up and reached out to take his hand.

"Fare thee well, Fitswilliam. Thank you for your friendship. I'll miss you."

Bowing low and with one last old, familiar brush against her cheek, he was gone.

Sonya sat down slowly in her chair. A whirlwind of newly fallen red leaves from the Sweet Gum tree flitted and did cartwheels across her lawn.

"Goodbye, Fritz," she whispered hoarsely and blew him a kiss.

Chapter 59

Two nights later, Sonya had a dream. She saw a lone bagpiper standing upon a rocky knoll playing the sweetest, saddest melody. An unearthly voice sang these words:

"Going home, going home
I am going home
Quiet like, some still day
I am going home"

"It's not far, just close by
Through an open door
Work all done, care laid by
Never fear no more"

"Mother's there expecting me
Father's waiting too
Lots of faces gathered there
All the friends I knew"

"No more fear, no more pain
No more stumbling by the way
No more longing for the day
Going to run no more"

"Morning star lights the way
Restless dreams all gone
Shadows gone, break of day
Real life has begun"

"There's no break, there's no end
Just a living on

Wide awake with a smile
Going on and on"

When she woke, she knew Fritz was gone. Her dear friend was on his way home.

Goodnight dear reader. Thank you for reading. May you have sweet dreams.

Sigrid Vansandt

A Ghost's Tale